the Day and the Hour

The Story

Lynn Andrew

CROSSBOOKS

CrossBooks™
A Division of LifeWay
1663 Liberty Drive
Bloomington, IN 47403
www.crossbooks.com
Phone: 1-866-879-0502

© 2012 Lynn Andrew. All rights reserved.

No part of this book may be reproduced, stored in a retrieval system, or transmitted by any means without the written permission of the author.

First published by CrossBooks 11/5/2012

ISBN: 978-1-4627-2274-7 (sc)
ISBN: 978-1-4627-2276-1 (hc)

Library of Congress Control Number: 2012920457

Printed in the United States of America

This book is printed on acid-free paper.

Because of the dynamic nature of the Internet, any web addresses or links contained in this book may have changed since publication and may no longer be valid. The views expressed in this work are solely those of the author and do not necessarily reflect the views of the publisher, and the publisher hereby disclaims any responsibility for them.

Scripture citations are paraphrases by the author.

All characters are fictional.

Composed in OpenOffice.org Writer.

The Story

Chapter 1

Officer Al Cypher and his son, Asher, are cleaning up the kitchen at Detention Suites. Asher insisted on preparing a gourmet breakfast for the seven homeless men who are being held for experiments. Al Cypher's idea of cooking for the inmates is to pour something from a box or heat something out of a can, but Asher enjoys cooking and is endeavoring to pass on a few things his mother taught him.

He constructed two quiches using three kinds of cheese. Perhaps the dish would have appealed to certain cheese connoisseurs, but it was a bit beyond the reach of the inmates' simple tastes. One by one, the men decided they were not quiche lovers, got up from the table, left the common dining area, and went back to their suites to forage in their private refrigerators.

"Your quiche missed the mark with those guys," remarks the senior Cypher. He is leaning against the freezer door, watching his son load the dishwasher.

"The cheese combination didn't work like I thought it would."

"You can't expect vagrants to appreciate good cooking, let alone a gourmet dish."

"I could make it better. I'd like to try it again. But I'm not sure I'll be around after tomorrow morning."

"I'm not worried about that. ... How would you like to make a real gourmet meal—for two?"

The cooking episode this morning has reminded Al Cypher about the boast he made to his boss when she called him up to her office and told him to expect customers to feed and look after in the detention center. She is the object of his passion, and he dreams of her joining him for a meal. Although he represented himself as one whose cooking she would appreciate, it is Asher he would depend upon should the dream materialize.

"A gourmet meal? For who?"

the Day and the Hour

"Me and my boss."

"I wouldn't feel right about that, Dad. How could I use what Mom taught me, to entertain another woman?"

"That's over, Asher. It's been a year. You like her, don't you?"

"Ms. Labaki? I guess. If she's half as wonderful as you say she is. I only know what you've told me about her."

"Everybody in the FSA is crazy about her. Well, not the women so much. But nobody has reason to complain about her, and that's unheard of in a federal agency."

"How do you know she likes you, especially?"

"Oh, it's just a dream, son, I'll have to admit."

What diminished the dream for Al Cypher was the fact that Leila Labaki would never take an interest in him as long as Earl Clark remained in the picture. But now he has hope. It is no secret among the security personnel within the Federal Services Administration that Clark is soon to be apprehended by the FBI. Cypher not only knows about it, he was not surprised by the news. He ventures to reveal it to his son:

"Can you keep something under your hat?"

"What do you mean?"

"Something not everyone knows about yet. But they will after Monday. It's a good thing this is your last game because Earl Clark is leaving town in the custody of a federal marshal."

"I don't believe it."

"Keep your eyes open, son. You'll see FSA cops following him everywhere he goes. Earl Clark is wanted by the FBI, and Leila Labaki has him under twenty-four-hour surveillance so he doesn't skip town."

"Then I don't think she's going to be well liked anymore."

"Clark would be gone already if she hadn't put them off. You can thank her for that. She got the FBI to wait until Monday, but she had to promise to keep him under surveillance."

"Whatever they have against him must be a mistake."

"Things go on behind the scenes. If you oppose the government, there's risk of getting caught."

The Story

"I'm sure whatever Mr. Clark was against needed to be stopped. What was it?"

"It's the reason these men are in here, for one thing."

"Are you going to tell me why they're here, now?"

"It's for a good cause, son, but Clark and others see only the short term, not the long-range benefits. The police rounded these guys up yesterday, so they can be taken to a Reorganization lab for experiments. Think of it this way: One day the world will be a better place, and your homeless friends here will have made their contribution. The Reorganization will clean up every city and neighborhood in the country. Crime will be a thing of the past. There'll be no more bombings, no gang wars, no drunk drivers."

"Yeah, I know, but we don't need it here. You said that yourself. And to pick up these homeless guys and send them off when they haven't done anything really stinks. I wish Mr. Clark could stop it. Maybe he still can, and it won't have to come here."

"All I'm saying is, it's dangerous business when you oppose the government. Unfortunately, Clark got caught."

"Who turned him in?"

"... It's hard to say. Everyone has an enemy somewhere."

"Not him. He's always doing things for people. Everybody loves him."

"Especially the women."

"So why haven't he and Ms. Labaki gotten together if they're both such wonderful people?"

"Son, ... Kenneth Clark won't be here after Monday. That's why I'm hoping I can get Leila interested in coming to our place for dinner. Then you'll see what I mean."

"Who's Kenneth Clark?"

"That's his name. Earl is his middle name. I happen to know more about him than anyone else in this town. I worked for his father when we lived in the city."

Having completed wiping the counters, Asher tosses the sponge into the sink. "Come on, Dad. He wants me there forty minutes before the game starts."

the Day and the Hour

Asher's primary passion is baseball. He is one of Earl Clark's best hitters and a buddy of Homer Foster, the home team's star pitcher. Maybe Asher's cheese choices were compromised by his thinking about the game soon to take place, the final game of the championship playoff. Or it could be that he was trying too hard to do something special for the inmates, these freedom-loving men, most of whom he considers friends.

Like everyone else, Asher has the Rapture warning to deal with as best he can. His church recently put a twist on its interpretation, making it fall somewhat in line with the earth-cleansing theories. He and Homer have debated the issue, Homer arguing for a hoax, Asher taking the position that it could be exactly what the Rapture-dreamers say it is, in spite of his church's advice. Asher's father refuses to discuss it, maintaining that it will soon be forgotten as has every Rapture prediction before it.

The young fellow now has this troubling news about Clark's imminent arrest added to the rest, but it does not weigh on him as much as his concern for people who are ignoring the warning. For all he knows, Earl Clark and Leila Labaki are believers, but Homer, who has abandoned the faith of his parents, holds to the original Rapture-denying doctrine of his new church. It is the same church that Asher attends, but Asher has lately abandoned the Church's teaching on this and other points and now has beliefs aligning more with those that Homer grew up with at Grace Bible Church. As for his father, Asher holds little hope. The man disapproves of his son having anything to do with religion. It had never been an issue between them until the new sponsor of the baseball team, who is rather old-fashioned in her ways, ruled that it would be an all-boy Catholic team. That drew Asher into the circle of religious instruction and opened a new dimension in his life: he had never before considered that God might take an interest in him personally.

After confirming that the inmates are in their own suites and making sure all doors are locked, Al and Asher exit the Federal

The Story

Building and drive down Hill Street to the athletic fields by the school. Al has no official leave for this, but nothing would keep him from watching the final game of the season. In view of his dual assignment as the security officer for the Federal Building and warden of its jail, he believes he is endowed with autonomy exceeding that of ordinary FSA employees. Furthermore, he is fully qualified as a law-enforcement officer with jurisdiction not limited to the environs of the building. No one would question his presence in uniform anywhere in the town any time day or night if it were not known that he had left his detention post during working hours.

And few would suspect that he had. This is the first time the suites have been occupied since the FSA moved into its ultramodern, lavishly appointed building. This town has little use for such a facility. None of the disruptive unrest that plagues the world has taken root here. Seldom is there a crime worthy of the front page of the paper. Earl Clark, whose primary job is writer and reporter for the local weekly, normally has to work hard to find something to make an attractive headline. Tuesday's issue ignored the Rapture warning (being initially suppressed, it was little more than a rumor) save in the religion column submitted by Earl's close friend Adam Murphy, pastor of Grace Bible Church.

Next week will be different. There will be plenty of material for the paper—assuming there will be an issue next week.

the Day and the Hour

Philip and Pamela Evans came to an important decision this morning. Earlier in the week they picked nine o'clock Saturday morning as the hour and day at which they would inform their unbelieving employees about the disposal of the hardware store. Their first idea was to give the business to them, but they remained open to any other plan that might come along as they waited on the Lord each day. No other plan came along.

Russell Tarr would be appointed manager. He had some executive experience and probably was not susceptible to the Rapture, having his own ideas about End-Time events, which did not admit of tomorrow's fulfillment.

The two professing believers on the staff were left in charge of the sales floor downstairs while the others gathered together in the upstairs room that Philip used for his office. When he presented the plan to them, he was surprised by the reactions he saw on their faces.

Since only three good chairs were in the room, various other objects had been pressed into service for seating. Only Lonnie, the senior member of the staff, remained standing. Philip was seated near his desk with Pamela beside him on one of the better chairs.

"It's not going to work, Phil," Lonnie said.

The others were silent, all looking at the speaker.

"I thought you might spring this on us, and it gave me the cold sweats when I contemplated the hodgepodge of obsolete and half-baked systems you use to run this place. One would have thought, since you knew you would be leaving in a week, that you would have spent your evenings in here getting things put in order instead of running all over town scaring folks."

Everyone seemed to think that was funny. They all had a good laugh at Philip's expense. Pamela perceived that something was amiss, and she correctly concluded that they were in collusion and had appointed Lonnie their spokesman.

"No. ... Seriously, Phil, I was a little concerned about that, but I'm not anymore. We all came in early this morning and had a

The Story

meeting before you got here. I don't know whether you realize it, but none of us is keen on running the store without you. In fact, we want to keep everybody together. Call it a family or whatever you want. We're going to hang together one way or another."

"I'm not sure I understand what you're getting at," said Philip.

"We're going with you. We figured if you invited the customers to go with you, in that ad you put in the paper, you wouldn't mind if we joined you too."

"Do you understand what you're saying?" Philip was understandably aghast.

"Good enough, I think. Russell explained it to us."

"It wasn't my doing!" protested Russell. "I just gave them your believe-and-be-saved line, and they all swallowed it like it was the gospel truth."

"You told us it *was* the gospel truth," said Lindsey with a knowing smile. She was sitting on a stack of doormats next to Russell.

"Well, it is. I just don't like admitting it to Phil after all these years."

"All right, I forgive you for being so stubborn," said Philip.

"Did he tell you what to expect?" Pamela asked. In her amazement and excitement, she had stood up, her long, flaming-red hair framing a face that seemed to be seeing a vision of heaven.

"Jesus!" they exclaimed in unison.

"It sounds like you all mean it," said Philip.

"When Pastor Murphy comes out in his column saying he's resigning, you take notice," said Jeremy, who was sitting in a yard chair with a broken armrest. Nods and "That's right"s indicated general agreement with the statement.

"I always knew there was more to life than we were taught in school," said Joanne, who was sitting in an inflatable camp chair. "It wasn't acceptable to associate with Christians, so I just let it go. But things started happening this week, and I knew I couldn't stay away any longer. When Russell told us the story about Jesus this morning, it was like, 'where have you been all my life?'"

"Did you tell them that Jesus is a person of the Godhead, Russell?" asked Philip.

"Yes he did!" said Lonnie.

Russell said nothing in his defense. He was staring at the floor, shaking his head.

"Did he tell you the bad news too or just the good news?" asked Philip.

"I'm not sure what you mean by the bad news," said Lonnie. "But if there's one thing about life that's obvious, it's that something is terribly wrong. How could anyone be as good as a guy who cuts his neighbor's lawn, yet as bad as when he turns around and slaps his own wife? I've done worse things myself."

"It's the stuff we all have to live with," said Frieda, who was sitting on a box of shop towels.

"If I were God, I'd wipe everybody out and start over again!" said Carl, who was sitting on a spool of rope.

"Good thing you're not. You'd wipe yourself out too," observed Clarence, who was perched on a stubby stepladder.

"That's where Jesus comes in. Only he could take the punishment for us and survive," said Carl.

"Not just survive! He's inherited everything!" said Lindsey.

"The best part is, he's willing to share it with us," said Vicki, who was sitting in a squeaky office chair.

"Not just willing: he does it because he loves us," said Francis, who was straddling an air compressor.

"It's not the kind of love you find anywhere else," said Frieda.

"I guess we don't have a better word for it. He actually yearns for us to be with him," said Carl.

"While he's the King and we're guilty rebels—or used to be!" added Clarence.

"The way he conquered our death and then captured our hearts is enough to think about for a thousand years," said Francis.

"I've a feeling nothing else will matter pretty soon," said

The Story

Lonnie.

"Russell, did you tell them all that?" asked Philip.

"No. I don't know where they got it," Russell replied.

"I thought you *did* tell us," said Joanne.

"I told them the basics, that's all. Now they're preaching to *me* as far as I can tell."

"I've seen some strange things this week, but this tops them all," said Philip. "Now, what are we going to do about the store?"

"Let's just leave it unlocked and go home," suggested Carl.

"Put a sign in the window that says *Free,*" said Clarence.

"I'm afraid the place would be mobbed," said Lonnie.

"I'd like to leave something in the account to help the bank recover the loan," said Philip.

"We could leave it unlocked and extend the fifty-percent-off sale. Everyone knows how to check stuff out with the self-service scanners," proposed Lindsey.

After batting similar ideas around for several minutes, someone found a sign board, and they made a sign for the window.

Then they all went home, promising to see each other in heaven.

> Gone-on-to-glory sale
> 50% off everything
> Open 24 hours every day
> until sold out
> Self service
> Honor system

Except Russell.

Russell had written up a bill of sale and handed it to Philip.

"Just in case I don't make it—would you make over the store to me, effective Monday morning?"

the Day and the Hour

*L*eila Labaki had been spending her morning hours reading and praying. She had discovered some of the purest gold in the world and was reading it over and over, underlining her favorite words and phrases.

> Blessed be the God and Father of our Lord Jesus Christ!
> <u>He</u> has blessed <u>us!</u>—in Christ—with every blessing in the <u>heavenly places</u>.
> <u>He chose us in love</u> before the foundation of the world.
> He predestined us to become <u>holy</u> and <u>blameless</u> before him.
> His plan, which is pure, glorious grace, is to <u>adopt us in the Beloved Son</u>.
> In Jesus Christ—<u>through his blood</u>—he redeemed us from the deadly grip of sin.
> He lavished upon us the riches of his grace, including the forgiveness of our sins, in all wisdom and insight,
> Even making known to us the mystery of his will—
> His purpose in Christ for the fullness of time—
> <u>To unite all things in him:</u> things in heaven and things on earth.
> When you heard the word of truth, the gospel of your salvation, and believed in him,
> You were <u>sealed with the</u> promised <u>Holy Spirit</u>,
> Who is <u>the guarantee of your inheritance</u> until you come into possession of it—
> To the <u>everlasting praise of his glory</u>.

In spite of the glorious message, which she sincerely took to heart, the nagging pain returned soon after she closed the book: it continued to grieve her that Earl Clark did not seem to be happy about the prospect of her being baptized—or of her being there at all. Perhaps he felt that things had gotten out of hand. It was *his* beach being used for the baptism and, as originally scheduled, only for Evelyn Newton. She could understand his attitude if he planned to be absent: boycotting the baptism would be in character; it would merely mean he did not care for religious ceremony. But judging from what he said last night, it seemed he planned to be there.

The thought of him possibly preferring Evelyn's presence to hers was troubling even as she firmly held to the explanation that

The Story

came to her last night. She told herself again that probably she had misinterpreted his evident disappointment. It was reasonable that he would be unhappy about her becoming committed to something that might take her away from him. It had little to do with Evelyn.

Either way, it amounted to the same thing: it had turned out that she was not what he wanted.

But she also considered the other side: He must give in or lose his freedom next week. The Translation was his only realistic hope. Why was he disregarding it? The danger that Earl faced distressed her greatly. She did not want him to suffer.

Seeking an additional dose of relief, she opened her Bible again—randomly. (It was all new to her.)

The Song of Songs. What is this about?

> Let him kiss me with the kisses of his mouth! ... Take me with you. Let us run.
>
> Behold, he comes leaping upon the mountains, skipping over the hills. ... There he stands, looking through the window. ... My beloved speaks:
>
> *Arise, my love, my fair one, and come away with me, for the winter is past, and the rain is over and gone. Flowers are opening upon the earth, and the time of the singing of birds has come. ... Catch the foxes, the little foxes that spoil the vines, for the vineyards now are in bloom.*
>
> My beloved is mine, and I am his. ... On my bed at night I dreamed and sought him whom my soul loves. I sought him and did not find him. I will rise now and go about the city, in the streets and in the squares; I will seek him whom my soul loves.
>
> *Come with me from Lebanon, my bride, from the dens of lions. ... You have captivated my heart, my sister, my bride. How beautiful is your love! ...*
>
> I sleep, but my heart is awake. My beloved is knocking!
>
> *Open to me, my sister, my love, my dove, my perfect one. ...*
>
> He puts his hand on the latch, and my heart thrills. I rise to open the door, ... but he has turned and gone.
>
> I sought him but could not find him. ... I charge you, O daughters of Jerusalem, if you find my beloved, tell him I am sick with love.

the Day and the Hour

Someday I'll ask him what it means.

Although the meaning was obscure, it was a comfort that the Holy Spirit knew what she was going through. Beyond that, it seemed to be about her in some exciting way. She turned to the last verse to see how the story ended.

> Make haste, my beloved. Be like a swift deer or a young stag coming down from the mountains of spices.

Leila had her phone at hand in order to follow the surveillance reports. She knew when Earl left his house; she knew he had stopped at the Burns-house rebuilding project. Again the phone vibrated, and she checked the message. Earl had left the Burns house and gone directly to the baseball field. But she waited and did not leave immediately. She was timing her arrival to be slightly before the game was to start. She did not want to risk being a distraction that he might resent when he was busy with his team.

So much will depend on these last few hours. There will be no making amends tomorrow for mistakes made today.

The Story

Chapter 2

*T*he sky was overcast. It had been threatening rain, but none had fallen. Leila parked in the school lot, walked by the track, and skirted the soccer field before coming to the baseball diamond.

She spotted Earl on the bench with the team. It appeared that the game was about to begin. Other than Filstein the surveillance officer, with whom she exchanged nods, she did not immediately recognize anyone among the seventy or so in the bleachers. Then she saw Al Cypher. She thought he would have been on duty at the detention center. He tipped his hat and smiled. She nodded slightly and looked away.

Leila picked out a space near the middle aisle about halfway up, next to a couple with two children. She guessed they were the parents of one of the players. Between them sat a girl of about twelve. The man held a little girl on his lap.

"Excuse me; are you saving these seats for anyone?"

"You're welcome to sit here," replies the woman. "I don't remember seeing you before. My name's Harrietta. Do you come to these games often?"

"Mine's Leila. This is my first time."

"Leila. ... Leila. Your name is somehow familiar. This is my daughter Holly, and my daughter Hannah is there with my husband, Harold."

Harold knows who she is. He leans forward, looking past Holly and Harrietta. "I don't think we've actually met. I'm Harold Foster. Earl has told me about you."

"I believe, sir, I owe you and your wife a huge thank-you for making your airplane available to Earl and me last night. It was the most fun I've ever had."

"You're Earl's friend?" exclaims Harrietta. "I'm so glad to meet you! We were just now talking with Earl—just before you got here. He was telling us you gave him a flying lesson!"

the Day and the Hour

"That man surprises me sometimes with his sense of humor."

"It's pilot humor," explains Harold. "He meant you surprised him with your performance."

"I surprised myself! They were elementary maneuvers of course. Oh—did you see the sunset last night?"

"Where were we, Harold? Did you notice the sunset?"

"That would have been about 6:30. We got to church at 6:15, so we missed it."

"Do you, by any chance, go to Adam Murphy's church?" Leila asks her new friends.

"We certainly do," replies Harrietta.

"I'm to be baptized by Pastor Murphy this afternoon."

"Oh, that's absolutely wonderful! Will it be at Earl's beach?"

"Yes."

"That's awesome! Will Earl be there?"

"I think so."

"We've been praying a long time for Earl."

"I've been praying for him too, but only since Thursday night when God finally got my attention—thanks to Earl."

"Oh, really? You mean ... the Lord used Earl?"

"He used a donkey once, so it's possible," puts in Harold.

"It was as unlikely as that," continues Leila. "Earl took the piece that Pastor Murphy submitted for the religion column and made it better. Did you see it?"

"Yes, I read it," admits Harold. "You're right: it made a much bolder appeal than usual—and well written. I was going to mention it to Adam but forgot. So Earl wrote that?—the rascal! But I think he would have told me if he'd given in and gotten saved. He must have done it to honor his friend. That would be just like him."

Play ball!

"Is there someone special on the team?"

"It's our son, Homer," replies Harrietta. "He's our pitcher."

Pitching for the home team is Homer Foster, number 11. And leading the batting order for the Hornets today is midfielder, number 58, Isabella Young.

The Story

"He's a fine-looking young man."

"Thank you."

> Foster checks his sign, stretches. Here's the pitch—over the plate! Strike one!

"Please excuse my ignorance: I'm afraid I've been cloistered away from the more important things in our community. Is Earl's team all boys?"

> Here's the 0-and-one pitch—a swing and a miss!—a sinker dropping over the plate. Strike two.

"It's a boys' team now. Earl's the manager. They've won all but one game this year."

"I've forgotten where the Hornets are from. The sports page isn't one I read much."

> Here's the windup, and down it comes—another sinker, and ... it's been called a strike! **Strike three!**

"Homer struck her out! *Yea Homer!* ... They're from Herne. Homer calls them the Hernettes. Isabella is a fast runner; he did a good thing keeping her off the bases."

> Left hander Sonya Stern, number 23, is up next for Herne. Sonya plays first base. She's also the Hornets' team captain.
>
> Here's the windup, the pitch—there's a swing and a hit!—a line drive to shortstop. Miles White, number 66, has it—he dropped the ball!—picks it up, throws to first .... It's wide; Jackson Moore reaches—misses. ... She's safe!

"What a pretty girl she is. Their team appears to be all girls."

"It's mostly girls. They do have some boys on the team, but I don't see any today. They don't seem to have any extra players."

> Amelia Young is stepping up, number 57. She plays left field for the Hornets. ... Amelia is Isabella's sister.
>
> One out now for the Hornets with a runner on first.

"She's a powerful hitter," declares Harrietta.

"And our team is called?"

"We're the Lakeside Leaders. The team used to be sponsored by the restaurant. Originally, it was called the Lakeside Lions, but animal names had to go."

"Samson would have liked the old name."

> Foster goes into the windup; here's the pitch—over the plate at the knees. Strike one.

the Day and the Hour

"Who's Samson?"

"That's what I call Earl sometimes."

"The Lions were before his time," Harrietta informs her.

"He had the part of Samson in the play."

> Here's the pitch—she swings: fly ball to right field! Number 49, Oliver Hernandez, has it. No! It's over his head! He's running it down. ... He's got it, throws to second—too high! Homer scoops it up, throws to third. ... Safe!
>
> Runners now on second and third: Amelia Young at second and Sonya Stern at third.

"The play—of course: Earl's play. We couldn't go this week, and now—I think we've missed it."

"The opening was postponed until next week, and we won't miss it after tomorrow, I'm sure. But Earl—I'm afraid ...."

"I know. There's still time," says Harrietta.

> In the cleanup position for Herne is second basewoman, number 34, Scarlet Reed.
>
> Still only one out with two runners on.

"This isn't the only team in town, is it?"

"It's the only one in the Autumn League. This is the final game of the season. The winner takes the championship."

"That young lady looks as though she could hit the ball out of the field," Leila remarks.

"If Homer gives her a chance, she will."

> Here's the windup, the pitch—a swing and a hit! Line drive to first base—in the glove of Jackson Moore! Scarlet is **out**. Amelia's on her way to third; Moore throws to Evan Carter on third; Amelia going back to second. Carter throws home. Stern turns back. Catcher Logan Thomas drops the ball! Sonya Stern is safe on third, and Amelia is back on second.
>
> Two outs now for the Hornets.
>
> Next in the lineup is Herne's pitcher, Victoria Martin.

"Victoria is Homer's girlfriend."

> Stern leading off. Here's the pitch—a fast ball, a swing, and a pop fly to short field! Second baseman Mason Rodriguez has it— had it—bounced out of his glove. He picks it up and throws to first. Stern **scores** crossing home base. Nice throw to first; Martin is **out**, and the Hornets go down at the end of the first half of the

The Story

first inning.
The score: the Hornets one; the Leaders zero.

"Now is our chance. *Go Leaders!*" cheers Harrietta, as the team trots in to the bench while the Hornets take their positions on the field. "I'm sure their catcher is a boy, though it's hard to tell with so much armor on. I remember him now."

Victoria Martin, number 21, is pitching for the Hornets today.

"Isn't it a bit ironic?" asks Leila.

"You mean because Homer's opponent is his girlfriend?"

"I wouldn't have thought they could be serious."

"About each other or the game?"

"Oh, I don't know. It's confusing. ... It's impressive that you have that announcer."

"It's a requirement: in case any blind people are here."

We're at the second half of the first inning, and Oliver Hernandez, number 49, leads the batting order for the Leaders.

"I had intended to attend the service at your church Thursday night. That was my crisis night. Then last night I had the flying date with Earl. Perhaps tonight I'll be able to come."

"There isn't any service tonight. The church is being used for a secular concert. It's really a shame. On this night of all nights. What was your crisis?"

"It's a bit complicated—what led up to my reading the article in the paper. ... That is too bad about the concert. I'll never hear Pastor Murphy preach. But I suppose Earl would not have wanted to go with me."

*Martin winds up. Here's the pitch to Hernandez—he swings! It's an infield grounder to second base! Scarlet Reed has it—throws to first. ... Hernandez is **out**!*

"You should have been there last night. There were twenty-four new faces—all FSA employees and their families, if you can believe it."

"Oh? ... That's wonderful."

Number 24, Mason Rodriguez, is next to bat for the Leaders with one out and no one on base.

"The chief executive officer—you know: the one sitting up there in those plush offices on the top floor of the Federal

the Day and the Hour

Building? By the way, I've never been up there, but my friend Dottie told me—she got it from her brother who used to work in maintenance; he's been all over the building—she said it has structural defects.

> The pitch is low. Ball one.

I don't think I'd be comfortable working there, especially up on a high floor like that. The view is spectacular though. It's all windows with rich draperies, a thick carpet, a lounge—even has a private bathroom that is out of this world."

Leila nods, letting Harrietta know she understands.

> Here's the pitch—low and outside. Ball two.
> Two-and-o for Hernandez.
> One out for the Leaders here in the bottom of the first inning.

"Anyway, the chief executive up there sent out a message to everyone in the building about the Rapture. It was a big surprise because religious speech in the workplace is strictly forbidden."

Leila nods her agreement.

> Martin is taking her time, ... gets her sign, winds up. The pitch —outside. Ball three.

"All the FSA personnel were talking about it yesterday, trying to guess what will happen when word gets out to the Free Speech Regulators. Somebody will complain, I guarantee you that. But I guess the new honcho is well liked. I don't know anything about him—really haven't heard a thing. The paper won't mention goings-on in federal agencies of course."

> Here's the three-zero pitch—a swing and a hit! ... Foul ball up on the wire.

Anyway, it made a big impact on a lot of the FSA employees, and a dozen of them showed up at our church last night along with some of their spouses and children. God moves in mysterious ways, doesn't he? Excuse me; I think Harold has been trying to say something."

> Here's the windup. Martin delivers—a curve ball to the outside.
> Ball four! Rodriguez walks to first.

Harrietta has leaned across Holly to her husband, who is whispering in her ear:

"She *is* the chief executive."

The Story

"She is? She's the chief FSA officer? Are you serious?"

"I'm serious."

"Why didn't you tell me?"

"I guess it didn't seem to be relevant at first. I'm sorry."

> Leaders' midfielder, number 48, Asher Cypher, is up next with one runner on base.
>
> One out so far.

"Leila, I owe you an apology. Harold just told me you're the chief executive. I'm so sorry."

"I am too, really."

"What do you mean?"

"It seems—it seems I've wasted my life."

> Martin looking—Rodriguez leading off first base; goes back. Here's the pitch—a swing and a hard drive between short and third! Amelia Young goes after it in left field. Rodriguez is rounding second. Young has the ball, throws to Violet Torres at third; Rodriguez sliding—safe on third! Torres throws underhand to second. Cypher going back to first; Torres throws to first, and ... Cypher is safe!
>
> Runners now on first and third—Asher Cypher on first and Mason Rodriguez on third.
>
> Still one out for the Leaders.

"How can you say that? Anyone would give anything to be as successful as you are. I'm flabbergasted! I feel honored to be sitting here talking to you."

"Thank you, Harrietta. But I liked it better before you knew. Can we go back to that and pretend I'm just that stranger who came to sit by you?"

"I don't know. I'll try. Are you sure?"

> Leaders' shortstop, Miles White, number 66, comes to bat.

"I'm sure. Thank you."

> Martin winds up. The pitch—a swing, a grounder to short. Number 76, Abigail Wilson, picks it up and throws to catcher Henry Baker at home base; Mason Rodriguez is **out** at home. Baker throws to second—not in time; Cypher is safe.
>
> Two outs with two runners on base: Miles White on first and Asher Cypher on second.
>
> Jackson Moore, number 13, is up next. He's first baseman for

the Day and the Hour

> the Leaders.
> The pitch—low and inside. Ball one.
> Low and outside. Ball two.

"Could Victoria be trying to load the bases for them?" Leila asks.

> The pitch—low and inside. Ball three!

"Homer is up next. I can't believe she's doing this," Harrietta confirms.

> The pitch—high and outside, ball four! Jackson Moore walks, and the bases are loaded with two outs.
>
> Homer Foster bats next. ... Homer is the captain of the team as well as being the starting pitcher today.

"Harrietta, I would give anything to have a son like that. I have no children. You have chosen a better way of life than I have."

Harrietta puts her arm around Leila. They are both teary.

> Homer swings and hits! It's a grounder between first and second. Emma Taylor, right field, is on it. She throws to first. Asher Cypher coming home. The throw to first is on time; Homer is **out**.
>
> And the Leaders go down with one run at the end if the first inning.
>
> The score: the Hornets one; the Leaders one.

Amidst the general cheering by the Leaders fans, Harrietta stands, wiping her eyes with a tissue and shouting, "*Good going, Homer!*" She waves, trying to get his attention, but he goes back to the bench without looking up and sits down with his back to her.

"Leila, I'm worried that Homer isn't ready for tomorrow."

"Is he not a believer?"

"He's not a believer in the Rapture."

"Perhaps something will happen to change his mind."

"It was a wonderful thing you did, writing that letter to your employees. I think some of them are going to be baptized today. In the next life—who knows? Maybe our spiritual children are the ones that matter. My Homer has turned his back on the faith he was raised in. I'm afraid he ...."

Leila puts her arm around Harrietta, who is taking out another

The Story

tissue.

Earl Clark has finished his inter-inning pep talk to the players, who are on their way out to their positions. He has turned around and is peering through the fence, surveying the fans in the bleachers. He ignores Filstein but spots Al Cypher with obvious displeasure. He acknowledges Harold and Harrietta; he waves and flashes a smile meant for Leila. Sizing up the situation, he guesses that she has been paying less attention to the game than to her conversation with Harrietta. He frowns again at Al Cypher and turns his attention back to the field, shaking his head.

> *We're at the top of the second inning, and next in the Hornets' batting order is shortstop Abigail Wilson, number 76. Returning to the mound for the Leaders is Homer Foster.*

"Leila?"

"Yes?"

"Tell me about Thursday."

> *Here's the wind-up, the pitch—Wilson swings: pop foul outside the first-base line. First baseman Jackson Moore is going for it and ... has it!* **Out!**

"Oh, it's a long, complicated story. ... He hasn't been very friendly since Thursday. I think he is upset over my becoming a Christian."

> *Violet Torres is up next. Don't be fooled, folks. This little girl can play ball.*
>
> *One out for the Hornets at the top of the second inning.*

"He never held it against anyone else as far as I know."

"Then I don't know. Apparently it's not about the Rapture because he doesn't believe in it."

> *Here's the pitch—there's the swing. It's a fly ball to left field! Grayson Green, number 47, was playing in close; he's going after it. It's rolling, rolling almost to the fence. Violet is going for second. Green picks it up—throws toward second base ... too late. Violet Torres is safe on second!*

"He is a complex man. How did you meet him?"

"I first learned about him as someone who was in violation of the regulation requiring licensing for residential maintenance work."

"He gives so much of his time to the community. The folks he helps can't afford to pay him for what he does for them."

"That's the first thing that impressed me about him. I couldn't allow someone to be prosecuted for benevolence, so I suspended the investigation and started going to his gym in order to get to know him in person. I discovered I wasn't the only woman who admired him."

"I know; several go there to be near him. But I'm sure none of them can compete with you."

"I don't know about that. I'm terribly naive about those things."

"So you haven't been married before?"

"Oh, no. I had never met a man I was thrilled about. In fact, I didn't know what it was to be in love until this week."

"He had a wife once, didn't he?"

"Yes. She got involved with a minister. After that experience, he vowed to remain independent of women and religion. It seemed I had become the exception—until he met Evelyn Newton."

"She came to our church and asked to be baptized. I heard she was here for the Reorganization. Nothing about her makes any sense."

"She's working temporarily for the Reorganization, on loan from the State Department—against her wishes."

"Forced? How could they do that?"

"Good looks aren't always a blessing. For Evelyn, it has meant extreme difficulties. That's why she has a bodyguard. Apparently, someone connected with the Reorganization wanted to use her beauty and charm to advance public relations. She was allowed to keep her staff; they always travel together—her secretary, a driver, and the bodyguard."

"I was wondering about the limousine. Now that part makes sense. Did she come on business or to see Pastor Murphy?"

"She came because she wanted to be baptized by Pastor Murphy. It was something she had wanted to do for a long time."

The Story

"He made it clear that they had been friends in the past."

"When they were in high school together in Appleton, Wisconsin, Evelyn picked a book from her father's library—from a forbidden shelf of books on arcane spirituality—and gave it to Adam to read. It was the type of thing that confuses evil with good, and he devoured it. Later, realizing what she had done, she repented of her disobedience and prayed for Adam's salvation. When she learned that he had become a pastor, she decided she would like to have him baptize her someday."

"It was Thursday when she came to church. You said Thursday was a crisis day for you."

"It was Evelyn's doing, really. Earl was quite taken with her. He invited her out to dinner, breaking a date with me, which I'm sure she didn't know about because she and I had met for lunch that day and become friends. Nevertheless, when I found out what he had done—that's when I went home and learned about the Rapture."

"Hadn't you heard about it before then?"

"No. I hadn't been following the news. I found I could survive two or three weeks without daily doses of disappointment. But at that moment, nothing could have been worse than my disappointment in Earl. As an escape, I checked to see what had been going on in the world. The first mention of the Rapture controversy got my attention, and I was able to get uncensored details that could be interpreted only one way."

"No one had told you? Not even Earl?"

"He did mention it in connection with the UN Bible confiscation scheduled for Monday, but I didn't understand what he meant. I was preoccupied with other things and didn't follow up with questions."

"So you became a believer in the Rapture. Then what?"

"What is left? It makes everything else almost insignificant."

"Then did you begin reading the Bible?"

"Yes. I had a Bible that someone had given me years ago. What really happened is, a faith I had in my childhood was reawakened."

"Were your parents Christians?"

"Oh, no. Not at all. It was through programs on satellite TV that I learned of Jesus. I was an only child born into a Muslim culture, and my parents, while not devout about their religion, were strongly anti-Christian. When I tried to tell my mother about our Savior, she took my computer and TV away."

"Then did they make you study Islam?"

"My parents were quite secular. My mother had become an atheist. I was young when it happened, and I acquired a fear of religion as a result. ... I was beaten. No, I was not forced to study the religion of my country."

"And where is that?"

"Lebanon. We lived in Beirut. I came to this country for college and did an internship with the FSA in Washington DC, after which I was hired full time."

"Do your parents still live in Beirut?"

"They were both killed in a bombing."

"I'm sorry."

"For the first time I feel that I belong somewhere besides the FSA—Earl, Pastor Adam, Evelyn, and now you. I never thought I needed a family before. It has happened so suddenly."

> *The score at the bottom of the second inning: the Hornets three; the Leaders one.*

"What happened to the second inning? The Hornets scored two more points when I wasn't looking."

"You were very attentive to my story."

> *Starting off for the Leaders, we have number 35, Evan Carter. Victoria Martin is back on the mound, pitching for the Hornets.*
>
> *Martin stretching. Here's the pitch—Carter swings! Strike one, a curve ball.*

"It was worth it."

> *Victoria is ready. The pitch—there's a hit, a grounder to left infield. Shortstop Miles White is on it—throws to first with Carter sliding in. ... He's safe!*
>
> *Number 22 is up next, catcher Logan Thomas.*
>
> *Martin winds—a fast ball. Strike! Thomas missed the inside*

The Story

*curve. Carter is stealing second. Baker throws to Martin; Martin to Scarlet Reed at second base. ... Carter is sliding in; Reed's foot is there first, and Carter is **out**!*

One strike now for Logan Thomas.

"Leila, speaking of new families, did you hear what happened at the Lakeview? On Tuesday around lunchtime, everyone there was instantly baptized in the Holy Spirit.

There's the pitch—strike two.

A new church family was born, and now they meet every evening at six for dinner and Bible study.

Victoria eying the batter. She delivers—a change-up. There's a bunt off to the left—the catcher has it, throws to Martin; she throws to first. ... Thomas is safe!

Pamela Evans was there, and they say that Clio—you know, the waitress? Well, she saw a light surrounding Pamela, and it was like an angel had appeared.

Grayson Green batting next. Number 47. Grayson anchors the bottom of the Leaders' batting lineup.

One out now for the Leaders.

Since then Clio has been on fire for the Lord. Apparently, she always loved history because she immediately delved into the Old Testament, and now she's teaching the adults while Pamela teaches the children."

*There's the pitch—a swing and a grounder between second and first. Scarlet Reed is on it—Thomas going by on his way to second. Reed throws to first. ... Green is **out** at first!*

Two outs for the Leaders. One man on base.

We're back to the top of the lineup: Oliver Hernandez goes to bat.

"Harrietta, may I ask you a Bible question about the day after tomorrow?"

... ball one.

"Okay, but maybe you should ask Harold. ... Go ahead. I'll ask him for you."

... ball two.

"What happens to those who are left behind?"

the Day and the Hour

The Story

Chapter 3

"Harold, what happens to those who get left behind tomorrow morning?"

... strike!

"Harold?"

"Yes, Harrietta."

The two-one pitch—ball three.

"What happens to those who get left behind?"

Strike two!

"They'll miss out."

"Leila wants to know. Can they be saved?"

"Yes."

Ball four! Hernandez walks to first.
With two outs, the Leaders now have two men on base—Logan Thomas on second and Oliver Hernandez on first.

"They can still be saved."

Next is Mason Rodriguez batting for the Leaders.

"Then why are we acting as though this is the end of everything?"

"Harold, if they can still be saved, then tomorrow isn't the end of everything, right?"

*... a swing and a hit. It's a fly over the infield. ... Scarlet Reed dropping back. ... The ball hits the ground. She picks it up, throws to Violet Torres at third. Logan Thomas has rounded third on his way home. Torres throws to Baker at home, and Thomas is **out**.*
That's three outs for the Leaders. At the end of the second inning, the score is the Hornets three and the Leaders one.

"Right."

"He says it isn't the end of everything."

"I'm glad."

At the top of the third inning now, Homer Foster is back on the mound for the Leaders. At bat is Scarlet Reed.

"Harrietta?"

"Yes?"

the Day and the Hour

"God still has a plan for them, just a different one. Is that right?"

> *... a swing and a hit. It's a high fly toward second. ... Mason Rodriguez has it!* **Out**!
>
> *The first out for the Hornets here in the third inning of the Autumn League championship game.*

"Harold, God has a different plan for them, right?"

> *At bat now is Victoria Martin.*

"Harold?"

> *The pitch from Foster—a fast ball over the inside corner. Strike one.*

"Yes, Harrietta."

"God has a different plan for them, right?"

"Watch, Mom," says Holly. "Homer is pitching to Victoria."

> *... a swing and a hit: a pop fly to the right, ... over the line. It's a foul, ... and Jackson Moore has it.* **Out**!
>
> *That's two outs for the Hornets with no runners on base.*

"Right."

"He says that's right."

> *Next at bat is Abigail Wilson.*
>
> *Foster winds up. The pitch—she swings and misses—a curve ball.*
>
> *There's the pitch—a swing! Strike two, fast and inside.*
>
> *The o-two pitch to Wilson—it's low, and she lets it go. It's been called a strike!* **Strike three**!
>
> *And the Hornets go down with no runs. The score: the Hornets three; the Leaders one.*

"Is one plan better than the other?"

"I always thought so. But let me ask him. ... Harold, is one plan better than the other?"

"One what plan?"

"You said God has a different plan for those left behind."

"God knows."

"He says God knows. I don't know if he knew what I was asking."

"Will the Great Tribulation start immediately?"

"I think so. ... Harold, will the Tribulation start immediately?"

"Yes, but not the Great Tribulation."

The Story

"How do you know?"

"Babylon isn't complete yet."

"He says no."

"Do you ever get impatient with Harold?"

"Always."

"Are men just like that?"

"Pretty much."

"I think so too."

> At the bottom of the third inning, Victoria Martin is returning to the pitcher's mound, and Julian Garcia is coming to bat as pinch hitter for Asher Cypher who has been retired from the game.
>
> The Leaders are trailing, three to one.

"That's odd," says Harrietta. "Asher is our best hitter."

Leila looks over to where Al Cypher was sitting. He is standing, obviously distraught. "This is not good," she says. "I think that's Asher's father standing up over there—the FSA officer in uniform."

"That's him," confirms Harrietta. "Al Cypher. He isn't thrilled about his son being taken out of the game. Do you know him?"

> ... there's a swing. Foul ball.

"Yes."

> Martin winds up—a swing and a foul to the catcher. **Out**!
>
> The first out for the Leaders in the third inning. No runners on base.

"Oh, look who's here!" Leila is waving to Adam Murphy, who has just arrived. "It's Pastor Adam. He sees us."

> Next at bat for the Leaders is Miles White.

Leila was already sitting close to Harrietta, leaving room on the bleacher seat. He comes up to sit beside her.

> ... there's a swing and a hit—a fly ball to left field. Amelia Young is reaching for it. ... The ball gets away from her. White is rounding first. Amelia gets the ball under control and throws to second. Miles White is **out**!
>
> Two outs in the bottom of the third inning, and no runners on base.

"I see the Hornets are ahead by two runs," he says.

"Still? I wasn't paying much attention. Harrietta and I were commiserating. She's worried about Homer; I'm worried about Earl."

"We're both worrying too much about both of them," says Harrietta, leaning forward to join the conversation. "How do you stop fretting about people?"

"That's what ballgames are for," he replies, giving Leila a wink. "Everything will work out in the end."

> *Next at bat for the Leaders is Jackson Moore. The score is three to one with the Hornets leading.*

Leila tries concentrating on the game, thinking, *Isn't this a bit incongruous? Here we all are, hours away .... I get it: we're trusting God.*

> *... It's a bunt! ... Moore makes it to first.*
>
> *At bat for the Leaders next is Homer Foster.*

"How did you feel Sunday Morning when you woke having had the dream announcing the day and hour of the Rapture?" Leila asks the preacher.

> *Martin looks, winds up, the pitch—he swings. It's a fly to center field. ... Dropped. Foster is on his way to second. ... No, he's going back to first. ... Too late: he's **out**!*
>
> *That's three outs for the Leaders, and at the end of the third inning, the score remains Hornets three and the Leaders one.*

"I thought it was nothing to be taken seriously. But it was so peculiar. ... I couldn't get it out of my head. I determined to say nothing about it, and yet I wound up telling the congregation in the middle of the sermon. A lot of people thought I had lost it, and I thought as much myself. I had always believed and taught that no one knew the answer to that riddle because it was a secret, just as Jesus had said. However, I won't deny that I, along with every other pretribulationist, was pleading for the answer because the enemy was threatening to destroy us. Our Bibles were being confiscated and the stage was being set for the Antichrist.

"When I got home, I called a friend who teaches at a seminary and found that he had the same dream. That was the biggest shock of all. It opened up the possibility of many Christian leaders having been given the same message.

> *Violet Torres batting for the Hornets.*

The Story

So I searched the Uninet and found there were others reporting the same thing. We all were given local times that reduced to the same universal time: four o'clock Sunday afternoon in London. After all the failed attempts by cultists trying to guess the riddle, here he came out and told us the secret almost at the very end. How sweet it was at first, but it wasn't long before the enemy knew, and he has been out this week like a roaring lion trying to bind us and blind people to the truth."

... strike one ...

"I don't understand how Earl can deny it," Leila says. "I don't believe he is blind to those things."

"A million Christian leaders agreeing on something is a miracle in itself," Adam remarks. "I don't know how anyone can deny it. ... It goes beyond natural apathy and misunderstanding."

... strike two ...

Looking back over the whirling events of the week, he perceives a vortex, a spiral becoming tighter by the hour, compressing possibilities to the point where corrections become impossible and repentance pointless. It forebodes little progress in the remaining hours, which precipitates bitter regrets.

... strike three ...

He reflects that he has not been as concerned for Homer as he might have been. *I've let Harold down. I should have reached out to that kid.*

Henry Baker is up next.

How many people out there—indeed, how many here in these bleachers—are whirling down toward the drain, ignorant or confused? Yet might they still be rescued from their delusions by just the right word spoken in time?

... infield pop fly ... ***out!***

He looks around at the little crowd made up of his townspeople, most of whose faces are familiar to him. He detects no apparent concern for tomorrow. *It's almost too much to accept; how could this be the last day?*

... Emma Taylor ...

It looks as normal as any Saturday morning at the ballgame—

the Day and the Hour

except the attendance is down a bit; and the visiting team is smaller than usual. It could strain one's faith to the breaking point.

> ... swings and misses ...

In all appearances Earl is right. For his and Homer's sakes I wish he were. And all these people—could they all be wrong?

In Noah's day they were all wrong.

Noah had years to preach the warning and discharge his obligation, not just a week. This is expecting too much.

> ... she lets it go—strike!

Is there anything I could do or say at this late hour?—if I weren't so committed to things that don't matter!

> ... **strike three**!

As the precious minutes pass, he sits incapacitated, doing nothing.

> ... Evan Carter is up for the Leaders.

After the game is over, he must spend his time performing predetermined and unavoidable tasks: the baptism of the saved, a wedding of no consequence.

> ... drive to the outfield.

If I were one of those old-time, salty preachers, I'd be standing on my seat right now ...

> ... right-field fence.

shouting warnings to these folks. But then ....

> ... safe on second.

It could turn out otherwise.

> ... Logan Thomas ...

The thought of going back to the way it was before Sunday is potentially petrifying and must be avoided at all costs.

Must the door be closed on doubts and locked absolutely? Does true faith need fear competition?

> ... fly to outfield.

Are not creative corrections shut out when faith blindly protects herself?

> ... **out** at home.

What is the proper attitude to this?

> ... runner on second.

The Story

Total trust in the word received must come first.

Trusting the Word, yes, but have I rightly read it? I think so, but I still worry!

Why not celebration? Is any worry worthy of unseating joyful anticipation of what lies ahead?

It really should be a time to celebrate.

　... Grayson Green ...

Then why be dejected, Adam? Why not let your witness to these people be your head lifted high with a happy countenance? You came in, in front of these folks, looking as though you were expecting to be tossed to the lions.

　*... line drive to third ... **out!***

The early saints may have been happier going to the lions, already tasting the sweetness of their salvation, than I have been today. I was under bitter conviction for escaping my duty—until I saw Leila waving!

So why, Adam? Why are you doing this?—submerging yourself in regrets over inevitable outcomes. If nothing went wrong, you would think you were dreaming of a different world!

He tries to imagine himself abandoned to the joy that lies ahead, mirth sweeping away sadness.

　... Oliver Hernandez ...

It doesn't work for me. He is unable. He would not feel free to act in a carefree manner right now. *I wonder why not.* The answer hits him as if it were the diagnosis of a deadly disease: he does not believe that the Rapture is certain.

　*... pop fly to the infield ... **out!***

Not with his whole heart does he believe it. Something is holding him back. O dreaded compassion that would wait forever and bolt the gates of hell!

　At the end of the fourth inning: the Hornets three, the Leaders one.

The fourth inning came and went, and Adam scarcely noticed what happened. Instead of taking in the drama of the game, making use of the diversion offered him, he dug down, turned over the rock of his soul, and played the game of startling himself

the Day and the Hour

with the creeping things beneath it.

"Pastor Adam?" Leila's voice is near his ear. "Are you all right?"

He swallows hard and struggles to bring himself back to his present company.

"I'm here," he says in a weak voice, "—just got carried away with regrets and forebodings."

She has turned toward him, and he is drawn to meet her eyes.

"I found the fourth inning a bit boring," she offers, relieving him of the need to explain. "The score stayed the same."

Her friendly face and intelligent eyes smite him from an entirely new direction. Here is a bright, cheerful soul freshly baptized in the Spirit and manifestly tinged with a holy light. The contrast between her hopeful radiance and his doleful brooding is the difference between day and night. He determines to make the best of what remains of this rare opportunity to enjoy her presence. It means renouncing his regrets. How easy she is making it already! There is no room for both Leila and his gloom. Or so it seems at this moment.

"We need some runners coming across that home plate," he says, stating the obvious in his eagerness to grasp the moment. "I thought Herne wouldn't do so well today against Earl's boys. And it appears they've barely scraped a team together."

Isabella Young, number 58, is leading off the fifth inning for the Hornets.

Harrietta leans over with a word of reassurance: "There's still plenty of time for us to win."

"Of course," replies Adam. "I'm sure Earl has everything under control."

... she swings and hits—a grounder out to right field. ... She's safe on first.

No outs here at the top of the fifth.

"Is that good?" asks Leila.

"For the team, I think so. But I know what you mean. We men have a lot of trouble with pride."

Sonya Stern, number 23, is at bat.

The Story

"It's not just men," she says evenly.

... It's a drive to left field. ... Isabella Young is safe on third.
*Sonya Stern is **out** at second.*

"You must be right."

Amelia Young, number 57, is up next.

"How do you manage to live with things being out of control?" she asks.

"It takes faith—lots of it," he replies curtly, determined to avoid revisiting the weighty subject.

... sinker—ball one.

"More than a mustard seed?"

"No," he replies, realizing that he owes her an explanation.

Leila marvels at the uplift of her spirits from being near the pastor. There is no room for him and her worry, or so it seems to her at this moment. She is feeling better about Earl already.

Ball two. Two-and-o for Amelia.

"I don't know anymore, Leila. I've had a terrible time accepting certain setbacks, but the game is helping me get over it." What began as an honest admission came out a lie. "No, that's not quite accurate," he confesses. "*You* are helping me get over it."

Ball three.

"I was thinking a while ago how incongruous it is of us to be sitting here watching kids play baseball when our time on earth is so short," she says.

Ball four. Amelia walks. Runners now on first and third.
One out for the Hornets at the top of the fifth inning.
Scarlet Reed, number 34, bats next.

Seeing an opportunity to switch the focus away from himself, he replies, "It's part of your job, isn't it?"

"Yes. I wouldn't want to be anywhere else right now. Am I wrong being primarily concerned about Earl, almost to the exclusion of everyone else?"

... strike one.

"It's exactly what I would do if I were you, honey," says Harrietta. "Same reason we're all here for Homer."

"The Lord hears your prayers and honors your dedication, Leila," replies her pastor. "Although Earl and I have been the best of friends, there is nothing I can do directly right now. I think he's a little sore about ...."

> *... strike two.*

"About Evelyn?"

"Yes."

"Is it my pride that hurts when I think about that?"

"I would have to say it is, but it's nothing to be ashamed of. It comes with love as we know it. There is a higher form of love that we will be experiencing more fully. In this life some of us are privileged to taste a little of it. It knows jealousy only for the freedom of others, not their bondage."

"That would be a great relief. I can almost imagine it. I'll try to be that way. I think Evelyn is one who knows that kind of love."

> *... pop fly ...*

"She has experienced a lot of disappointment and loss. That seems to be what develops the capacity for *agape* in people. It's one of those paradoxes."

"I loved her immediately, but I didn't know why or what to call it," says Leila.

"It can be infectious."

"I'm afraid Earl didn't catch any of it from her. I think duty is more on his mind than anything, and I'm not sure where that leaves love."

> *The bases are loaded, and Victoria Martin comes to bat for the Hornets.*

"Watch Homer strike her out," enthuses Harrietta.

"It would be ironic if she hit a homer," says Adam.

> *Homer winds up. There's a swing and a grounder up the middle—hits the pitcher on the leg. ... Homer has it, throws to first.*
> *Isabella Young, coming in from third, **scores**. Victoria tagged **out** at first.*
>
> *Homer appears to be unhurt.*

"You're a prophet," remarks Leila.

Adam laughs, which delights her, and she laughs too.

> *Abigail Wilson is up next.*

"What's funny?" asks Harrietta, demanding her share of the merriment.

The Story

"I'm sorry," says Leila. "It was a little play on words is all. I'm glad Homer wasn't hurt."

"He should have thrown home," Harrietta explains. "He was getting back at his girlfriend. Now they're leading the Leaders by three."

*... grounder inside the first-base line; Jackson Moore has it, and Wilson is **out**.*

At the end of the half inning: the Hornets four, the Leaders one.

"Harold just said we only have twenty-one hours," Harrietta announces. "Pastor Adam, have you had time to think of the glory of it?"

"Such knowledge is too wonderful for me; I cannot attain unto it."

"Isn't it true that people longed for this day hundreds or even thousands of years ago?" asks Leila.

Mason Rodriguez is up for the Leaders.

"Yes. We're incredibly privileged," replies her pastor. "If we were given the choice of when to live, out of all of the ages of mankind's existence, I'm sure we would choose today. But I pity those who will remain here through tomorrow."

*... a drive to shortstop—**out**.*

"What about Earl? Will he have to endure the wrath to come?"

Julian Garcia is up next.

"I think not, but it's something I can't explain. Earl is unable to desire heaven right now, and that compels him in the direction he's going. But it could turn quickly."

"Will he change before it's too late?"

"I hope so, Leila. It will be a miracle."

"And if he doesn't .... Is everyone who gets left behind cut off from being with us?"

"Jesus Christ is coming for his bride. That includes us as well as all who have died in Christ."

"Could there be exceptions?"

"I suppose there could be. Most rules have exceptions."

*... pop fly to the infield. ... **Out**.*

"Before you came, we were saying that tomorrow isn't the end

the Day and the Hour

of salvation," says Harrietta.

> *Miles White, number 66, is up.*

"That's true; the game isn't over tomorrow," the pastor replies. "Tomorrow starts the interlude before the seventh inning. It's appointed that many will be saved; others will be immersed in severe delusions."

> *... grounder to second. Scarlet Reed has it, throws to first—out.*
> *At the end of the fifth inning: the Hornets four; the Leaders one.*

"I hope he doesn't have to suffer," says Leila.

"Most all of these folks we see here will be suffering a great deal. Some of them have heard of the coming calamities; a few have read the book of Revelation. Some have been led to disbelieve what it says about the future by teachers who have been misled themselves. Others are indifferent. It has been a constant desire of mine to find a way to communicate the urgency of taking God's Word seriously. Now, here we are, and time has run out."

"I know it breaks your heart," says Leila.

> *At the top of the sixth, batting first for the Hornets is number 45, Violet Torres.*

Adam falls silent, brooding again, but on a happier note: *What an enormous blessing to belong to this family—these dear people: the miracle of Leila and her testimony, my faithful wife spending her morning visiting her hostile sister, ...*

> *... strike one.*

Harold over there—what a stalwart guy he is.

He feels overwhelmed by this blessing, the privilege of being a member of this family.

Was that you, Adam, so downhearted during the fourth inning?

What a difference it makes to be thankful.

> *... strike two.*

Yet that setback was real. Was it a reality check?—to alter the tone of your ministry?

If there was any value in it, how late it was!

Or was it a partial truth inspired by the enemy and put there to discourage you? You need not answer: it's too much to attempt

The Story

to comprehend right now.

That's one reason to be thankful that the time is short!

*... **strike three**!*

However, the concert this evening, mandated by the government, is such an unfortunate event that he continues to resent it. The church is required to present something of interest to the entire community once each month. Tonight's concert was scheduled months ago.

Henry Baker comes to bat.

"Trust me, Adam."

"Who said that?"

"Who said what?" asks Leila.

... throws to second—safe!

Emma Taylor is batting next for the Hornets.

"Somebody said, 'Trust me, Adam.' It sounded as if it came from the PA system."

"I didn't hear it."

"It was clear as a bell."

"Was it timely?"

"Bless you, Leila, it was timely!"

*... **out** at third. Taylor slides to second—safe!*

"I heard a mysterious voice last night," she says softly. "It seemed to come from the airplane's radio, but I don't think it did. Has anyone mentioned last night's beautiful sunset to you?"

"No. Did we miss one?"

"I'm not sure. I heard this voice say it was for me. I thought I was seeing the colors of heaven. But Earl didn't see the same thing, though he was right there. I would be afraid to tell that to anyone else."

Back to the top of the order, Isabella Young, number 58, is up.

"Tomorrow morning we'll find out, won't we?"

"Whether we're both crazy?"

Homer gets his sign.

"Um-hm."

*... **strike**! It was a high, wide curve.*

"I'm excited to be baptized."

the Day and the Hour

"Did anyone tell you that fifteen more will be joining you?"

"Are they FSA people?"

"Ten of them are your employees, two are their spouses, and three are their children."

... ball ...

She brought all these folks to the Lord in one day, and I haven't made one convert all week. "Leila, whether it's right or not, I'm proud of you, and I wish you were my daughter. It will be my joy to baptize you. There's nothing I would rather be doing."

... the one-one pitch—strike!

"Thank you. Don't forget Evelyn. Without her, there would be no baptism tomorrow."

... grounder to second.

Adam is quiet.

"Did I say something that's troubling?"

*... **out** at third.*

"Evelyn will not be coming. She was notified last night that they're taking her to Baltimore today. It's a government flight, and it couldn't be changed."

"Excuse me," says Leila. "I have a call. ... Evelyn, nice to hear from you. ... That's wonderful! I've been wanting to talk to you. ... No, we went flying instead. ... Earl's upset about something—hasn't been himself since Wednesday night. ... Pastor Adam happens to be right here sitting next to me. We're all at the baseball game."

The Story

Chapter 4

"Evelyn wants to talk to you. She didn't have your phone number."

Number 13, Jackson Moore ...

"Adam, I'm coming! I talked to the mechanic who is taking care of the plane while we're here. I told him I needed to keep an appointment to be baptized. He's grounding the plane until this evening."

... fast ball—strike!

"How did you manage that? Did you smile at him?"

"No. I didn't even see him. All it took was a phone call. I told him where I needed to be at 2:30, and he said he would come up with a reason to ground the plane until late this evening."

"Did you get his name?"

"He said his name is BJ."

... strike!

"I know him! He used to have the maintenance shop here at our airport, back before general aviation got regulated into near extinction. He still comes over occasionally to service the mayor's plane and the few others we have left. He's a good man—comes to Grace Bible Church when he's in town."

"So you see, it wasn't my charms at all."

... fly ball to center field.

"Don't be too sure about that."

***Out*!**

"I know. But you love me anyway. Earl's place is on Beach House Road, is that right?"

Homer Foster batting ...

"That's right. Turn at Shore Drive off Mountain Highway; then turn right onto Beach House Road. It's the first driveway on your left."

"I'll see you there about two o'clock. Is that too early?"

"I'll be there."

43

the Day and the Hour

"What do I need to bring?"

"Bring a change of clothes or a swimming suit and a towel if you have one."

"I can't wait."

> *... a swing and a miss.*

"Our waiting is nearly at its end."

> *... Hornets four, and the Leaders one.*

"Thank God for BJ, Leila." Adam's gloom is gone altogether.

"Who's BJ?"

"He's the mechanic servicing Evelyn's plane. He's grounding it until tonight."

> *... hard crack to left ...*

"It's wonderful how things turn out," Leila says, her voice betraying doubt.

> *... second baseman ...*

"It will become more wonderful each hour from here on," Adam assures her with soaring optimism.

> *... **out** at first.*

"What do you have planned after the game?" he asks.

> *Number 35, Evan Carter ...*

"Earl invited me to join his sailing class, which starts at one o'clock. Maybe I will have some time alone with him if I go early."

> *... low inside—strike.*

"It sounds like the sailing class will be getting over just as the baptizing starts. ... And after that?"

> *... strike.*

"I don't know what will happen. I want to be with him, but I don't know what he has planned. What will you do after the game?"

> *... strike.*

"There's a wedding at one o'clock. I'll have to be there a little early, of course. That reminds me: I need to unlock the church for those folks as soon as the game is over."

> *... four; the Leaders one.*

"Pastor Adam?"

"Yes, Leila."

"Do you think adoptions will be allowed in heaven?"

The Story

"That's an interesting thought. I don't know. But I don't see why not."

At the top of the seventh inning ...

"What happened to the sixth inning?" Adam asks.

"They played it," says Harrietta.

"Apparently, I'm losing my grip on the world already," he says.

"At least we kept them from scoring another run," says Harrietta. "If Homer can keep up the good pitching, we still have a chance. Victoria doesn't have as much stamina as he does."

Sonya Stern comes to bat. She scored the first run in this game back in the first inning.

Homer has his sign. There's a big windup—a fast ball over the outside corner; she lets it go. Strike one.

"There's Alice!" Harrietta is on her feet, waving. Alice Murphy sees her and is hurrying up to join them. "Scoot over and make room for Alice," she instructs everyone.

*Here's the pitch—down the middle. A hard hit to third. Carter blocks it, recovers the ball, throws to first; Stern is **out** by a narrow margin.*

One out; no runners on. Top of the seventh; the score: four to one.

Alice comes up the steps, smiling and obviously happy to see them but also expressing surprise at finding a pretty woman sitting between Harrietta and her husband. She sits down next to Adam and reaches for a hug and kiss.

Amelia Young, number 57, comes to bat.

"How was Lavelle?"

"My poor sister—I don't know what we can do. Her minister was there when I arrived."

"That must have been interesting."

"It was indeed."

... lets it go, but the pitch was good—strike.

"I would like you to meet Leila. Leila, this is my wife, Alice."

"Oh, I'm so glad to meet you. I understand you're being baptized this afternoon. Welcome to the family of God. How is it with Earl?"

"He's still all Earl, I'm afraid. There, he's waving at us."

the Day and the Hour

... foul ball ...

"How did you manage with two disbelievers against you?" asks her husband.

"It turned out to be the other way around. She had seen the light and embraced premillennial theology as well as our pretribulation Rapture."

... strike.

"That's fantastic. ... What did her minister think about that?"

*... **Out**.*

"It was the *minister* who made the turnaround. Lavelle was furious! They were in a big argument when I got there. Then I went into the kitchen with the reverend, and we had a friendly talk. She is extremely excited about tomorrow.

Scarlet Reed, number 34, ...

But Lavelle was yelling from her bedroom the whole time, so she left before long."

"How did Lavelle treat you after that?"

"She clammed up and wouldn't say a thing. Is there any hope for her?"

... straight to center ...

"I believe there is. She might have died peacefully with her cancer, but now ...

*... **Out**.*

she's struggling against something,

... end of the first half of the seventh, the score: still four to one.

and it could well be the Spirit of God."

Logan Thomas, number 22, is up. He had two balls and a strike his first time at bat.

"Has it been a good game?"

"I got here late, but I think Leila and Harrietta have seen the whole thing."

"I'm not much of a sports fan," Leila says. "But it has been fun to watch these kids play. Homer is quite the pitcher."

... hit hard into short field—fumbled, recovered. The throw to first ... is too late. Logan Thomas is safe on first base.

"I see they're playing the Herne girls," Alice remarks.

"There is one boy on the Herne team, that's all," Adam says.

The Story

"And they barely have nine players. Fortunately, none of them has been injured."

"Nevertheless, they're winning," Harrietta adds.

Grayson Green, number 47, comes to bat.

"We need three points to tie the game; we can do it," she continues. "Grayson will get a hit, I'm sure."

*Victoria winds up; here's the pitch—it's a bunt! Green is off to first. Baker gets the ball, throws to Garcia; Garcia throws to first —Thomas on his way to second—Green sliding: he's **out**. Thomas is safe on second.*

One out for the Leaders.

The Leaders fans are cheering wildly.

... number 49 is up next.
The pitch—low. Ball one.
Victoria waiting. ... The pitch—ball two.
The two-and-o pitch—ball three! Low and outside.
Here's the windup and the pitch—low. Ball four.

The fans are standing, shouting encouragement to the next batter, Mason Rodriguez.

Runners now on first and second. One out.
Eli Davis, number 14, coming, replacing Mason Rodriguez.
Bentley Williams, number 28, will be replacing Julian Garcia.
Eli Davis now at bat. Eli is fresh and eager. Let's see what he can do for the Leaders.

*Martin wiping the ball, getting her sign. The windup, the pitch —Eli swings: a hit into deep right field. Emma Taylor going back for it. ... It's over her head. Thomas rounds third. Hernandez rounds second. Emma is after the ball, picks it up and throws. Shortstop Abigail Wilson goes for it. Thomas crosses home and **scores**. Hernandez rounds third. Wilson is on the ball, throws to Martin—Davis on his way to second. Martin throws home to Baker; Hernandez sliding; Baker has the ball ... safe! Hernandez **scores**, leaving the Leaders with three runs and a runner on second.*

The Fosters are all on their feet, except little Hannah who is on Harold's shoulders. Leila, Adam, and Alice stand up, as it is the only way to see. The fans are screaming and stomping on the bleachers.

Still only one out now. The score: four, three.

the Day and the Hour

The coaches have gone to the lines at first and third.

Bentley Williams, number 28, is coming to bat.

Everyone remains standing, but there is sudden silence in the home stand. It seems that no one dares take a breath.

"Now I can see the game, Daddy," says Hannah from her perch on her father's shoulders."

Here's the windup and the pitch—a swing and a hit to short field; Scarlet Reed has it, drops it, throws to first—Davis going to third. Good throw to first, caught by Sonya Stern; **out** *at first. Stern throws to Martin, Martin to Violet Torres. Davis is safe on third.*

The home crowd, tense and hopeful, is letting off steam again with shouts and whistles. Nearly everyone believes that the Leaders will not be left behind.

Miles White, number 66, coming to bat.

Cheers go up: "Miles White, Miles White, Miles White ...".

Davis is leading off; Martin throws to Torres; Davis goes back and is safe.

The ball goes back to Victoria. She winds up; here's the pitch— a fast ball, wild and outside. Ball one.

*Davis leading. Victoria eyes him, fakes a throw; Davis steps back. ... The pitch—a swing and drive up the middle. Scarlet Reed has it—Davis closing in on home—Reed throws to Evan Carter; Eli Davis sliding home—***out!**

The final score: the Hornets four, the Leaders three.

The winners of the Autumn League Tournament this year of two thousand—a loud horn blast comes from behind—*the* **Herne Hornets!**

"Thank you for letting me sit with you," Leila says to Harrietta.

"I'm so glad to have met you, Leila. I don't think of you as the FSA chief."

"Thank you. Please don't ever because I'm not anymore— except ...."

She looks to see where Earl is. He is in a heated discussion with Al Cypher. No doubt, Cypher is arguing that they would have won if Asher had been left in the game.

"Except, I still have to finish one duty: I'm supposed to be keeping an eye on Earl."

The Story

"You will be seeing him at the baptism," Harrietta reminds her. "Goodbye. God bless you."

Leila waits to see what will happen with Earl and Al Cypher. *It's a good thing there's a fence between them.*

Earl looks past Cypher to Leila and winks. Cypher turns to look and sees her watching them. He says something to Earl, nods to Leila, walks a few paces, hesitates, gets a signal from his son to go ahead without him, and heads for the car marked *FSA Security*.

Leila goes to the gate in the fence to wait for Earl. While standing there, she notices a woman with flaming-red hair step down from the bleachers and go chasing after Al Cypher. (Almost everyone knows Pamela Evans. Leila remembers seeing her before—who would not!—but does not know who she is. The name meant nothing when Harrietta mentioned her in connection with the Lakeview church.)

"That's highly irregular," Leila remarks under her breath. But she has no desire to inquire about Al Cypher's actions today.

Earl is talking with the coaches. Finally, he picks up his bag and comes to the gate, looking dejected.

"I blew it, didn't I?" he says to Leila.

She turns to walk beside him and puts her hand on his shoulder.

"You sure did. But I enjoyed the game."

"I noticed you were sandwiched right in there between those church folks."

"Yes, I enjoyed that too. And I'm looking forward to sailing with you. Will the weather be suitable?"

"It's hard to say what it will do."

"I'll be there anyway. One o'clock, right?"

"Yeah."

Earl goes his way, with Officer Filstein following a few paces behind him. Leila lingers on the spot where they parted, watching him go, her car being in the opposite direction. Harrietta and the girls are getting into the Fosters' Chinese Electric 240, which is parked next to Earl's antique military jeep. Homer, Victoria, and Asher are walking together with a couple she guesses are Victoria's parents. Harold intercepts Earl while Filstein continues on to his patrol car parked not far away. Apparently, Harold and Earl are engaging in serious discussion.

Leila turns around and walks back toward the school parking lot. Having lingered after the game longer than others, she is the last one to go in that direction. Adam Murphy had parked in the school lot too, and she sees his unique little car driving away. In spite of her anxiety, she cannot help chuckling at the comical "brickmobile."

†

Pamela had nearly caught up with Al Cypher.

"Are you ready to meet the Lord, Al?"

He turned to see who was following him.

"Not in public, Pamela."

"You'll regret it if you don't turn to Jesus Christ now. He's the way, the truth, and the life."

"Look, Pamela. I can put you in jail for saying that."

"There is only one way to escape the wrath of God, and that is to believe Jesus Christ died for your sins and accept his offer to save you. Otherwise, you will be guilty of ignoring this great salvation."

"That may or may not be true, but *you* are guilty of breaking the law, and I'm going to lock you up!"

The Story

On his way to unlock the church for the wedding party, Adam Murphy caught a radio news report.

    These results just in from the latest Pulpit poll:
    10% believe the classical Rapture will occur.
    15% believe it will be a mass UFO abduction.
    20% believe in the earth-cleansing Removal.
    15% believe nothing will happen.
    25% believe nothing.
    10% don't have an opinion.
    20% never had heard of the Rapture.
    3%   believe they will be included in the Rapture.

    These statistics were compiled from a survey of three thousand clergypersons from three hundred denominations and nondenominations, combining data from thirty polling agencies.

†

Adam is having an early lunch with Alice, which will allow him to be back at the church for the wedding preliminaries well before one o'clock.

"I'm afraid this is all we have left. I've cleaned out just about everything," says Alice. "It isn't much."

"That's all right. It's better than having food go to waste. Where did these cookies come from?"

"I think you know."

"I never saw them before."

"There was a dozen of them in the refrigerator behind some old items I got rid of. They were in a glass bowl with **EAT US** on the lid, laid out in currants. I thought you put them there as a joke."

"Not I. There must be some mischief here."

"The refrigerator hasn't been as cold as it should be. I had to reboot it again. It's getting worse and worse. Maybe they grew there."

"That didn't have anything to do with it."

"If you're sure they're not fungi, I'll eat one," says Alice, taking a nibble.

Not wanting to be outdone by Alice's famous daring, Adam

takes one of the cookies and bites off half.

"Not bad," he says. "Tastes like a cake baked with oil. What is it?"

"I don't know. Am I growing taller?"

"It isn't a mushroom. You'll have to take more than a nibble if you expect it to have drastic effects."

"You're right: they are good. ... Did you ask Felix about dinner tonight?"

(Yesterday, they decided to ask this man Felix, whose real name is Paul Christian, to join them for their last meal on earth. Who Felix is and why he is here is explained in another book.)

"I forgot. I'll call him right now. ... He's not answering or taking messages. He may be visiting someone. I've never seen anyone so bent on evangelizing the neighborhood. He's not wasting any time."

"If we're having company for dinner, I'll be fetching some groceries. It will take a little time to prepare it too. I planned to go right after the wedding."

"I'll let you know as soon as I'm able to reach him. Wouldn't you need to pick up a little food for us anyway?"

"I planned to have pancakes. I thought you wouldn't mind."

"It would be okay with me."

"There's nearly a full bag of flour; I have two eggs left and a can of beer. There's a quarter pound of butter in the freezer, and that bottle of maple syrup Earl gave you for your birthday still has some in it."

"It sounds like we would have enough pancakes for Felix too."

"I'd die before I'd serve pancakes to company for dinner! That would be as bad as leftovers."

"You're right. Perhaps Felix wouldn't care too much, but I agree: we should treat him as well as we can for all his efforts."

"Have another what-is-it."

Adam's phone rings.

"Hi, Philip. How did the meeting with your employees turn out? ... No kidding? ... No kidding! ... Wow. ... That would be fine

The Story

—if you're sure they're sincere and they understand. ... All right, brother. I'll see you soon."

"How refreshing!" exclaims the pastor.

"What happened?"

"Philip's employees are all confessing Christ, not in spite of the Rapture but because of it. He's pretty sure some of them will want to be baptized. He wanted to check with me first before asking them."

"Oh, this is grand, isn't it?" exclaims Alice.

"Earl will be surprised. ... I think we best leave it that way."

the Day and the Hour

Following tradition, members of both teams repaired to the Lakeview after the game. The rule is that the managers share a table, and the manager of the losing team buys lunch for the manager on the other side.

Victoria Martin's parents went to sit with another couple while she and Homer took a table together. Victoria invited Asher to join them.

There had been discussion in the car on the way over about the outcome of the game. Various theories explaining why the manager replaced Asher with an inferior player were put forth. Only Asher was silent; he alone knew of the animosity his father held for Earl Clark, and he suspected that Clark had reason to dislike his father. Nonetheless, that he should be caught in the middle of the conflict seemed unfair. While walking into the restaurant, Earl had spoken to him and offered his sympathies, which lifted his spirits a little, but as recompense for what seemed to be unfair treatment, it was insufficient.

While waiting for their lunch orders to be taken, the discussion resumed:

"I'm not a natural baseball player," Asher admitted. "I work hard to keep my batting average up. So I score our first run and then get replaced by a guy who doesn't practice and can't hit."

"Garcia didn't last long," said Homer. "A foul, a pop-fly out, and he never got to base or caused a runner to advance."

"He hesitates in his swing," said Victoria. "It's like he doesn't have his heart in the game."

"So Mr. Clark put Williams in, who isn't much good either," said Asher.

"One swing and he was out, but at least he got Davis to third," said Homer.

"Little good it did: he never made it home," said Asher.

"I liked pitching for Williams," said Victoria. "Did you see the grin on his face? He was thrilled to be in the game. But I'll have to agree: he didn't merit such favor. I think your manager had some

The Story

other purpose in mind besides winning the game. Maybe it was to give more of your guys a chance to play."

"I know what it is," said Asher. "He has something against my dad."

"Victoria's lunch is on the house for pitching a winning game," said Clio. She was reaching over the table, pouring water.

"Thanks," said Homer. "I was going to pay for it."

"If you're not going with us tomorrow morning, you need to be saving your money, kiddo," Clio replied.

"I'll have one of these," said Asher, as he pressed the Select button next to the picture of the lamb gyro being featured on the tabletop display.

Clio put the pitcher down next to the picture and took out her dinerPad to take orders from the pitchers. Victoria was tapping the tabletop, paging through the menu.

"Homer?"

"Just bring me a ham sandwich," he said, leaning back with his arms folded.

"I'd like the chicken-salad sandwich," said Victoria. "Do you want me to select it here?"

"I've got it," Clio replied. She picked up the pitcher. "Hold on to what you believe, dear. Don't let Homer fill you with doubts." She started to walk away, and then she turned and added, "Listen to what she says, Asher."

"How did she know?" Homer demanded, as soon as Clio was out of earshot.

"The Spirit is moving," said Victoria.

"I thought she was a witch," said Asher.

"Don't you know what happened here on Tuesday?" Victoria asked. "Everybody in Herne heard about it."

"I know because my aunt was involved," said Homer. "But that doesn't have anything to do with it. Everyone knows about the rule for being on the team, so how did she know Asher isn't committed anymore?"

"I haven't told anyone but Homer," Asher confirmed. "But I

don't care who knows. We need to listen to the prophets."

"There's no way for it to happen," countered Homer. "The laws of nature don't allow it."

"There are spiritual laws that are higher," said Victoria.

"That's right," said Asher. "There's a new nature."

"They can't just come along with something that goes against what's always been taught," maintained Homer.

"The Spirit can," said Victoria. "Your church no longer rejects it, so why do you keep saying it's a hoax when everyone believes it isn't?"

"I don't think everything that gets reported is true," Homer replied.

The Story

Chapter 5

By the time Al Cypher had checked Pamela into the last unoccupied suite in Detention Suites, his anger had cooled. His dislike for Earl Clark was nothing new, of course, and Clark's taking his son out of the game was predictable, for the feeling was mutual. Under normal circumstances he would have brushed off Pamela's indiscretion and simply driven away, leaving her standing on the sidewalk, rather than enforcing the law she was violating.

Now it struck him: he had jailed one of the town's leading citizens over a triviality. He had been consumed with evil thoughts about Earl Clark and had made a dreadful mistake with a foreseeable outcome.

"Pamela, I'm sorry about this. You caught me at a bad time. I would take you right back to the ball field if I could. But the system has picked up your biometrics, and I won't have the means to cancel your residency until Monday. In other words, you're logged in as a prisoner, and all kinds of bells and whistles go off if you try to leave by yourself. You can go out with me as your escort for a limited time, but you have to stay with me until we come back. I think you would rather remain here. But if you have an errand to do, let me know, and I'll take you. Call Phil if you like, and I'll let him in to visit you. But the bell goes off after an hour, and then he'll have to leave for the day.

"I'm really sorry this happened. At least the jail is a pleasant one. But I'm afraid you have some bad company. The other suites —I almost said cells—are occupied by a bunch of rough guys: the homeless gang the cops rounded up yesterday morning.

"It's time for the noon meal, and since I'm warden, cook, and waiter, I'm going to be taking the food to the table. I'll let the guys out into the dining area to eat. It works better that way and keeps the rooms clean. You can join them if you wish. So make yourself at home if you can, and let me know if there's anything you need."

the Day and the Hour

Having finished his discourse, Cypher walks out, leaving Pamela alone. Her door closes with sounds of secure latching.

She takes out her phone and calls her husband.

"... It's plush. In fact, it's nicer than our house."

"When can I come up to see you?"

"Whenever you can get away."

"I'll need to go to the baptism since nine of our employees plus one spouse and a child want to be baptized; so I really should be there. I'll come right after that."

"That's wonderful! ... I see you're back at the store."

"It's giving me a chance to explain things to customers. I'm having a conversation with one of them right now."

"You can tell me about it when you get here. I'll let you go now. Don't forget to find yourself some lunch."

She picks up the remote control for the entertainment center and sinks into the easy chair.

The News button produces a menu of stories:

> Poll: Majority Say Something Will Happen
>
> Media Planning Live Coverage
>
> Celebration Parties Scheduled
>
> Olympia Shrine Mobbed
>
> Pope Announces Full Cooperation with UN
>
> ET Threat Focuses on Evangelicals
>
> Flights Canceled
>
> Gridlock in LA

She points to the third headline. It brings up a woman at a news desk reporting on this growing phenomenon:

> *Around the nation, politically active people on the left are waking up to the likelihood of the removal of the remnant of the religious right. The awareness is spreading rapidly, and we're seeing hundreds of websites announcing massive cannabis parties tomorrow afternoon.*

The *Live Coverage* menu item brings back the same

The Story

newswoman:

> All major media outlets are making arrangements for live coverage of the Rapture event—which is no longer being called the Rapture but rather the Removal, keeping in line with the Vatican view and also the majority interpretation of the apparent UFO presence.
>
> As one would expect, it is proving difficult to find individuals who are both sure of their disappearing and willing to have reporters capture their convictions on camera. Consequently, the focus will be on the three largest East-Coast churches where regular services are scheduled at times that include the Hour.

The audio cuts out, and Cypher's voice comes over the speakers: *"Your soup is ready, Pamela. I'm unlocking your door."*

the Day and the Hour

Grace Bible Church's fellowship hall has become a banquet room. Ellen Miller, the bride's mother, is fussing about the flowers being late even as Flo is bringing in vases with the blooms fully arranged and setting them on the linen-clothed cafe tables. With only half an hour before the ceremony begins in the sanctuary, Ellen is striving to have everything perfectly in order before the first guest arrives.

The string quartet is setting up after she had them move to a different corner of the room—again. She has just discovered that artificial strawberries are part of the table decorations while chocolate-covered strawberries are included in the dessert, and she is pressing the caterer for an immediate remedy while keeping an eye on what the florist is doing. She wants to rush over and advise Flo, but she must first make sure that the caterer will be following through with a suitable solution to the strawberry conflict.

Ellen's husband is in the foyer, where it is relatively peaceful, passing the time with the ushers. They are standing by the glass-paneled entry door, watching the parking lot for early arrivals, some of whom will have come a long way.

The Story

The cloud layer that dominated the sky earlier today has thinned and is becoming broken: small patches of blue have expanded and are merging together. A freshening breeze out of the south promises good sailing.

Leila arrived early, as she planned. Expecting that Earl is readying the boats, she walks around to the side of the house. From her vantage point there she surveys the bay and lake. There is a spit, a low point of land, jutting out from the shore on the right to form the harbor, and just beyond it, in the main body of the lake, is a police boat. Down on the dock, Earl is stepping off the float onto one of his sailboats.

The brick-paved walkway that Leila is on leads from the driveway down three broad steps under the sprawling limbs of a yellow-leaved maple tree. From there the path branches to the right, sweeping around the corner of the house to the side yard and on down to the beach.

The house is known as the Beach House. Earl rents it from Ken and Karen Martin, who reside in the other dwelling on this little bay at the north end of the lake. The Beach House was built by Ken's grandfather in 1930 when the town was thriving on timber and gold and when no building restrictions were in effect. The back of the two-story structure is barely twenty yards from the water's edge. To the right are the dock, a sandy swimming beach, and the shop in which Earl builds his boats. It is a delightful property, and the beach makes a perfect baptistery in good weather.

Earl is bailing rainwater from the cockpit of the boat as Leila steps onto the dock, and as she approaches the floating portion to which his boats are moored, he stands up, squeezing water from a sponge.

"Hi. I came a little early to see if there's anything I can do to help you get ready. If not, I'll understand and stay out of your way."

"Leila, you're something. Sure, you can help. It looks like

the Day and the Hour

you're dressed for it too. Boat shoes?—great. Here, take the sponge. There's a bit of rainwater in each boat—not enough to use a bucket for; the sponge works fine. It's against your environmental rules to squeeze it overboard; but since I'm already a rulebreaker, I'm not concerned about that. Shall I get you a bucket?"

"No. It's an insulting rule. I'll ignore it too even though they're watching us with telephoto video."

"They've been out there since I got back from the game. Can't you call them off for a while?"

"I could try, but I don't think it's worth the risk of getting them into trouble for violating procedures. My surveillance officer is on board, and he will discourage the policeman from taking note of our illegal bailing activity."

"I'm going to get the oars. After you finish sponging, I'll let you remove the mains'l covers."

Earl expects to be using four boats. He likes to have two students in each one. Five have signed up for the lesson today. If they all come, it will work out just right for Leila to be paired with one of the more capable women.

The Story

The bride is late, and Ellen is frantic. It is one o'clock, the hour of the wedding. The stream of guests has dwindled to a trickle, and all have either been seated or are being seated. Ellen has come to the foyer. She is looking in at the doorway to the auditorium, surveying the audience. Her husband is staring out through the entry doors, watching for the bride.

"Adva thinks if she's on time she's early," Ellen whispers to the usher standing beside her. "The groom is here, I assume."

"I think he's with the pastor."

"Go and find out," she commands.

She goes to help her husband watch the parking lot.

"Do you see her car? That girl! Late for her own wedding!"

The usher reappears.

"Apparently, the groom isn't here yet," he reports.

"That explains it," Ellen declares. "They're together against my orders. She's always late for everything."

"I'm sure they'll be here in a moment," her husband assures her.

"Go tell Asaf he can start the music," she instructs the usher. And to her husband: "I hope she's wearing her dress. There's no time for dressing now."

"She had it on this morning," he replies. "I told her she looked nice. But I won't be surprised if she comes in wearing pants after all."

"It wouldn't surprise me either. I'll bet that's what she's doing: leaving her dress at home and coming late so there will be no time to change."

"We should have insisted she wear dresses to church when she was younger," says her husband as if his insight solves the problem.

"I know. But she always hated dresses."

Alice appears, smiling brightly. Alice loves weddings.

"Ellen, you look delightful. ... Is there a problem?"

"Kids are so irresponsible. The bridesmaids should be out here

the Day and the Hour

right now. Would you please go see what's taking them so long?"

"You know how it is, Ellen. Every hair has to be in place. I'll be right back."

"Is Adam ready with the groomsmen?" Ellen inquires of the usher.

"I don't know."

"Please go make sure they're ready."

"They're here: there's her car," Adva's father announces. "Probably, you could be seated now, so folks won't be wondering."

Ellen walks briskly across the foyer to the sanctuary doorway.

"You may escort me to my seat," she says to the remaining usher.

As Adva's father watches, a strange couple emerges from the car and heads for the door.

"Uh-oh," he mutters.

Adam comes around the corner from the hallway.

"Have you seen the groom?" he asks. Adva's father is peering out more intently than ever, trying to find another car like his daughter's.

"No, we haven't," he answers, without turning to look at the pastor. "We haven't seen the bride either. We think they're together."

Alice is back.

"I can't find the bridesmaids. I don't know where they could be."

Asaf is repeating the prelude.

Adam has the groom's number in his phone and is trying to call him: no answer. Adva's father is calling his daughter's phone: no answer.

Both ushers are watching them, and Adam can see through the doorway that people are looking around and talking in whispers. He sees Ellen sitting stiffly in the front pew, her head motionless.

None of the groomsmen is known to Adam. "Can you call the best man?" he asks Adva's father.

"I don't remember what his name is."

The Story

Adam is about to ask Alice to try to contact one of the bridesmaids, but she already has her phone to her ear.

"Janie, this is Alice at church. Where are you? ... You're at home? ... It's canceled? ... Who told you that? ... Adva did? ... Oh, no!"

She drops her phone into her purse and bites her lip.

"It sounds like they called it off without telling their parents," observes Adam.

Asaf has turned up the volume of the music. The whispering in the auditorium has broken out into chatter. Family members in the front rows are looking back and trying to explain the delay to each other. Except Ellen. She remains as still as stone.

Adam motions for one of the ushers to come over.

"It appears that the wedding has been called off by the bride," he informs him. "Please go tell Ellen, and ask her if she would like you to escort her out." Turning to Adva's father, he asks, "What shall we do?"

"Might as well go ahead with the reception—er, let's call it the party."

Ellen is coming back up the center aisle with the usher. Her face appears to be carved stone. If anger and embarrassment rage within her, there is no sign of it.

Pastor Murphy walks down the side aisle on the left and takes the microphone as Asaf quiets the music.

"We have had a change of plans," he announces. "The wedding ceremony has been called off but not the party; the best part is still going to take place. I've seen the tables and the food, and I assure you that you will not be disappointed. The ushers are coming to conduct you out."

Asaf launches a rousing recessional as the ushers march down the center aisle to release the family.

The word whispered and somewhat embellished has spread from the ushers to the ears of everyone: the bride and groom eloped. Reactions are mixed. Some of the women are sympathizing with Ellen and are nearly as stern faced as she. The younger folk are taking it lightly, some of them apparently extolling the wisdom and courage of the couple in their secret rapture. Some of the older men are shaking their heads; others are grinning.

Ellen and her husband have been seated at a table for four at the far end of the banquet room where hors d'oeuvres have been brought to them. Adam and Alice hurry in ahead of the crowd and join them. The strings are playing a baroque piece as family and guests file in and take places at the tables. The caterers are bustling in and out, bringing trays of food and arranging the buffet table. The omission of the ceremony is having no effect on the way people respond when food is present. But Ellen's stony face has not softened, and she will not eat.

It is an awkward time for Adam and Alice. Ellen's husband is silent as well. Regardless, the spirit in the rest of the room is undampened. The brief catastrophe has bound the guests to a single purpose, which is to let Ellen know that they have forgotten the original reason for being here and are appreciating the party. It is beginning to affect her a little. She takes a bite of an olive and a sip of water.

Everyone has been fitted into the hall, and Ellen realizes for the first time that nearly all who declared intentions of attending have indeed come and have stayed for the banquet. She expected that her decision to go ahead with the event on the eve of the Rapture would not be respected by everyone. While most of the groom's family is unchurched, many others are believers and have made a sacrifice to be here on their last day on earth. These thoughts are bringing a little life to her broken heart as she stares at the centerpiece on the table. Occasionally she glances up.

One of the women of the church catches Ellen's glance, and she cannot restrain herself: She gets up and goes to express her sympathy. Bending over Ellen's chair, she puts an arm around her. Ellen does not respond outwardly, but she is moved a little by the gesture.

It did not go unnoticed. Others follow. More goodwill is being

The Story

shown to her in this very personal way than she has experienced in a long time, if ever. A major cord of her personality has been stretched to its limit, and it snaps: Ellen suddenly loses her concern for appearances.

She is experiencing something new and of great worth, a thing far removed from the propriety and precision that was her life. Ellen never much appreciated a hug since those long-forgotten days of her great disappointment before her own wedding. Each one she now receives is priceless, worth more to her than her system would have admitted was possible. A trial smile comes to her face, and she cares not that tears are marring her makeup, for a burden has been lifted. The new freedom leaves her feeling at first as though she cares about nothing. Her heart was severely damaged, and it can no longer hold the cold, heavy stuff of her perfectionism. That has drained out and is being replaced with a light, warm, airy substance made of touches and embraces, tender eyes and kind words.

Men and women of all ages are stopping by on their way back from the buffet table with second helpings and new findings on their plates, complimenting her on the fine food, the exquisite music, and the fun company. Their sincerity is partially proven by their laughter heard above the sounds from the musicians. She finishes the food on the plate that was brought to her.

Pastor Murphy is curious about something. He asks Ellen whether Adva talked about the Rapture.

"All the time. I got tired of hearing about it."

"What about her fiance?"

"He was just as bad."

The pastor picks up his glass and a spoon and stands up.

Most people in the room remained conscious of the corner in which the bride's parents sit, and they notice Adam's standing and tapping the glass. Others hear the ringing, and the banquet hall becomes quiet.

"Friends, I would like to say a brief word. I'm Adam Murphy, Ellen's pastor. As we can well understand, her heart was broken.

the Day and the Hour

What you may not know is that it was broken not by her daughter, but by God. Sometimes he does that. Tomorrow, he will be breaking into the lives of every one of us in one way or another. In many cases it will be painful. In the years of my ministry I have seen many broken hearts. One thing I have observed is that when God breaks a heart, it always turns out well. If you belong to Jesus Christ, as Ellen does, you never have to fear what God will do to you. If he breaks your heart, he will mend it, and someday you will be happier than you ever thought was possible as a result of it. Thank you for listening."

Ellen stands up as the applause dies, and the room falls silent. She is drying her eyes with a handkerchief as she begins to speak.

"I would like to apologize to you all. I wanted to go ahead with the wedding because I thought it was my right, and God had no business interfering with it. Adva, however, did not see it that way. It was her hope of a happy marriage and children, not just a wedding ceremony, that was wrecked by the Rapture announcement. Yet she was happy about the prospect of seeing the Lord, and she could talk of nothing else. I should have known she was right. She had the better attitude.

"So first I'm asking for your forgiveness. I want to tell you that I don't care about appearances anymore, and I wish I had time to pay you back with kindness for all the stress I have caused by my striving to make everything and everyone perfect."

Ellen pauses. She knows what the second thing is that she wants to say, but if what she just said was uncharacteristic of her, the next thing is totally out of character. Yet she feels a burning desire to say it. A glow descends upon her, and the words come easily:

"Secondly, since Adva is not here, I'm going to take up her cause and tell you that tomorrow morning at eight o'clock, my family and I are going on an adventure that is beyond anything you can imagine. In fact, we are married to Christ in a way that we can only call mystical now; but when we are with him, every joy we have known will pale in comparison. There will be a wedding

The Story

feast that will make this one seem like we've been eating ... dog food."

Ellen surprised herself with the entire speech, but this final expression—the outrageous incongruity of it is a hit. She breaks out laughing, as does the rest of the party. Cheers and whistles complement the loud applause.

"Your wife hit a home run," the pastor remarks to her husband. James is his name—it just came to me.

the Day and the Hour

The Story

Chapter 6

"We will row out toward the middle of the harbor before putting up the sails—one sailor at the helm and the other on the oars. First, get well away from the dock and the shore; then turn, row into the wind, and raise your mains'l.

"*Willow* will go first, so you ladies step aboard. One of you go up to the bow to receive the mooring line, and the other get your oars ready. I'll cast off your lines.

"I'm releasing your bow line. The wind will swing the bow away from the float. Here's the line; keep it out of the way and out of the water. Now, get those oars into the rowlocks and pull away from the dock. Here's the stern line, helmswoman. You do the steering and let your shipmate concentrate on pulling the oars. I know, they take a little getting used to, but you will soon have the boat moving steadily forward."

Four students had come for the sailing lesson—two women and two men—out of the five expected. That meant only three boats would be needed.

Earl's fleet consisted of four sister sailboats, nearly identical except for their names: *Willow, Winner, Wind Chaser,* and *Walter.* They were seventeen-foot, classic, wooden, pocket-cruiser sloops with cuddy cabins and ample cockpits. *Winner* would be left at the dock today.

All students except Leila had attended Earl's shore school a week ago. They knew how to handle the sails, in theory at least. This would be their first time on the water. Lacking the benefit of any prior instruction, Leila would accompany Earl in the instructor's boat and learn whatever she could absorb as an observer. The two ladies, as we have seen, were assigned to *Willow*; the men would sail *Walter*. Earl would sail *Wind Chaser* with Leila being his passenger.

The lesson, as Earl had explained it, would consist of beating

the Day and the Hour

to windward and then running home before the wind. Each boat had an intercom radio, allowing the students to hear the instructor from a distance.

"*Walter,* you're next. You saw how it's done. Here we go."

"*Willow!*" he shouted, for *Willow* was already several boat-lengths away, and the breeze made noise in one's ears. "When you get a chance, bring the fenders in and stow them under the cockpit seat on the starboard side.

"I'll hold onto the bow line while you get those oars ready. Okay, here we go, *Walter*—swinging away from the dock. Take the bow line back to the cockpit with you. ... Dig those oars in and pull; try to keep the blades vertical when they're in the water, or they won't do any good. Here comes the stern line. Now, get some headway on.

"Okay, Leila, let's get aboard *Wind Chaser.* You can operate the tiller if you like, and I'll do the rowing. Don't worry: I'll tell you what to do. Go ahead and step aboard while I cast off. I'm going to sit facing the bow, so I can see the other boats."

"*Willow,* keep rowing!" he shouted. "And helmswoman, turn up to windward now, and hold your course straight into the wind.

"*Walter,* lift your oars clear of the water then reach forward, letting the blades swing toward the bow; then dip them in, keeping the blades vertical, and *pull hard.*"

Wind Chaser, having come around from the opposite side of the float, was leaving *Walter* behind under Earl's powerful stokes with the oars.

"*Willow,* now raise your mains'l!" Earl called out to the leading boat. "Keep heading dead into the wind!"

Looking back over his shoulder, he directed more encouragement at the lagging vessel: "*Walter,* keep pulling! Steer a little more upwind because you're drifting sideways!"

Earl was closing in on *Willow,* enabling him to give them directions without shouting so loudly.

"*Willow,* now turn to port slightly, heading off the wind just enough to steady your mains'l, and sheet it in. ... You're sailing!

The Story

Bring your oars aboard. ... Now, quickly unfurl your jib. ... Now, sheet the jib in, but not too tight, and haul the main in as close as you can."

Earl shipped his oars, letting *Wind Chaser* coast.

"Leila, see the intercom there on the seat next to you? Would you hand it to me?" He reached behind his back, and she placed the device in his hand.

"*Willow*, head off the wind, a bit more to port, but not too much," he said over the intercom radio. "You want to keep those sails pulling you forward. Ease the jib sheet if you fall off too much. It's okay to have it luffing a little: you want to hold close to the wind until you get to open water."

He looked over his shoulder, back at *Walter*.

"*Walter*, you're doing fine. Concentrate on making long, steady pulls with those oars. And steer upwind more: toward me. We want to get you more to windward, away from the lee shore.

"I'm going to turn around and face the stern now, so I can row more easily," he said to Leila. "Also, I get to look at you. Keep an eye on *Willow*. Here, take the intercom and hang the lanyard around your neck. Channel one is *Willow*; channel two is *Walter*. We need to get *Walter* to where *Willow* was when they raised her sails, but they should be a little more to windward in case they have trouble."

"Aye-aye, Captain. ... *Walter*, you will need to steer toward the middle of the bay. And hurry! You don't want the girls to get away from you, do you?" she taunted, smiling at Earl.

"That should have some effect," said Earl, grinning.

"I'm not sure they heard me. ... Oh, I see: they're switching positions. Evidently, the helmsman thinks he can do better at the oars."

"How is *Willow* doing?"

"She's off to a good start, making progress toward the lake."

"*Walter* is coming along better now," he observed.

"Shall I bring the fenders in?"

"Yes. Go ahead, please."

the Day and the Hour

Leila left the tiller, scrambled over the oars as Earl continued to row, and collected the fenders from the port side, tossing them into the cockpit; then she stepped back over the oars and resumed her position at the helm.

"Tell *Willow* to come about before getting too close to shore."

"*Willow*, be sure you leave room to come about. Remember, you will drift downwind fast if your sails are not filled, so be quick and always keep an eye on the shore."

"When did you teach sailing?"

"It just seemed the thing to say. I must be absorbing it from you."

Leila located the fender stowage under the starboard cockpit seat and put the two air-filled tubes away.

"Are they coming about?" Earl asked her.

"*Willow*, are you thinking about coming about?" she prompted.

"What do you call it when you switch over to the other side of the wind?" she asked Earl.

"The other tack. It would be the port tack."

"*Willow*, go ahead and switch to the port tack. Put the tiller hard over to the port side; then when the bow comes across the wind, release your port jib sheet and quickly sheet the jib in on the starboard side."

"Don't tell me you figured that out by yourself."

"It seemed simple from here, but I thought they might be forgetting what to do. That's the way it always is with my employees before I get them trained."

"Where did you learn about coming about?"

"I was watching you on Monday afternoon, remember? I heard you say, 'Coming about.'"

"Let's see if we can get *Walter* to put up her main."

"*Walter* helmsman, go ahead and raise the mains'l. Rower, pass the—"

"What do you call it?"

"Halyard."

The Story

"—halyard to him; then keep rowing. Helmsman, keep steering while you hoist the sail, and keep your bow pointed into the wind."

"How was that?" she asked. "It's just what you told the other boat."

"Except you embellished it considerably."

"That's because I thought *Walter* needed everything spelled out as you were doing with them when they were having trouble with the oars."

"You did fine, Leila. You were right to keep them rowing, under the circumstances. How is *Willow* doing?"

"They're trimming the jib on the port tack and picking up speed. I think the girls have gotten the knack."

"I'm going to raise our sails. Keep an eye on *Walter*."

"Shall I unfurl the jib while you raise the main?"

"Go ahead."

"*Walter* has her main up," Leila reported. "But it doesn't look right."

"The luff isn't tight. It looks like they didn't use the winch."

"*Walter*, you need to get the sail all the way up. Rower, turn around and use the winch on the halyard. Helmsman, try to keep the bow pointed straight into the wind until the luff is tight."

Wind Chaser's sails filled as Earl and Leila adjusted the sheets. Leila was thrilled at the sensation of the boat's response, gliding forward so easily, being pulled by the invisible wind—drawn by the wind into the wind itself.

"*Walter*, that looks better. Rower, keep pulling on the oars a little while longer. Helmsman, steer a little off the wind to the port side just until the sail starts drawing."

"Nice call, Leila. Now, let's see if we can get them to unfurl her jib."

"*Walter*, ship your oars and haul your main in tight. Helmsman, unfurl your jib, but hold your tiller steady too. Use your knee."

"Earl, please hand me the winch handle when you're through,

and I'll sheet our jib in closer. We're picking up speed already."

"You're really getting into this."

"It's fun! ... *Walter's* jib is flailing, and their main is luffing too."

"We had better go back. Tell *Willow* to slow down because they're leaving us behind, *Walter* being so poky here. Tell her not to point so high."

"*Willow*, you're leaving us behind. You don't have to point quite so high now that you've cleared the point. Ease your main and turn away from the wind a bit. You will go faster without making as much progress to windward, but keep an eye on the lee shore too."

"Let's jibe and sail back to *Walter*."

"Turning to port?"

"Affirmative. We'll be on the opposite tack. Say 'jibe ho' and watch your head."

"Jibe ho!"

The breeze having become brisk, the little boat shuddered as the boom quickly swung across the cockpit to the starboard side, and the mains'l filled again with a *crack*.

"Let the jib out; we're going to be running downwind," commanded the captain as he payed out the main sheet, letting the boom swing wide over the starboard side.

"What happened to the wind?"

"It's amazing, isn't it? Going with the wind, we're subtracting from its speed rather than adding to it."

"I see. We're still moving right along, but it's not quite as thrilling. ... *Walter* has gone over to the port tack, and her jib is back winded."

"Tell them to let her main out a bit. We need to get her moving ahead through the water."

"*Walter*, pull your jib sheet in on the starboard side, and release it on the port side. Then let your boom out a little more. Keep your present course until you pick up speed."

"As soon as we get even with them, we'll come around to a

The Story

reach."

"What's a reach?"

"Across the wind. How's *Willow* doing?"

"She's disappeared behind the point—all but the tops of her sails."

"Have her switch to the starboard tack now."

"*Willow*, we can't see you. Come about now to the starboard tack. Try to keep us in sight.

"Coming up to a reach!" she exclaimed to Earl excitedly. "I'll trim the jib."

"You're not leaving much for me to do," complained the captain.

"I'm having too much fun. Just haul that main in, and we'll see how fast we can go. Does it look like *Walter* is ready to get back on her course for the harbor exit?"

"I would say so. They could point higher first, but that might be too hard for them. Just have them come about."

"*Walter*, come about now—helm to the lee: to your right, turning to port. ... Now, release your starboard jib sheet. Keep the helm over, and bring your bow across the wind. ... Hold it there! Now, sheet in that jib and make those sails work!"

"Good job."

"Hey, Captain, we're sailing now!"

"You're getting the hang of it, Leila. Soon you'll have the rail in the water."

"I'd better come about first. I wouldn't want to ram the dock! Ready about?"

"Why did you say 'ready about'?"

"Are you ready? I hope so because here we go. Helm's alee! ... I thought it sounded good. What should I have said?"

"'Ready about' is correct, you sailor. So's 'helm's alee.'"

"*Walter*, haul your mains'l in closer now, and steer as near the wind as you can while keeping it full. Sheet your jib in close too. Try to make the mouth of the harbor without spilling any wind."

"I can see *Willow* now. They're cooking," she reported.

the Day and the Hour

"Let's hold back until we get *Walter* out to the lake."

"*Walter*, round up a little. You don't need to have the rail in the water. I know it's fun, but you're not pointing high enough to make the entrance."

"I'll head off a bit; I'm easing the jib," she announced to the instructor.

"No, not yet—unless you want to sail circles around them. Let's remain close hauled and point high enough to let the sails luff some, which will slow us down. ... I think *Walter's* main isn't nearly flat enough. See how the top is twisted? It looks like they're not making use of the traveler."

"Is that the track where the main sheet attaches to the boat?"

"That's right."

"*Walter*, look at the top of your mains'l. See how it's luffing? Move your traveler outboard, and put more tension on the main sheet. The top of the sail is important. Try to keep it full."

"Now, look at *Willow*. She has the same problem with her jib. Tell them to move the fairlead forward."

"*Willow*, since the wind has picked up, you can move your jib fairlead forward to flatten the top of the sail and keep it from luffing."

"*Walter* is zigzagging. Tell the helmsman to hold it steady."

"*Walter*, you're doing better, but you're oversteering. Try to keep your heading steady. Don't move the tiller so much at a time. Just make little corrections."

"Let's go ahead and cut downwind of *Walter* on a reach; then we'll take a port tack out of the harbor."

"*Wind Chaser*, we're going sailing now!" Leila exclaimed.

"Ease into your reach; I'll let the main out gradually."

"We'll need a jib-sheet fairlead adjustment too," she observed.

"You're right. Give me a little slack, and I'll slide it forward."

"Look, *Walter* thinks we're racing her."

"Tell them to keep on the wind."

"*Walter*, we're not in a race. Your job is to get out of the harbor. Keep heading as close to the wind as you can without luffing your sails. And try to *steer straight!*"

"I think *Walter* envies our speed," Earl said. "Will you run my boat for me in the next race?"

"I'd love to, you know that. Bring our main back in a little, just with the sheet; leave the traveler fully extended."

"Now you're showing off."

"I'm sorry. This is such fun. How far is safe to tip over?"

"Don't say 'tip over,' that sounds like 'capsize.' Say 'heel over.' These boats will come back up even if they're knocked down—as long as the cockpit doesn't get swamped."

"I can let the rail go under, then?"

"Sure. But not too much, or we'll be making too much leeway. The keel loses much of its effectiveness when we're heeled over too far."

"So we drift sideways?"

"Right. I'm surprised you're not a little bit afraid, leaning way over like this."

"Why should I be afraid when you're my captain?"

Leila was on the starboard side of the cockpit with a foot braced against the opposite seat, holding the tiller with both hands and halfway standing due to the angle at which the boat was heeling.

"How's the pressure on the tiller? It looks like you're having some difficulty holding her down."

"I love to see the water rushing by; I'd hate to let up on it."

"I'll try to balance the sails a bit better. I'm going to winch the jib in tighter to make the center of effort move forward."

"That's better: I can feel the difference. Do you think if we came about now we could clear the point?"

"No, I don't. It's deceptive. The boat will make more leeway than you think. But we can always take another tack if need be."

"If we came about now, we would cross *Walter's* course—behind her, I think," Leila said.

"I agree. We can always fall off if we come too close. We definitely don't want to cross her bow. So let's come about now and give your arms a rest."

"Shall we round up into the wind first on this tack?"

"That's a good idea. Go ahead. You may be surprised."

Leila turned up to about sixty degrees off the wind, and the sails started luffing.

"We weren't on a reach! Is that the surprise?"

"We were, but you were making so much of your own wind by going fast that you were almost close hauled on the reach."

"I was wondering about that, but it was exciting; I didn't want to change anything."

"As we slow down, you can follow the apparent wind and turn closer to the true wind."

"Got it."

"How is *Walter* doing?"

"Look at you," she said, ignoring his question, "sitting there all relaxed with your back to the wind. You *could* turn around and look for yourself!"

"I'm enjoying watching you. For me it's more fun than sailing."

"If you're trying to make me your slave, you're doing it well. ... *Walter* is bumbling along; at least she's on the same tack. *Willow* is out in the middle of the lake again."

"Are we going to cross behind *Walter*?" Earl quizzed her.

"It will be close."

"Hopefully they remember they have the right of way and will hold their course."

"Shall I come about now?"

"Go ahead. Do I have to do anything?"

"Maybe not; we'll see. The main is already pretty well close hauled. Ready about?"

"Ready."

"Helm's alee."

"Here, let me take in the jib sheet. I was just teasing. You won't be my slave."

"I wouldn't mind."

The waves from the body of the lake were coming directly into

The Story

the bay at that point, and while they were on the reach they rode over them slowly. Now, as they turned, heading directly into the wind for a moment, the bow of the boat lifted, cresting a large wave, and then splashed down into the next trough, sending spray back to the cockpit.

"Did you get wet?" asked Earl.

"Just a little."

"We'll see how it is when we settle into the groove. There's foul-weather gear below if we need it."

"Is this what you call foul weather?"

"No, not really. But I want you to be comfortable."

"I'll let you know. So far I'm not cold."

"That's because you're sailing the boat. I'll be getting cold before you will at this rate."

"You're right. I can see we're not going to clear the point."

"Can you tell whether we'll collide with *Walter,* the way we're going?" It was a question he would ask a student after covering the technique in shore school.

"Her angle to us isn't changing, so we'll be coming close. Is that the right answer, teacher?"

"You're acing the class, Leila. It's still hard to believe you haven't been sailing before."

"If it isn't you, then it must be the author. That's the only way I can explain it."

"Just in case *Walter* would become alarmed, let's fall off and let ourselves pass behind them by a good margin."

"Aye-aye, Captain."

"You don't have to call me captain."

"What shall I call you, then?"

"If we weren't out here with so much to do, I would tell you. I guess it will have to wait."

Every few seconds, a wave smacked the port bow and sent a plume of spray back, wetting the deck and sprinkling the cockpit.

"*Walter* is coming about, or trying to," she informed him.

"It's a little early. It means they might have to take an

the Day and the Hour

additional tack in order to get out of the harbor—if they ever do get out."

"Shall we close haul again?"

"Yes. We'll scoot out of the bay and out of their way. They're far enough from the lee shore not to get into any real trouble."

The wind had been gradually gaining strength, and *Wind Chaser* seemed to like it better. She leaped from wave to wave, throwing spray at every impact. Earl smiled broadly as Leila found just the right tiller pressure to keep the speed at maximum. In almost no time, it seemed to them, they were closing in on the point. They came about with the finesse of a racing crew and soon passed the point with the lake opening up on the starboard side, revealing the buildings on Lake Way arrayed along the shoreline and the little police boat bobbing like a cork a hundred yards distant.

Willow was not in sight. Earl leaned back to see more on the left side ahead, for a great segment of the view was blocked by the headsail. As he leaned back, the wind caught the bill of his hat and carried it away.

"Hat overboard!" he yelled.

Leila saw it fly by, and she immediately shoved the tiller to port, which swung the bow to starboard, into the wind. The sails fluttered and rattled violently, sounding as though they would shake themselves to pieces.

"See if you can hold her in irons," Earl shouted above the racket. "I'll furl the jib."

Leila had never heard the term *irons* before, but it sounded like something preventing the boat from turning right or left, so she endeavored to keep the bow pointing straight into the wind as *Wind Chaser* coasted to a stop.

The tiller became lifeless. Earl had sheeted the main tight and was attempting to steer by moving the traveler and forcing the boom by hand to one side and the other.

"Keep the helm in the middle," he said as the boat began to drift backwards.

The Story

Leila was looking for the hat. She was standing on the cockpit seat, steadying herself by hanging onto a backstay, and keeping a foot on the tiller. The wind whipped her hair into her face.

"It's back there quite a ways, I'm afraid!" Earl shouted. "It won't stay floating for long."

"I see it!" Leila exclaimed, pointing to her left with her free hand.

"You can help me steer with the rudder. Turn it just a little: not too much or it will get away from you."

She was already feeling a renewed force on the tiller. She jumped down and grasped the long handle, holding it in the neutral position, and then tested the reaction as she moved it a little to the port side of the cockpit. It had an immediate effect, forcing the stern to starboard. She could not see the hat from her lowered position, but she thought she knew approximately where it was, and she gently nudged the stern toward the spot as the boat began sailing backwards.

"Can you see it from where you are?" she shouted to Earl.

"Not yet. It may have sunk."

The shaking and rattling of the mains'l was nearly constant.

"There it is!" he exclaimed. "We're backing straight toward it."

"I see it!" She needed to turn a little to the left. Then she had a decision to make: whether to back straight to it or attempt to come alongside of it. She decided it would be better if the hat came to the middle of the transom even though there was a possibility that the rudder might snag it first and cause it to sink.

The hat was now only a few feet away, but it had become submerged. Still, she could see it through the backs of the waves. She tossed the intercom aside and stretched herself out, hooking the tiller with her feet and hanging over the transom as far as she dared. She could reach the water but not far below the surface. Closer it came. In a few seconds, there would be an instant when she might be able to grab it.

Just then a bright aluminum shaft came down before her eyes. Earl had a boathook and had thrust it below the surface with its

the Day and the Hour

hook positioned perfectly to intercept his hat. The boat was swinging off course, but the hat was now in contact with the hook, and Earl raised it up. It slipped off. It was about to be run over by the drifting hull. He took a swipe at it, and it went to one side and then quickly disappeared under the transom.

"It's gone now," he said. "Nice try."

"Won't it come out on the other side?" she gasped.

"I'm sure it'll be too deep by then."

"Can you help me get back up?"

Leila was still hanging over the transom, precariously close to falling overboard herself.

Earl stepped back into the cockpit, dropped the boathook, and put a strong arm around her, lifting her gently up onto her feet. She tried to turn around and almost fell over, but he had grabbed a backstay to steady himself, and with the other arm he held her to his side. She looked up into his face, and he kissed her on the forehead. She put her arms around him, and he still held her close with the one arm. She stuck a foot back onto the cockpit seat, and raising herself up, she reached his lips and kissed him.

"That's all right, Samson. You have another hat at my place. What was it you wanted me to call you?"

"I'll tell you when we get to shore. We're still in the classroom, you know."

The Story

Chapter 7

Philip Evans anticipated that parking at the Beach House would be a challenge, and he considered it his duty to do something about it since he was responsible for as many as nine additional vehicles potentially vying for a place in Earl's driveway. (After checking with Pastor Murphy about inviting his employees, describing the experience in his upper room this morning, he telephoned each of them and got an enthusiastic response in every case, excepting Russell who considered himself already well baptized.)

Philip knew about the original arrangement, as everyone did. The mysterious beauty, an old friend of the pastor's, would be returning to town in order to be baptized in the lake. He assumed that she would arrive in her limousine, for such people once accustomed to their amenities are loathe to give them up. He also knew that Leila Labaki had decided to piggyback onto the occasion and be baptized too.

He was not sure that Earl knew about the extras. He thought it likely that he had not made provisions for managing the parking for such a crowd. Therefore, Philip assigned the job to himself.

Philip knew nothing of the FSA employees responding to the invitation during last evening's meeting at the church since he and Harold were out dispensing warnings of the wrath to come. His wife had not told him about it since Pamela did not know about it either, she being involved with the Lakeview church at the same hour. A total of ten FSA employees had requested that Pastor Murphy baptize them along with two of their spouses and three youngsters. That meant ten more cars would likely show up at the Beach House in addition to the nine driven by the store employees plus Philip's own car and the Murphys' car and the two vehicles of the original baptizees, making a total of twenty-three. Philip had forgotten about Earl's Saturday sailing class, so those four cars had been omitted from his accounting. The grand total would be twenty-seven vehicles, assuming no other friends, relatives, church members, etc. would be driving in.

Philip assumed that the limousine would be expecting to use the driveway. Therefore, his preliminary plan was to have all others park on the road and let everyone walk down the winding drive to the Beach House.

As Philip arrives, he finds a car with LEILA on its license plate, parked on the shoulder of the road just past the Beach-House driveway. He goes fifty feet beyond it and parks with his right wheels in the weeds.

The weather has been adjusted for the baptism: The remaining fragments of the overcast have risen to form puffy white clouds drifting by the sun. The lively wind that drew the sailors forth has driven them home again; and after completing that task, it slacked off and became a breeze for a short while before going elsewhere, leaving only occasional rustlings in the bright maple leaves.

†

Down on the bay the remaining waves, having nowhere else to go, are washing up and dying upon the shore while out on the spit the stronger waves of the lake continue to break on its far side, making a hollow sound apart from the rushing wind that called them forth.

On the docks, *Willow's* crew has neatly flaked her sail, the little ship being safely moored back in her place at the float. *Walter* is coming in with splashy strokes toward her own mooring spot, her mains'l hanging in an awkward lump on one side of the boom. Earl and Leila are ghosting in close to the dock, unwilling to lower the sails while any trace of the breeze remains, coaxing *Wind Chaser* to catch every stray current of air that wanders by.

†

Beach House Road consists of one narrow lane, and its shoulders are nearly nonexistent. Philip estimates that he can provide all of his employees (former employees, but he is not used to that yet) parking spots along the road even if some have to be scrunched against the bushes. What does one care about a few scratches on a car soon to be left behind?

As Philip walks back toward the driveway, his right-hand man arrives. He motions Lonnie to park just behind him.

"Glad you made it, brother," says Philip. "I get to call you 'brother' now, you know."

"I was thinking you'd be my son—if we're in the Lord's family together. But if you want me to be your older brother, that's fine."

"We'll have to work that out later. ... I think that's Lindsey's car coming, isn't it?"

"Looks like it."

"Would you stay up here and have our people park on the shoulder as far over as they can? We don't want to block the road in case Karen needs to get her truck out. Also, we'd better leave the driveway clear for the limo. I'm going to go and check the situation down there. Maybe there's enough room for the pastor's car too."

Lonnie directs Lindsey to park behind his car, leaving space for perhaps two or three more between hers and Leila's.

Philip hurries down the long, curving driveway. Near the end he discovers the four cars of the sailing students parked well to the side. Fortunately, they are all very small cars. It appears that there will be enough room for the limousine to squeeze by if the driver is careful. Earl has put a sign on the door of the main garage.

> **DO NOT PARK HERE**
> **LEAVE DRIVEWAY CLEAR**

Up on the road, Jeremy is arriving, followed by Joanne. Lonnie has them park behind Lindsey's car.

Having seen all there is to see, Philip walks back up the driveway. He is familiar with every turn since he lived at the Beach House himself for nearly nine years, well before Earl came to town. There is a straight section about mid way where the hedges are farther apart and the pavement is wider. It would easily accommodate the pastor's car—actually, three or four of the pastor's cars. Alternatively, it could accommodate the limousine without preventing passage around it. Philip decides to use the latter arrangement, confirming his original plan. Otherwise, the limo would have to park some distance down the road, for the spot behind Leila's car that he is reserving for the pastor is not spacious enough for anything but a compact vehicle, being limited by a large cedar tree.

Conway, from the Drinking Water and Wells Department of the FSA, is arriving with his wife, Coral. These being unexpected guests, Lonnie is unsure whether they should be allowed to go down the driveway. The driver is likewise unsure; he turns tentatively into the drive, stops, and lowers his window because Philip is walking up the middle, blocking his way.

Lindsey comes around the corner from the road to the driveway with a roll of towels and her change of clothes in a bag. She beams when she sees Philip and tries to hold up her arms for a hug, but it does not work well with what she is carrying. She manages a hug with one arm. As she continues on down the hill, Philip turns back to the car.

"Are you here for the baptism?" he asks Conway. He has recognized the man and knows about his capacity in the FSA.

"We are. We're here to be baptized by Pastor Murphy. Are you managing the parking?"

On the road, Frieda is arriving, closely followed by Carl. Lonnie directs them to park farther down beyond the others.

Jeremy and Joanne come striding around the corner into the driveway, carrying towels and bathing suits.

"Hi, Phil," calls out Jeremy.

Jeremy is full of questions.

"Is there a place we can change?"

"Earl generally lets us use the house," replies Philip. "There's a bathroom just inside the back door. Lindsey is down there

The Story

already."

"Would you mind parking along the road?" Philip asks Conway, having finished answering additional questions from Jeremy. "We're trying to keep the driveway clear."

"Sure, Phil. No problem."

As Conway begins to back out, a car goes by carrying Clarence and his wife, Clara. Philip hopes she is here as a believer, and he makes a mental note to alert Pastor Murphy. He can vouch for his ex-employees but not for their families.

Philip walks beside Conway's vehicle as it backs up out of the driveway. Lonnie is trotting over, and he directs Conway to find a place on the road beyond the other cars.

Seeing there is more room on the shoulder in the other direction, Philip turns right and walks that way to catch the arrivals sooner. Looking back, he notices Frieda and Carl approaching with their baptism bags in hand. The girl holding Frieda's hand causes him to pause. She appears to be about five years old, and he assumes she is Frieda's daughter, Fritzi. The little girl carries a towel and a bag, also. He makes another mental note to have them talk to the pastor and then continues on to greet the next car.

It is another one he does not recognize, driven by a woman he suspects is visiting the Martins. He lets it go by and then looking back sees her turn into the driveway.

"Why don't these women use their turn signals before it's too late?" he mutters.

Lonnie was not close enough to catch her either. He is greeting Clarence and Clara, who are walking from their car, both carrying bags.

Yet another strange car is approaching. Philip waves it down.

"Hi. I'm Bennie. I work for the FSA in Behavioral Health. Is this where Pastor Murphy is baptizing?"

"This is the place. I'm Philip Evans. Welcome to the family of the Lord Jesus. That's the driveway to the Beach House, but we're trying to keep it clear. Would you mind parking up here on the

the Day and the Hour

road?"

"Funny you ask that. Normally, I would park wherever I pleased. But since last night I feel like a new man. Tell me exactly where you want me to park."

"Anywhere you can find a spot along the road here. You could back up—wait, here comes a truck. It might be better if you pull ahead and find a place beyond the other cars."

"Good thing I came early! Thanks, Philip."

The truck, it turns out, is driven by Brutus of the FSA Child Weight Division. Philip catches him in time and gets the jumbo rig to park far enough off the road to let the limousine pass. Its right wheels go well off the raised roadway, and it tilts to an alarming angle. The driver struggles and squeezes out with difficulty but shows no concern about his truck getting stuck.

As Brutus swings down the road toward the driveway, the car that turned into it reappears, its driver having realized that parking on the road is to be preferred. She is hesitating, wondering which way to turn. Both Philip and Lonnie are motioning to her to come their way. Finally, she turns right and stops by Philip, lowering her window.

"Sorry about the congestion," he says. "Are you here for the baptism?"

"Yes, thanks to Leila and her message. I'm Sanela from the Healthy Retail Stores Project."

"Oh, I remember you now. We had some disagreements with your department back when we were in the old building."

"I'm really sorry I caused you so much trouble."

"I forgive you. I think we're sister and brother now, is that right?"

"That's right," she agrees. "Aren't you excited? I can hardly wait!"

"Now that you're headed this way, see if you can find a place to park off the side of the road along here. ... Here comes someone else. Stay right where you are for a minute."

It turns out to be Vicki, and Philip has her park behind Brutus'

The Story

truck.

"Okay, now you can go ahead and park on this side," he says to Sanela. "It looks like there is a spot you can get into up there. I'm trying to keep the space behind Leila's car open for Pastor Murphy."

Realizing that more cars are coming than predicted by his calculation, Philip decides to send all of his people on to Lonnie. Francis arrives, and he points him down the road to where Lonnie is standing.

Close behind Francis is a car Philip does not recognize, and he steps out to meet it.

"Are you here for the baptism?"

"Yes, I'm Felice. I worked for Leila in Forms and Permits. This is my daughter, Faith."

"Welcome, both of you. Your best place to park would be up here on the road. Pull as far over as you can to keep it passable for larger vehicles. It might be easier if Faith gets out now since there won't be any room on your right side after you're parked."

Another strange car is approaching. It stops for Philip's advice.

"Hi. I'm Amna from the Safe and Active Routes to School Department."

"Welcome, Amna. I'm Philip. You're here to be baptized, is that right?"

"That's right. I heard the gospel at Grace Bible Church for the first time last night. I mean, I understood it for the first time. I can't believe I missed it all my life. Thanks to Leila, who invited us to reconsider, some of us have just made it under the wire. I feel like my new life has already started, and I'm halfway to heaven, and I haven't even been baptized yet!"

"It looks like Pastor Murphy and Alice are here, Amna. Could you back up? I see a place where we can fit you in behind the car that's behind the truck."

"Hi Philip!" calls out the pastor. "You've gotten yourself quite a job here. Has the limo shown up?"

the Day and the Hour

"Not yet. I'm trying to keep the driveway clear for it. I've reserved a spot for you behind Leila's car."

Adam is relieved to hear that Evelyn has not yet arrived, since he had told her he would be here at two o'clock. Now he can start worrying about the possibility of her being detained again. He lets Alice out near the driveway.

Everyone is stepping back onto the slender shoulders wherever they can find places to stand, making way for an approaching FSA patrol car. Adam is glad to see it, since it tells him that Earl is still here. The officer stops and waits while the pastor maneuvers Alice's little electric car into the slot reserved for it.

Adam and Alice are marching down the driveway when a sound makes Adam look over his shoulder. The gleaming grill of the limousine is right there, nudging them from behind. They step aside to let it pass. Evelyn has her window down. She is trying to maintain a dour composure, but when she looks up at Adam, her face breaks into a smile. The driver having slowed to a crawl, she has time to reach out and squeeze Alice's hand.

"So that's Evelyn's smile!" Alice whispers. "Why didn't you tell me?"

"What didn't I tell you?"

"You told me her looks gave her a lot of trouble, but you weren't specific. Why didn't you say she's a beauty queen?"

"You met her at church Thursday."

"Does she like stories?"

"I believe so."

"How surprised she'll be when she finds out who I am."

"Wait until you find out who she is."

"How old is she?"

"The same age I am, almost."

"No! That can't be right."

"She does look a lot younger when she smiles."

Philip, who had been walking behind the limousine, slows his pace to stay in step with Adam and Alice.

The Story

The long car comes to a halt in front of the no-parking sign. The bodyguard emerges and opens the door for Evelyn. She gets out and stands by the car, tall and straight, waiting for Adam and Alice.

The Murphys and Philip round the last bend to find the limousine with Evelyn watching for them. She rushes to them and links her arms with Adam and Alice. They remain there, talking, while Philip instructs the driver about parking.

Hugo from the Historic Designation Board is arriving. Lonnie greets him as he exits his antique roadster, and sends him ambling down the driveway to join the others.

Adam, Alice, and Evelyn are proceeding to the steps under the golden-yellow maple boughs. Evelyn's bodyguard follows, carrying two canvas bags. Looking back, Adam notices that Evelyn's secretary is coming too, and she too is carrying a bag. The limousine is backing up the driveway under Philip's direction.

†

Down on the dock, having completed *Walter's* mooring to everyone's satisfaction, Earl's sailing school stands on the float, marveling at the crowd that gathered in their absence. They are reluctant to mingle with landlubbers after being in the fellowship of wind and wave. It is like returning from a successful military campaign and finding your homeland occupied by the enemy. Earl expected to see Adam and Alice—and Evelyn. But he does not know why the others are here. Regardless, it falls on him as commander of his navy to see his sailors safely home.

"Fall in behind me," he commands. "Forward! ... Harch!"

Leila grabs Earl's arm, the *Willow* ladies follow, and *Walter's* crusty crew takes up the rear. Earl surveys the enemy lines ahead and notices several hardware-store employees.

As the fearsome force steps off the dock, the baptism occupation gives way, shuffling off the path. Leila spies Evelyn coming down the walk, linked together with Adam and Alice, and she breaks away from Earl, dashing up to greet her, while Earl turns aside and disappears into his shop. The remaining four, led

the Day and the Hour

by the intrepid ladies, hold their formation, not turning right or left, marching up the walkway. The bodyguard sees them coming and responds to the challenge, whirling out in front of Evelyn with a fierce look for the insurgent sailors who simply swerve around this flotsam, snubbing the lubbers and proceeding to their cars.

†

Up on the road, Naenia of the Office of Neighborhood Commercial Revitalization is the last to arrive though Lonnie does not know it yet and continues to wait for others.

†

Evelyn is making introductions.

"Pastor Murphy, this is Ruth, my secretary, and Benayahu, my faithful guard and companion of many years."

"Thank you both for coming. This is truly a great day."

"Pleased to meet you, Pastor Murphy," says the bodyguard.

"When I told Ben about you, he asked me whether he could be baptized too," says Evelyn.

"That means you know Jesus Christ as your Savior and Lord, Benayahu?"

"Yes, sir. By his grace I received him on Monday when I first heard about the Rapture. I was home with my wife. She had been praying for me most of her life. I was just stubborn. I always knew she was right, but I was stubborn. When I heard about those dreams, I knew I had to admit she was right.

"I asked forgiveness first of my wife for causing her so much worry, and then I got down on my knees and asked God to forgive me for having insisted on my own way. And that was it. He did the rest. I reckon I'm a new man by the blood of Jesus Christ according to his proimise, and I think Ms. Newton knows it. I'm hoping, if I be real nice to her, she will let me be her bodyguard in heaven."

"Yes, I do know it, Benayahu. The Lord looks wonderful in you."

"Does your wife know you're being baptized here?" asks Adam.

The Story

"Oh, yes. She would be here if she could. But we had no transportation. We're still under the rulers of this world for a little while."

"And Ruth would like to be baptized too," says Evelyn. "We spent some hours last night sharing. She has a remarkable testimony."

"Please tell me about it, Ruth. If you would like, we can go to those chairs near the water and be a little more comfortable.

"By the way, everyone!" Adam says in a louder voice. "Earl is letting us use the house to change into whatever you will be wearing into the water, and you can change out of your wet clothes there afterward."

†

Philip, having completed overseeing the limousine parking, is back on the street with Lonnie. After several minutes without traffic, they conclude that their task is over. He sends Lonnie down the driveway to join the party. But for himself he walks to his car for a little rest and calls Pamela.

†

Earl is working on the boat hull under construction in his shop. He was intending to correct the mistake he made nearly a week ago—the planking-sequence error he discovered yesterday. He thought this afternoon would be an ideal time to get it done while Leila and Evelyn were being baptized. He is rechecking plank widths on both sides of the hull and comparing them with a table in his notebook. He keeps making mistakes; it is not coming out right.

the Day and the Hour

The Story

Chapter 8

Not wanting to miss the ceremony and thinking he may be of some service to the pastor, Philip emerges from his car after a conversation with Pamela and hurries down the driveway. He is approaching the limousine when he hears the voice of the driver quoting the prophet Isaiah:

> He was oppressed, and he was afflicted, yet he opened not his mouth;
> Like a lamb brought to the slaughter or a sheep before her shearers is silent, so he opened not his mouth.
> In his humiliation he was denied justice—who can explain his generation? They took his life from the earth!
> It was for the transgressions of my people that he was stricken.

Coming alongside the car, Philip sees the driver reading from a large Bible propped against the steering wheel. Philip stops. The driver stops reading and looks up, recognizing the one who was directing the parking.

"Do you understand what you're reading?" Philip asks.

"How can I?—unless someone explains it to me. Please—would you mind? Can you tell me what this means?"

"I certainly will try," says Philip.

"About whom is the prophet speaking? About himself or someone else?"

"He's prophesying about Jesus Christ."

"I thought so. That is amazing, is it not, sir? I know this is the Old Testament, which was written long before it happened."

"Would you like me to tell you more?"

"Sir, if you would be so kind. We can sit in the back where it will be more comfortable. Here, let me get out. This Bible belongs to Ms. Newton. She left it and said I was welcome to read from it."

"My name is Philip, by the way. I should have introduced myself earlier."

"My name is Melech. Here, hold the Bible, and I will get in

the Day and the Hour

first; that will make it easier for you."

The look, feel, and smell of the luxurious interior is a new experience for Philip, but it holds little interest for him compared to the priceless privilege of being the one to explain the Word of God to a hungry soul. Melech extends the desk and lays the Bible on it. Philip observes that the book is well used and that the particular page at which it is open bears copious underlining, including the portion Melech was reading.

"Isaiah knew that Messiah—that is, the Christ—was coming," Philip begins, "—the one anointed by God to be King not only of Israel but every other nation as well. That much they got, but they didn't quite understand how it had to happen. They didn't realize that in order for this kingdom to come, there would have to be a big change in the hearts of men and women. The world has never seen a government that didn't become corrupt—because the mind of man is desperately wicked. God's remedy for that was so radical that nobody really understood it back then. Probably, nobody understood it until Jesus explained it. Even then it was like his words fell on deaf ears. It wasn't until after he died and was resurrected that they understood. That's when the Spirit of God opened their eyes, and *then* they saw that he had *already* revealed what he was going to do. It was right there in the Scriptures; it was in front of their eyes all along. This fifty-third chapter of Isaiah is one of those passages. Let's look at it. Here, let's start with verse five:

He was wounded for our transgressions.

"This means it was for *our* sin that Christ suffered. It wasn't for any wrongdoing of his: it was for *our* disobedience—that is, for us who are sinful."

"Why does it say 'he was'—like it happened in the past—when Christ had not yet come into the world?"

"That's the way the prophets spoke. It means it's a sure thing, just as sure as if it already happened. In other words, it was already done in the mind of God. It's the grammar of certainty. What comes next?

The Story

It was a punishment that brought us peace.

"Everybody wants peace, but hardly anybody finds it, and nobody keeps it for long. There's no lasting peace in this world. Now, the amazing thing is that here God is saying peace is possible, and it comes through the punishment of Christ."

"How could that be? How could his punishment be of any help to me?"

"There is one answer to that. Here's how I explain it: Peace must be made with God before it can happen anywhere else. There's a score to be settled with God, and until it is, there can't be any peace. This statement by the prophet reveals that God is willing to let the punishment of Christ settle the score. It's as if *Christ* paid the price to get *us* off the hook with God."

"That doesn't seem fair. Christ himself was not the sinner. It makes God look unjust, but I know that cannot be."

"Yes, it does look that way, but we aren't left with a paradox. There's one way it would not be unjust of God to settle the score between him and me without taking it out on me. And that would be for him to take it out on himself. In other words, he could write off my debt by paying the price himself. He isn't penalizing anyone else: he's paying it himself. Since it was owed *to* him and paid *by* him, the payment isn't unjust to anyone else. And the law demanding punishment for sin gets satisfied."

"But are you not confusing Christ with God? That would work only if they were one and the same."

"They *are* one and the same. We say that Jesus Christ is a person of the Godhead. God is more complex than we are, as you would expect. He's one being, yet he's three as we perceive him. It's like he has three distinct roles: Christ is God the Son. He spoke of his Father as God. And the Spirit of God is known to us as the third person.

"What's next?

By his stripes we are healed.

"He was wounded, and we are healed—another way to look at the exchange. It isn't only that Christ settled the score on our

the Day and the Hour

behalf; he's also restoring us to a kind of health that we can scarcely imagine now. But he promised it. There are other places in the Bible where he speaks about that more fully. The summary of it is this: we'll not only be cured of our tendency to sin and be given peace, but we'll also be glorified in order to live and reign with Christ himself. We know this is true because Christ was raised from that awful suffering and restored to glory. He was buried, locked in a tomb, and soon after reappeared to many witnesses as a testimony to the power that God has to raise *us* to glory.

> We all went astray like sheep, each going his own way, and the Lord laid our sin upon him.

"You see, we've all been disobedient: we've all been living for ourselves, oblivious to the claims our Maker has on us. The penalty is an extreme one because in the economy of heaven no disobedience can be left standing. It's a sentence that we can pay only by dying—unless we take the gift that we're being offered. The Lord laid our sin on him. We must quit thinking that we can somehow make ourselves righteous. We need to simply accept what he's done for us. He won't force the issue because that would destroy our ability to respond to him in true worship—which is essential to our fulfillment if we only knew it."

"Is that what it means to be Christian?—to accept this gift from God and worship him for it?"

"That's the start."

"What then?"

"Then we owe him everything. He owns us, actually. We become his slaves for a while, which is not bad at all. Let me tell you, it's delightful. There's nothing better than to be in the service of God."

"And if we don't accept?"

"The devil already owns you and has a plan for your life that's not as wonderful as you may desire."

"Is there any reason I cannot be baptized now?"

"As long as there's water in the lake, there's no reason I know

The Story

of. Let's go see Pastor Murphy."

†

Alice sees them coming. "Here comes Philip ... with another man," she says.

"Melech wants to be baptized too," Philip announces.

"Adam is over there talking with Ruth," Alice informs him. "As soon as they're through, he will want to talk with you, Melech. I'll go see if I can talk Earl out of a pair of shorts you can wear into the water."

†

"I met Ms. Newton in Amman," Ruth was saying. "She did not have a permanent secretary at that time; she was using general staff personnel when she needed to have something done. I was employed at the US embassy and happened to be free during one of her visits. I worked for her for two weeks, and we got along so well that I asked her to hire me permanently. She hesitated because it would take me away from my country. I had no family ties that would keep me from traveling, and I wanted to see the world. That's what I told her anyway, and I think that's what I believed at the time. In reality, I had become attached to her as though she were my mother.

"'Please do not urge me to leave you,' I told her. 'Where you go, I will go, and where you stay, I will stay. Your people shall be my people, and your God shall be my God. Where you die, I will die, and there I will be buried. So help me God, nothing but death will part me from you.' When she saw that I was determined, she hired me.

"However, I didn't truly know her God. I thought I knew God through the religion of my country. I was a Sunni Muslim like nearly everyone else, and I thought that Allah was Jehovah and Jehovah was Allah by a different name. But it wasn't long before I knew without a doubt that the God of Ms. Newton was not Allah. So I began to study the Scriptures. As a Muslim, I had a certain reverence for Jesus, but I couldn't reconcile the statements in the New Testament that made him appear to be one with Jehovah. So

the Day and the Hour

I adopted Judaism as my religion, and I thought I had come to terms with my promise to Ms. Newton that her God would be my God.

"I went on that way for several years and brushed aside comments she made from time to time about Jesus being her Savior. It was not a concept I was familiar with. I knew about Messiah, but the concept of a personal Savior was incomprehensible because I thought in terms of obedience to the laws of religion.

"Then the shock came on Sunday when rumors of the Rapture dreams turned out to be true. Both Ms. Newton and I were driven to examine where we stood with God. It was then that she gave me the piece of the puzzle I had been missing. How I had missed it, I don't know; it is the most obvious thing in the world. Almost everything I had learned about winning a place in the kingdom of God was a lie because I thought it was attainable through enough effort."

"What did she tell you?" asks the pastor.

"She told me that my heart was deceitful and desperately sick, and I had no chance of improving it to please God in just one week."

"Evelyn told you that? I can't believe she would be so blunt."

"I nearly died when she said it. It was as though she had thrust a dagger into my heart. I broke down. I couldn't understand what had happened. It was awful."

"Did she apologize?"

"No. She opened her Bible and showed me Jeremiah 17:9:
The heart is deceitful above all things and desperately wicked.
She was being gentler with me than the Scripture was."

"What else did she say?"

"She gave me her Bible and told me to read the Gospel of John. I hesitated because of my Judaism. She said it was an order, and she would fire me if I didn't do it."

"So you read it?"

"I did."

The Story

"And what did you find?"

"I found Jesus. I had never known him before."

"Did you decide he is God?"

"He can be anyone he wants to be as far as I'm concerned. I found that he was speaking to me through the Scripture. The essential thing is, he loves me unconditionally. It doesn't depend on me being perfect or even good. I took him at his word, and now I'm free for the first time in my life.

"It's the most obvious thing in the world, isn't it Pastor Murphy? I mean the fact that the hearts of men and women are sick beyond any healing. It takes a miracle of God, not human effort. God had this all worked out from the beginning, and I was kept from knowing it by my religions that were supposed to bring me peace. There is no peace apart from the saving grace of God."

"I'm assuming you told Evelyn all that?"

"We talked about it a lot. She explained many things to me. We read Ephesians together. Isn't chapter one glorious?—especially the first few verses?"

"Blessed be the God and Father of our Lord Jesus Christ," quotes the preacher.

"He has blessed us in Christ with every spiritual blessing," responds Ruth with a smile.

"In the heavenly places!" he declares, completing the verse.

"He chose us in Christ even before the beginning of the world," she quotes, raising her hands.

"In love, he predestined us for adoption through Jesus Christ," he adds enthusiastically.

"According to the purpose of his will," she responds, rising from her chair and reaching for his hand, inviting him to stand.

"To the praise of his glorious grace!" Halfway shouting, he stands with her.

"In Christ, we have redemption through his blood—the forgiveness of our trespasses!" she declares, turning around in the manner of a Mideast folk dance.

"Thus are we blameless before him," he says, facing her and

raising his hands together with hers.

"According to the riches of his grace," she says slowly, making each word sound holy.

"I'm sure she was delighted with your response," says Adam, ignoring the silent stares he feels. (Their brief rhapsody did not go unnoticed.)

They are standing at the water's edge with their backs to the onlookers. Ruth continues:

"She said she had become desperate when she heard the news about the Rapture. Even though she wasn't sure it was true at first —it was awfully hard to believe—she was worried not for herself but for me. She said she could not stand the thought of being separated from me; she had been praying for my salvation since we met. Finally, she felt that she must become stern with me though she did it with fear and trembling. It is what God used to break down the walls of the prison that held me."

†

The FSA and hardware-store ex-employees are talking and laughing. Ruth goes to join Evelyn and Leila who are standing with Benayahu and Melech. Alice informs Adam about Melech wanting to receive baptism. The pastor takes him aside.

"So you were reading from Isaiah when Philip came by?"

"Yes, sir. Ms. Newton had lent me her Bible, and I was reading from the page where she had left the marker. There were some underlined verses, and those I was reading when he stopped and asked me if I understood it. I told him I needed someone to explain the meaning to me, and he said he would. He sat with me in the car and went through it verse by verse."

"What impression do you have of Jesus Christ?"

"Well, it is truly amazing, sir. That prophet knew about him hundreds of years before he ever came and died on this earth. He knew that this man would die not for his own offenses but for those of others and that his death would bring healing. Now, that is *not* something which makes any sense for a man to do. Philip explained how it *does* make sense because he is God."

The Story

"So you believe that Jesus was God come in the flesh and that he died for the benefit of others?"

"Yes, sir."

"Was it only for his own people?"

"No. Philip showed me it was for sinners, and in case I thought I was no sinner, he showed me what God thinks about the human heart. I knew then that I needed this Savior just as much as anyone else, and I asked him if I could be baptized. He said we should talk to you about it."

†

Alice is entering the house, looking for Earl. She passes through the kitchen, the dining room, and into the parlor where she finds Philip. It occurred to him that the warmth of a fire would be appreciated by some of the ladies after coming out of the water into the crisp autumn air. Being familiar with the arrangements in the house, he wasted no time locating wood and laying the fire, which is already producing lively flames.

"Have you seen Earl?" she asks Philip.

"No. I checked upstairs. He's not there."

†

No one other than Evelyn noticed when Earl went into his shop. It is as though he is a prisoner at his own house. True, he does not own the Beach House—indeed, it is regarded as a community treasure. Nevertheless, he is used to having it to himself.

Earl peers out of the shop window at the improbable multitude. He surmises that they are not merely spectators: apparently, the baptism roster inflated unexpectedly.

People are going in and coming out of his house, no doubt using all of the rooms for changing into their sundry and scanty attire for the sacred occasion. It all looks exceedingly profane to him.

†

Adam is searching for Clara. He does not know her and would not recognize her, but he recognizes Clarence from the store and makes the reasonable assumption that the woman hanging on his arm is his wife.

"Hello, Clarence. I don't believe I've met your wife."

"This is Clara."

"I'm Adam Murphy. It's wonderful to have both of you here. Are you both wanting to be baptized?"

"We're ready," declares Clarence.

"I was wondering if I could have a word with Clara in private before we start."

"It's fine with me," he says.

Clara lets go of her husband's arm and looks at the pastor rather sheepishly.

"Lets go over to those chairs on the beach and have a little talk," he suggests.

"How long have you been a Christian, Clara?"

"Just since this afternoon."

"Did your husband lead you to the Lord?"

"I don't want to be left alone."

"It's a little scary, isn't it?"

"Yes."

"Have you ever read the Bible?"

"No."

"Would you like me to show you the plan that God has for you?"

"Okay."

"I have some portions of the Bible here."

He brings up Romans 3:23 on his phone.

"Would you like to read this?"

> **All have sinned and fall short of the glory of God.**

"Does that mean anything to you?"

"Does 'all' mean everyone?"

"It really does. I could show you the context, but if you'll take my word for it, it does say that everyone falls short of what God expects."

"That isn't good, is it?"

The Story

"You're right. It's telling us what we probably already knew.

"Here's another one: Romans 6:23. Would you read it, please?"

> The wages of sin is death. But the free gift of God is eternal life in Jesus Christ our Lord.

"Does that mean anything to you?"

"It means that—it means ... um. ... It means—there is a gift. Is it for anyone?"

"No. Only for sinners. That's why it's put like that. It's assuming the readers know they're sinners. As it said, all fall short of the glory of God. You see, in God's book just falling short of perfection is as bad as any sin. It's really a tough place for us to be. We wouldn't have any hope if it weren't for the gift."

"Now, here's another one: John 3:3. Would you like to read it?"

> Jesus said to him, "Unless one is born again, he cannot see the kingdom of God."

"Do you think that could be the gift the other one was talking about?"

"Like being born?"

"Right. That's a gift, isn't it? Now we've found out that the gift for sinners is being born again."

"Let's look at another verse. This is John 14:6."

> Jesus said to him, "I am the way, the truth, and the life. No one comes to the Father except through me."

"Do you see any connection with being born again?"

"I'm not sure."

"First, Jesus said no one can see the kingdom of God except by being born again. Now he's saying that he himself is the only way. So, receiving the gift is being born again, which means coming to God through Jesus."

"How do we do that?"

"Let's see what the Bible says. Here's Romans 10:9-10."

> If you confess with your mouth that Jesus is Lord and believe in your heart that God raised him from the dead, you will be saved. For with the heart one believes and is justified, and with the mouth one confesses and is saved.

"What does it mean that God raised him from the dead?"

"Jesus was crucified."

"I know that."

"He was put to death. Do you know what for?"

"No."

"The religious leaders of that day were a jealous bunch, just like we are today. Jesus came along saying that the only way to approach God was through him. That made it sound like he was claiming to be God himself, and they couldn't or didn't want to believe it. He seemed to be leaving them out of the process, making their professional services unnecessary. So they got the Romans to crucify him. But as it turned out, they were playing into God's hand, and he raised Jesus from the dead."

"But what does that have to do with us?"

"Jesus died not on account of his own sin; it was the sin of others that put him to death. It turned out that God used this in a big way. Because Jesus actually was God—that is, the Son of God—when he was put to death, it also put to death the sins of his creatures, for he is our Maker, and the offense of our sins was against him in the first place. He made a way for us to escape punishment by taking the punishment on himself! But that wasn't the end of the story: Death could not hold him. He overcame death and escaped the grave, walking the earth again and finally rising to heaven where he sits at the right hand of God. And just as he took our sins with him to the grave, so he is taking us to heavenly glory with him—as a gift!"

"Doesn't everyone have the gift?"

"No. Here's another verse: Second Corinthians 5:15. Would you read it?"

> And he died for all, that those who live might no longer live for themselves but for him who died for their sake and was raised to life.

"That's the catch?"

"Right. Those who receive the gift no longer live for themselves but for Jesus."

"I'm not sure I would know how to begin."

The Story

"Let me show you. Here, read this verse; it's Revelation 3:20."

> "Behold, I stand at the door and knock. If anyone hears my voice and opens the door, I will come in to him and eat with him and he with me."

"How do you hear his voice?"

"I think you already have heard it—because you're reading this."

"How do I open the door?"

"It means he is not going to force you to do anything against your will."

"What does it mean to eat with him?"

"It's a way of saying that he wants to be close to you, one on one. If you invite him into your life, you will get to know him. He has promised."

"What is heaven like?"

"It is a safe place to be. The earth is becoming dangerous, and soon there will be dreadful disasters. You are fortunate to be chosen for heaven."

"Is it because Clarence works for the Evanses?"

"I think it is just as likely that he saved the Evanses in order to reach you."

"Me?"

"Yes, you. God has a different way of looking at people. His favorites are sometimes ones that would surprise us if we knew."

"Does he know me?"

"Yes, I'm sure of that. He knows all about you, and he thinks you are a delightful person. He has called you to come to him; if it were not so, you wouldn't be here. There are many people who will not listen to his voice. But you have, and he knew you would, and the angels in heaven are rejoicing right now because you have opened your heart to receive him."

"Is he in heaven how?"

"Yes, and he will be coming tomorrow morning to take us to heaven to be with him."

"Will Clarence live with me there?"

"It will be like one big happy family. Clarence will be there, but

the Day and the Hour

Clarence will no longer be your master. Only Jesus will be your Master, and you will love the way he treats you, and you will love serving him. In fact, he has a special place prepared for you to serve him that no one else in the world would be able to fulfill. Aren't you thankful that he has saved you?"

"When will I meet him?"

"In his Spirit he is here right now."

Clara straightens up, sitting tall in her chair. The timid look has left her, and a smile transforms her face. It appears that she is seeing something far out on the water or above it.

"He says he's coming for me," she says.

†

Earl peeks out and sees Adam sitting with yet another of the crazed company.

Is he going to interview all of them? This will take the whole day!

The Story

Chapter 9

Adam and Clara have gotten up from the chairs; he has delivered her back to her husband and gone looking for the remaining person he needs to interview.

"I'm Pastor Murphy. I know you from the store, but I'll have to confess I can't remember your name. I relied too much on your name tag."

"Frieda. And this is my daughter, Fritzi."

"Philip told me a little about your meeting this morning. I know it was heartwarming for him to have his entire staff come to the Lord."

"It was the Spirit who did it, that's for sure. But I'm not sure about Russell."

"He's a worry for me too. He's a peculiar man. Is Fritzi going to be baptized?"

"She wants to be."

"Have you explained salvation to her?"

"No. ... She's already memorized Scripture."

"That's wonderful, Fritzi. If you will allow me to be your pastor, I could listen to you say it. Would that be a good idea?"

"She's a little shy around men. She never saw her father."

"Maybe we could sit down on those chairs next to the water, so she won't have to tilt her head back so far to look at me."

"Fritzi, would you like to go talk with Pastor Murphy? ... She's not sure."

"Well, I don't blame her at all. Fritzi, I can tell you're a very special girl. You have a Father in heaven who loves you very much."

"I know that!"

"Would you like to tell me about him?"

"Okay."

"Come on, we'll go sit with Pastor Murphy and you can recite your psalm."

The pastor sits down on one of the chairs, but Fritzi wants to remain standing. She stands before him, and with her hands folded and her head bowed, she prays to her Father:

> O Lord, our Lord, how excellent is thy name in all the earth. Thou has set thy glory above the heavens. Out of the mouth of babes and sucklings has thou ordained strength because of thy enemies, that thou might still the enemy and the avenger. When I consider thy heavens, the work of thy fingers, the moon and the stars, which thou has ordained—what is man that thou are mindful of him and the son of man that thou visits him? For thou has made him a little lower than the angels and has crowned him with glory and honor. Thou made him to have dominion over the works of thy hands: Thou has put all things under his feet: all sheep and oxen, yea, and the beasts of the field, the fowls of the air, and the fishes of the sea, and whatsoever passes through the paths of the sea. O Lord, our Lord, how excellent is thy name in all the earth!

"Did you pick that out for her?" Adam asks her mother.

"No, she picked it out herself."

"Can she read, then?"

"I can only read the Bible," says Fritzi.

"She reads some. She looks at it and seems to get something from it," her mother explains.

"My angel always sees the face of my Father who is in heaven," declares Fritzi.

†

Earl is pretending to busy himself in the shop while continuing to steal glances outside. Evelyn and Leila are holding hands. He sees Evelyn's Ethiopian driver wearing his Bermuda shorts.

Evelyn is aware of Earl's awkward position.

"I'm going to speak to Earl," she tells Leila.

She goes to the shop door and knocks. Earl opens it and steps back, saying nothing. She steps inside and closes the door.

Much has changed since she spoke to him last. That was before Leila was saved, and Evelyn was then much more concerned about Leila's future than she is now. At that time it was

The Story

critical that the resistance effort succeed for Leila's sake so that she would not need to be in the middle of the Reorganization whether opposing it or implementing it's draconian devices as her office would have demanded. (Although her own assignment was to promote the Reorganization, Evelyn had undermined it at every opportunity and had advised Earl's resistance committee about forestalling installation of the infrastructure.)

"Earl, I'm truly sorry you won't come with us."

It was not the best way to begin. Evelyn meant to let him know that she values his company. She is aware of the gulf separating him from fellowship with her and the others, but there is no longer a reason that she knows of for his remaining on the far side of it.

However, there is a reason; there is something that has not occurred to her.

"I've had enough of women running everything," Earl says. "It appears that your kingdom of heaven will be no different. It's no place for me."

Evelyn is silent while she visits his point of view and processes this information. Seeing it his way, it strikes her that untold damage followed the bold intrusion of women into areas formerly dominated by men—not that the world is any worse for it, but what about heaven? How many men have thereby been repelled from taking the gospel to heart, being effectively sent to hell by their women? It was not always like this. There was a time when men were allowed the illusion of being leaders. She had never before considered how that subtle difference operated on the male psyche.

Evelyn sees Earl in a new way. For all his male fortitude, he is a product of his reactions to the women who have dominated him. What good is there in this war between the sexes? She knows it is a remnant of the fall. It was unknown in Eden. Still, paradoxically, it has in no wise ruined him. Quite the contrary, here is a man who would be willing to lay down his life for his friends. She loves him more than she can say. The tragic hero may not win the golden cup or the jeweled crown, but he wins the heart.

"Earl, remember, society in heaven is different. You have to put away your earthly concepts. The competitive spirit in this world is of the animal side of human nature. It serves the ends of self-preservation and procreation. In the kingdom of heaven, you leave that behind. You enter a new kind of life. There, we all belong to one another in our Lord. You may even see a bit of it here this afternoon."

As she spoke, she became more beautiful than ever. It was not her smile: she is not smiling. The beauty radiates from an inner light. It tears his heart: he yearns to embrace all that she is, but he knows he cannot get there from where he is. It seems that she has forgotten his mission.

She speaks again, reminding him of the option he will not accept:

"When you are apprehended, you leave the resistance effort to others, so why not claim your victory before that happens?"

With her connections in government, Earl is certain that she *could* find a way to get him out from under the FBI investigation, behind which looms a likely prison sentence. It seems that she is merely taunting him. He refuses to look at her. She may be a prophetess, but if she will not help him, he will go it alone. Earl vows to outwit and defeat the enemy without her aid; he will not let the responsibility pass from him.

Evelyn perceives his agony. She knows that she has brought it about. She waits for words of wisdom in order to save him from feeling excluded, and she comes out with a bold statement:

"Leila is the one to satisfy your soul. No power in heaven or earth will separate you from her for long. Earl, we love you."

He has turned his back to her and is facing the wall.

Evelyn has done all she can do, for better or for worse. She steps outside and closes the door. As she leaves, Earl turns, and looking out through the window, he meets Leila's sad eyes. He must not be moved by these women.

The Story

There will be time to sort things out. There is a time for everything.

He goes around to the far side of the unfinished boat, to a spot where he is out of their sight, and sits down on a stool.

†

"Do you know how late it is?" Alice says to Adam.

"Yes, it's time, isn't it?

He walks to the water's edge and steps onto the dock.

"If you will all gather around me here," he calls out, "I would like to make a few remarks before we begin your baptisms."

Everyone moves toward the pier, and they all crowd around the preacher.

"I would like to explain the meaning of baptism.

"You are all here because you have responded to the call of Christ. Is that true? Is there anyone who still has doubts? ...

"This is a believer's baptism. That means you are submitting to being immersed in the water as an expression of your faith. You are telling the world that you remember the pattern set down in the Scriptures. That means you respect the Scriptures. As you are immersed in the water and then lifted up, it symbolizes your being in Christ who died and was raised again to life and to glory.

"There is nothing magic about baptism. It does not wash away your sins: it is the blood of Christ that washes away your sins. It does not make you holy: this is not holy water; only the work of the Holy Spirit in our hearts makes us holy.

"Here is what I like best about this kind of baptism where we get all wet and come out with our hair plastered down and dripping and our clothes clinging to our bodies: It makes us look much worse than we would want to be caught looking in public. In other words, it's humbling. Being humbled is bad for our pride, which means it's good for our souls. If you take this the right way, it can be a reminder that we have nothing to boast of in ourselves. It's only in Christ that we boast. Not that we're proud of ourselves for having chosen him or even for being chosen by him. *We* are all wet. *He* is the one we boast of. Never stop praising him. He is the

the Day and the Hour

only one worthy of our boasting. And what a joy it is to boast of Christ! Boast of yourself, and it may give you a brief lift, but it lets you down afterward because it damages your soul. Boast of Christ, and it heals and purifies your soul.

"When you come out of the water and you're tempted to be embarrassed about the way you look, remember that Jesus was nailed to the cross and hung there naked for you. He was not humbled: there was no need for that. He was humiliated. Now is the time to realize that he took your shame upon himself, took it to the grave, and rose holy and victorious over shame and death. The life you now live is holy only because you live in him.

"Now, I will call the order. Some of you are eager and want to be first. Some of you remember that Jesus said the last shall be first, so you want to be last. Therefore, I will call the order.

"First will be Evelyn since she was the first to request to be baptized today. Next will be Leila since her request came next. Then will come Melech since he was last to ask and after him Ruth and then Benayahu.

"Now, Benayahu, will you be able to let Evelyn out of your sight long enough to have your whole self immersed in the lake?"

"Yes, sir. I'm trusting the Lord to watch over her. He doesn't need me as much as I thought he did. He was just humoring me. In fact, I don't think I was necessary at all. But I'm not complaining about that. I'm trusting him to make everything come out right just as everyone else here is."

"God bless you, sir. Let's all say amen to that."

"Amen!"

"Next, let's have the FSA folks come. Then will come Fritzi and Frieda. You can both come into the water together. Then Clara and Clarence. Philip, you can arrange the order for the rest of your folks."

Adam steps off the dock, turns around, and takes off his shoes. He will go into the water dressed. He empties his pockets and puts his wallet and keys in his shoes.

Evelyn is standing ready, wearing a robe over her swimming

The Story

suit. She pulls it tightly around her to keep it from floating as she follows Adam into the water. They go out twenty feet or so until the water is up to their waists.

"Evelyn, my sister in Christ, I baptize you in the name of the Father and the Son and the Holy Spirit."

Leila is wading out as Evelyn comes back in.

As Evelyn turns around to watch Leila, Earl slips out of the shop. While the pastor is lowering Leila into the water, symbolizing her dying to herself and being immersed in Christ—while everyone is watching—Earl walks briskly up the brick path to the garage and quietly opens the door with the sign on it, revealing one of his three automobiles.

Leila wades back and steps out of the water, her swimming suit dripping, and takes the towel offered by Alice. She wraps herself in it and immediately goes to the door of Earl's shop, gently pulling it open and quietly stepping inside while Earl backs his Thunderbird roadster out of the garage.

Discovering his absence, she knows intuitively that he has fled the premises. Nevertheless, hoping to be wrong, she hurries out and runs all the way up to the garage without caring who may be watching and careless of the sharp pains on her bare feet. The door is open, the T-bird is gone, and the smell of its exhaust hangs in the air. She feared this would happen. A weakness and dizziness comes over her. She steps inside and reaches to the forklift to steady herself.

Thoughts are racing through her mind: *I must find him.* But she doubts that her surveillance team will be able to keep up with him if he wants to escape. *Maybe he went to his office*—at the paper. *Maybe he went to the Burns house*—to play horseshoes. *No.* She understands him. He has been pushed too far. *He won't be coming back.* The thought is paralyzing but not to the exclusion of tears. *Who ever cried of a broken heart immediately after being baptized?* She is glad that no one is nearby, and she lets the tears flow. *Tears can't make me look any worse.*

After some minutes she regains her equilibrium and pulls the

the Day and the Hour

towel tight about her shoulders. The cold, clammy wetness of her clothing is causing her to shiver. She walks deliberately back down the stairs, passing under the golden leaves, back down the brick walkway, and into Earl's house. The bathroom door is closed; Evelyn's bodyguard is standing near it. Leila's heart is too heavy to bear company; she wants to be alone. She passes through the kitchen, through the dining room, and comes to the parlor where flames are leaping in the fireplace.

She stands at the hearth, absorbing the warmth of the fire. But the cold, numb feeling in her breast will not be relieved by anything in Earl's house but Earl himself. If only he were here, she would pour out her anguish to him. He would then understand and not reject her love. In spite of the fire, her teeth are chattering.

The sound of a footstep and the creak of a floorboard warn of someone's approach. She looks up, and in the mirror above the mantle she sees Evelyn standing in the doorway. Leila turns, shivering, and by her desperate look invites Evelyn in. The older woman wraps her in a hug, careless of the wet hair and damp towel.

"He ... left," Leila says shakily.

"It's my fault, not yours," Evelyn replies. "I tried to coax him to join us, but I'm afraid it had the opposite effect."

Leila does not answer immediately. Talking is difficult when your teeth are chattering. But the combined effect of the fire and the warmth of Evelyn's embrace is beginning to subdue the shivers.

"No. ... It's ... my doing. ... I tried to show him how I feel. He must have taken it the wrong way. ... I don't blame him. He wasn't expecting anything like this many people. I should have warned him candidly instead of trying to bind him. Now he's gone. I'm afraid he's gone forever."

Evelyn is silent, giving Leila time to spend the excess of her grief.

"How could I have been so foolish? ... Of course he would

The Story

resent this intrusion! ... I should have told him all I knew; then we could have gone somewhere together and saved him from having to be here."

"But what then?" Evelyn asks.

"I know. We would be followed everywhere by the surveillance squad. He hates them! How can I blame him for that? And they're out there because of me. If I were an ordinary woman, I wouldn't be a threat to him. But I can't escape being who I am even if I don't want to be who I am. I would rather be a cleaning woman working for him than one who wields authority over him. Then he would have been comfortable with me. We were doomed from the beginning."

"My dear, there is always hope. Nothing is impossible with our Lord in heaven. He put you and Earl together for a reason. Never doubt that. This is your test of faith. Though hope seems desperate, it never is desperate in him. I will hope for us both until you regain some courage."

Leila's shivering has subsided. Evelyn is her comforter, and the fire is warming her legs. She needed something tangible to replace her worthless scheme to stay with Earl as long as the day lasted. Now she has it. She would have clung to Evelyn with her arms if they were not wrapped in the towel. She will trust Evelyn's trusting for her. Like a child being consoled by her mother, she forgets her fear and drinks in the comfort, counting it the grace of God.

"Dry clothes will make a difference," Evelyn says. "Let's get your clothes and find a place to change."

Evelyn takes her up the stairs where they find Earl's office door open. She leaves Leila there, bidding her farewell for the last time.

"We will find you in heaven—very soon; it won't be long."

†

Melech had gone after the limousine with Ruth accompanying him. Down the driveway it comes, parking in front of the gaping garage.

the Day and the Hour

Adam and Alice are proceeding up the brick walkway, accompanied by Evelyn and Benayahu. Slowly, they mount the three steps. The bodyguard opens the door for Evelyn, and she turns to Adam.

"I'll see you in heaven—tomorrow. Don't forget me."

The Story

Chapter 10

Earl Clark stopped at the top of the driveway. Although no patrol car was in sight, he expected to see one shortly. It made little difference: he had taken into account that he would not get far before receiving some attention from Leila's surveillance team.

He got to Mountain Highway without picking up an escort. There he turned left, heading toward town using the route he always took when going directly to his office at the newspaper. He hoped to avoid arousing suspicions that he might be leaving the area, for leaving the area is what he had in mind—a trip to the city to be exact.

He had his phone with him, which would permit them to locate him easily. Before he reached the Creek-Street turnoff, he noticed an FSA patrol car in his rear-view mirror.

On Creek Street, Clark drove down the hill to Lake Way, turned right, right again on Howard, and pulled up to the espresso window. There he waited, pretending to be deciding what flavor to get, while checking his mirror in order to catch the surveillance car going by without appearing to be concerned about it. He waited a few seconds after it passed, handed a tip to the confused attendant, and pulled out to the street again, stuffing his phone into the specially shielded glove box, which would keep it from communicating with satellite and regional phone systems and thereby preventing his position from being tracked.

He had observed the patrol car turning left on First, no doubt to go around the block and come up behind him again while his espresso was being prepared. Therefore, he turned right on Second, went over to Creek Street, sped up the hill, and veered left onto Deer Drive. At the foot of Deer Drive he turned left onto Highway 321 and headed south without having attracted another escort.

the Day and the Hour

In less than an hour, Clark was into the outskirts of the city and still had not been trailed, thanks to his car not having any of the equipment that enabled the highway sensors to gather information from later-model cars. While his license plate might be detected, that was unlikely: it was mounted low on the car and had an anti-scanner coating applied to it.

He wound his way through the city, arriving by devious routing in a highrise business-and-residential area where he disappeared down a ramp to an underground parking garage. He punched in a code, and the door lifted to admit him into an unmanned facility where most of the parking spaces were assigned to tenants. He noticed that the spot where he usually parked was vacant, but he passed it up, circled back, and eased the T-bird into the remaining guest parking space.

Clark was bound for the residence of a friend whom he had not seen for several weeks. Prior to that he had visited her nearly every Saturday. Since she neither had nor needed a car (her place of business being within the same building), her parking spot was usually vacant.

His decision to come here was made on the spur of the moment while he sat in his shop after Evelyn had visited him. There was no opportunity to send a warning of his coming that would not have put too much information into the hands of the enemy. He had considered leaving a cryptic voice-mail message and had gone as far as composing it in his head:

> *Dr. Hayrab, this is Earl Clark, one of your patients. Look, I have a terrific toothache, and I need your help. Is there any chance I can get an appointment? I need your help today, really, but I would need to make arrangements before I can leave here since I'm under constant surveillance. Please keep an opening for me.*

There was a chance that Carmen would receive and decipher the message. Although she was a dentist, she had never been *his* dentist; therefore, she would know that the toothache was a ruse. Since he was clearly stating that he needed her help *today*, he

The Story

thought she would understand "Please keep an opening" to mean he was asking her to expect him at any time. Anyone else would think he was willing to endure the pain until next week.

After all that effort he had finally rejected the idea because it could lead to her being interrogated, and he did not consider it worth causing her that sort of trouble. The value of it was doubtful anyway since it would only slightly reduce the risk of her being away or being busy with something or someone else.

That risk was what he was contemplating as he rode the elevator up to the nineteenth floor of the Vineyard Building.

For all I know she's out of town. Maybe she has a date tonight.

the Day and the Hour

When her officers failed to find Earl's car after it disappeared from the espresso drive-in, Leila decided to take an active role in directing a more thorough search.

She had been at her desk on the top floor of the Federal Building for nearly an hour when she finally conceded that he had eluded her watch, broken the bonds of her security net, and gotten away. Her team had scoured the town and its environs while she maintained a map marking where they had searched. Although they had checked the airport for his car, when she heard the sound of an airplane's engine and saw Harold's 172 going by over the lake, she nearly panicked. She called Harold and was relieved to learn that a former student of Earl's had taken the plane up.

Thus it became clear that Earl had left the area. If he were about some business, on some errand, or attending some meeting in town, they would have found his car. Mountain Highway, Crossroads, and First Avenue had been covered all the while, but there was a possibility that he had slipped out on 321 and gone south. Chances are he went to the city.

The fact that his phone seemed to have disappeared from the planet made it certain that he intended to be out of her reach; and if that were his intention, she had a feeling that was the way it would be. Nevertheless, she considered it her duty—even while admitting to herself that it signified a lack of trust in what God might be doing—to keep trying.

In a few minutes the two-hour grace period would expire, and she would have to file a report with the FBI. She had already prepared the message, and it was ready to go in an instant. She was of a divided mind with regard to that too. Why not forget the surveillance protocol? In fewer than fifteen hours she would no longer be here, and hopefully he would be leaving too. The answer, of course, was that she was in love with him and harbored a desperate desire to communicate with him somehow—even that she might have an opening to plead with him to yield and be

The Story

saved for the Rapture and avoid any future complications. At the very least she must speak with him before going away, possibly leaving him forever.

As a practical matter it would change nothing to notify the FBI. The only thing they would do would be to have the city police look out for him. She had already initiated that. Other than going out looking for him herself, she had run out of things to do.

It was tempting.

Why not? Why not drive to the city?

If love could lead her, she would find him.

"I will rise now and go about the city, in the streets, and will seek him whom my soul loves," she quoted.

A message appeared on her screen. It was from Al Cypher down in Detention Suites.

> I noticed when you came in to your office – also that Earl
> Clark eluded our surveillance team. It looks bad for
> Clark. Is there anything I can help you with? -AC

I'll be glad to be rid of him. ... No, that's wrong. The poor man is in the detention of Satan.

She dictated a response, which appeared on the screen:

> Did you ignore my memo yesterday? Earl will soon be
> with me in heaven. Don't you miss out. -LL

I wish someone could bring the good news to those men down there. Lord, have mercy on them.

Ms. Labaki, chief executive officer, hit the key on her keyboard to send the report to the FBI. Lovesick Leila picked up her jacket and purse and turned her back to the panorama of lake and mountain that had been her delight during the few months that she had worked there.

I'm out of here.

At the foot of Hill Street, at the stop sign where it meets the highway, she hesitated with her left-turn signal blinking.

What are my chances, really? The sun will go down about the time I get there. ... What if he comes looking for me? I think

the Day and the Hour

there's a slightly better chance of that.

She switched the blinker to the right and headed toward home. As she passed the Garden restaurant, she recalled her thoughts of a day ago: Last night when making plans for today, she had every expectation of being with Earl tonight. They would be going to dinner together, probably to the Garden since it was the best restaurant in the area. So she had heard. She had never been there.

The Story

Earl pushed the bell and waited. He knew that Carmen would have received an automatic notification of someone coming into the garage using her code—if she were there. And she would see him standing at the door in her hallway monitor. If his visit would be awkward for her, or if she simply did not want to see him, she would not answer the door.

There was a click. The door was being unlocked. It opened slightly, revealing a woman's face. It was Carmen.

"I need a place of refuge," he said as he stepped inside and closed the door. "The feds are after me; but as long as I get back by Monday, I think nothing will come of me being here."

"Are you under surveillance now?"

"Yes, supposedly, at home but not here—I hope. I had to get out of there: I couldn't stand it anymore. I slipped away in the T-Bird, which is hard to track. I don't have my phone on me; I left it in the shielded glove box in the car."

"What about the cameras? They record every vehicle going by."

"That's under city traffic control, and I think it will take some time for the cops to get the information. At least it's not instantaneous. And they probably were not able to pick up my license-plate codes. So I think I'm safe here for a while." (He was not aware of the extent to which information systems had lately been integrated.)

"If we're that safe, I'm sure you intend to take me to dinner for putting up with you."

"Any place you would like to go."

"Close is fine. Let's go to Peter's."

"Good. We always liked it there, and Peter is our friend. I'll have him alert us if anyone comes snooping around. It could be that the cops have already gotten an order to look for me, but I doubt that they'll hunt all over the city. I'm not that important. They'll wait until some information comes up, and hopefully it won't be tonight."

the Day and the Hour

"Give me a few minutes to get ready. There's coffee in the kitchen."

"Thanks. I need some."

"You can call and make a reservation for six o'clock."

Being familiar with the apartment, Earl went into the kitchen and poured himself a cup of coffee; then he picked up her residential phone, requested Peter's at the Vineyard, and made the reservation.

He was too wound up to sit down and relax. He paced from the kitchen to the living room where there was a view out onto the courtyard, and back to the kitchen where a sliding glass door opened onto a balcony patio. He was thinking of various scenarios of possible encounters with the police.

Finally, he turned his thoughts to Carmen in order to relieve his mind of worry. She would be his refuge tonight. Her company would be a comfort after all he had been through since he saw her last.

Carmen emerges from her bedroom dressed for dinner, rendering Earl, who wore the clothes he wore sailing, an unlikely escort.

"Do you have a hat I could wear?—in case they get access to the traffic photos and figure out where the T-bird went. A bit of disguise might be prudent. It's possible that they will be checking restaurants in this building."

Carmen opens a closet door. "Would you take down that box?" She searches through the box of hats. "How about this beret?"

"That will do fine. ... How do I look?"

"Goofy. It's a woman's hat and too small for you. You look like a kooky jazz musician."

"Good. I wouldn't want to deceive anyone."

"I know you always like to have a hat on, but you can't wear that inside the restaurant!"

"Don't worry, I'll take it off. But if we get word of the cops coming around I might have to put it on."

"All right. Have it your way. Let's go. It's almost six o'clock."

The Story

Chapter 11

Alice Murphy is preparing the last supper for her husband. It will be just the two of them since Felix declined Adam's invitation. He was on a roll, he said, and wanted to continue calling on people who had been recommended by those attending his lectures.

In spite of his good intentions, it seems to the pastor that his own ministry this week came out half baked, and it does not feel right to be sitting back now and letting the enemy devour the last fourteen hours. It is an anticlimax. The humble pancakes Alice is making are a fitting symbol of this flat ending that things have come to.

Mercifully, a mellower thought comes to mind: *Why not be glad to be spending these last hours alone with Alice who has cheerfully shared so many mishaps with me in this world?*

Alice is presenting the first spatula load of pancakes to his place at the kitchen table. On her way back to the stove, the doorbell rings.

"I'll get it," she says.

She goes down the hallway and opens the front door. Two tall men are standing there, men whom she has never seen before. They are similar in appearance—perhaps twins. Though there is nothing sinister about their presence, she trembles and almost cowers. She is looking up at stern faces, yet they are not unkind. Piercing intellects seem to be weighing her and measuring the stature of her spirit, even reading the secrets of her heart. She lowers her eyes and finds the spatula still in her hand. Although no uniform, badge, or anything of that sort sets them apart from ordinary humanity, they are obviously men of importance. There is an uncanny emanation of authority. Their right to be there is beyond questioning, and their purpose is not something to be inquired of casually. Certainly, she is not one to stand in the way

the Day and the Hour

of whatever they have come to do.

Presently, her unease melts away as quickly as it came, and her eyes are drawn back to their faces. They are not permitting her to be afraid. They have made peace with her without speaking a word.

Adam, wondering about the delay, gets up from the table and comes to see who might have arrived in such profound silence. Hearing his footsteps, Alice turns to face her husband. She is still speechless. He takes in the strange scene, and at once a passage from the Bible comes to mind, opening a door to a possibility. On an impulse, he urges all his sensibility through the door and embraces the possibility as fact.

"Alice, please go and set two more places at the table. We have guests for dinner."

Glad to have her impasse resolved, she hurries back to the kitchen.

"Please come in," Adam says to the men. "We have little food left in the house, but you are welcome to all that we have."

"Thank you, Adam. This will be our last meal on earth for a while," says one of the visitors. "We're tired of lobster, and we're hungry for pancakes," the other says.

"I would tell you my name," says the first, "but it's a complicated affair. You can call me Jack."

"Likewise, my name would be inconvenient just now," the other says. "You can call me Flap."

They both grin, and Adam knows he can let down his guard. But more than that, what he knows from Scripture coupled with his commitment to apply it in the present case elevates his expectation to a level that is truly out of this world.

"You have come to the right house, as I believe you must know, because pancakes are on the menu tonight!"

They follow him into the kitchen where Alice is rearranging the table.

"I'm so embarrassed about the pancakes," she says.

"We love pancakes!" Flap cries.

The Story

"Indeed, that's why we're here," Jack says with a wink.

They take their places at the table while she goes to the stove to pour the last of the batter onto the griddle, to the cupboard to get out the remaining flour, and to the refrigerator to get the last egg. The beer can is sitting on the counter, and she slides it out of sight behind the mixing bowl. She used some of it in the first batch of batter but is afraid it will not be acceptable to these spiritual giants.

"Was that a can of beer?" Jack asks.

"Yes," Alice replies, blushing.

"You're not wasting it in the pancakes are you?" Flap asks.

"Well, yes, I was," she admits.

"Oh, well, go ahead and put it in," Jack says. "You don't have more, do you?"

"No, this is all I use it for," Alice says.

"That's a pity," Flap says.

"Their beer isn't much good anyway, Flap," says Jack.

"That's true," he replies. "But I wouldn't refuse a can if she offered me one."

"Don't tease her so! You know she doesn't have any more, Flap."

"You're right. I'm sorry, Alice—a little."

"Don't mind him," Jack says. "We should tell you right now why we're here."

"We've been working with Paul Christian," Flap announces.

"Paul has been telling folks who want to be baptized to go to the Beach House tomorrow morning before eight o'clock," Jack adds.

"Why didn't he tell *me* that?" asks Adam. "Please help yourselves to the pancakes."

"The reason is he wanted to wait until he had a headcount, so you would know what to expect and be able to adjust your timing accordingly," Flap explains, picking two pancakes off the pile.

"He wasn't even sure the Beach House would be available," Jack says, taking the next two hotcakes. "He was telling people to go there, trusting that he could get permission from Kenneth Clark. But he's been unable to reach Clark."

"So we're here to tell you that you need to be at the Beach House tomorrow morning," Flap says.

"There will be forty-nine souls for you to baptize," Jack adds.

"Forty-nine? Felix made forty-nine converts?" exclaims the pastor.

"Not yet, but he will before the night is over," declares Flap.

"Did Felix send you here?"

Both Flap and Jack have mouths full of pancake. Adam takes a big bite himself while he waits for an answer, and Alice delivers another batch to the table.

"No. ... He hasn't seen us," Jack says, finally. "But he's well aware that the Lord is working right along with him."

"Do you know where Kenneth Clark is?" Adam asks, being confident that his visitors have paranormal powers despite their manifestly mundane appetites.

"He's in the city tonight," Flap replies.

"Will he be back in time? He's my friend, you know. I'm still hoping he will ...."

"We're not permitted to say too much," says Jack, cutting him off.

But Adam is too excited, being in the presence of these heavenly personages, not to avail himself of whatever knowledge he can get them to divulge.

"Can you at least confirm the event we're all expecting at eight o'clock tomorrow morning?"

There is silence while Flap and Jack continue to demonstrate their genuine love of pancakes.

I guess I wasn't supposed to ask that.

"We're not permitted to say too much," Flap says, finally.

"The end of the age is at hand," says Jack.

"That means the Rapture, am I correct?"

"You had the dream," Flap replies. "Was it not the thundering voice of a lion?"

The Story

"I understand the thunder now; at first I attempted to emphasize the sweetness that came from it, but many in my congregation were unprepared to receive such an answer to the Rapture riddle, and it has become a bitter controversy. In fact, I was as unprepared as anyone. What determined the end of the age? Were there signs we missed?"

"Signs? What do you mean by signs?" replies Jack.

"The closing of free markets," mumbles Flap through a mouthful.

"What?" The preacher puts down his fork. "That has nothing to do with completing the church!"

"We're almost out of syrup. But here's some honey I found," says Alice, taking her place at the table. "The next batch will be ready in a moment."

"Perhaps you shouldn't have mentioned that, Flap," says Jack. "Now you will have to explain it to them. You will have to explain it to me too."

"The development of humanity was essentially the development of civility," says Flap.

Adam looks puzzled.

"You will have to explain that too," says Jack.

"The treatment people give to each other and receive from each other is not only a measure of their humanity, it's a measure of their rising above the Fall," says Flap, waving his fork. "That's the best way I can say it without using technical terms."

"By civility he means the free exercise of kindness toward all people," says Jack, just before stuffing the last of a pancake into his mouth.

"Not just to one's household or clan," says Flap. "That's the key to understanding what I mean."

Alice gets up from the table and goes to the stove. Everyone watches as she flips two nice pancakes onto a plate.

"It worked hand in hand with true religion," says Jack.

Alice drops a fresh pancake onto each of Flap's and Jack's plates. They knife globs of butter and lather the golden bread, eying the syrup bottle, which is nearly empty. They seem to be ignoring the honey.

"Let me see what else we may have to put on your pancakes," Alice says, and she goes to the refrigerator.

Adam hardly knows what to say. He is pondering Jack's statement.

It's the strangest theology I ever heard.

Adam's puzzlement plainly shows on his face.

"The exercise of civility was the surest escape from the stupefying culture of warring competition caused by the machinations of Satan," Flap explains.

"I found a full bottle of syrup in the refrigerator," says Alice. "I don't have any idea where it came from."

"From your point of view, it's part of sanctification," Jack adds.

"Also, here's a little strawberry jam and a little whipped cream left in this can," she says as she sets her offerings on the table.

"I thought sanctification was the work of God within the heart of the individual," Adam says.

"From heaven's viewpoint," Flap replies, "it involves both individuals and culture: you can't separate the individual from the culture. The culture in which you developed remains with you: it's part of you, and most of your personality is wrapped up in it." He was making a spiral of whipped cream on his pancake as he spoke.

"One aspect of sanctification is compensating for corruptions embedded in both your genes and the culture you inherited but doing it without destroying your essential characteristics," says Jack. "It's a relatively straightforward process; however, the results vary depending on how much corruption you came with." As he spoke, he was trying to copy Flap's spiral with little coming out of the sputtering spout.

"He refers to the ultimate perfection you must attain to before you're fit for eternal bliss," says Flap.

"All the hereditary wrongs—whether in culture or biology—

The Story

that are routinely blamed on God are due to the corruptions of the original creation by satanic parasites and genetic hacking—the results of the devil's attempts to be creative in his own diabolical way, much like your cyber-hackers exercise their creativity to pervert and cripple good computer code," says Jack.

"But the more difficult aspect of sanctification is lifting the man above the mores that the secular and religious elements of his culture have led him to believe are acceptable," says Flap. "As you know, sanctification, in order to be complete, must go beyond removing blemishes. But do you know what that entails?

"Becoming charitable, primarily," Adam replies.

"Yes, but what does that mean in practice?" Jack presses.

"Loving the needy, those from whom one cannot expect repayment or advantage, is one example."

"That's fine here and now, but have you ever considered that there will be no needy people in the Kingdom for whom some arrangement has not been made?" asks Flap.

"I see. Charity will be a little different then," Adam acknowledges.

"That's right," says Jack. "What you will find is the need to dwell cheerfully with all sorts of incredibly strange people. No longer will you be confined to your own church and family and town."

"Do you know how difficult it is to get people to let go of the idea that they're justified in shunning certain classes? It takes a great deal of training to get them to that point," Flap testifies.

"To get them to give up quarreling among their close associates is hard enough," Jack declares.

"Of course, there's no alternative but purgatory for the hard cases, which is most of them," Flap adds.

"Shall I make more pancakes?" Alice asks.

"If you don't mind. They're the best I've had since the Middle Ages," says Flap.

"I've told you a million times not to exaggerate, Flap," says Jack. "You said the same thing to a lady in England in 1842."

the Day and the Hour

"Oh, yes. I suppose I did. But I remember her pancakes well. These are better than those."

The pastor's perplexities are piling up. He sets the purgatory question aside for the moment. "I see that we did not aim high enough in our Christian culture. We were ingrown, definitely."

"Almost every culture and subculture in the world is at war with fabricated enemies," remarks Jack.

"There is one exception," says Flap.

"Not the market," Adam says.

Alice is at the refrigerator. "Where did these come from?" she asks, holding up two large eggs.

Flap points at Jack, who shrugs his shoulders and points back at Flap.

"Think about it," Flap says to Adam. "Whoever walks in the door is a potential customer and immediately becomes the object of unmerited kindness."

"Seldom is *that* the case," says Alice, breaking the eggs into the mixing bowl.

"True now, but it used to be common," says Flap. "Two things are essential: that the customer has other alternatives and that the merchant stands to profit from kindness exceeding that of the competition—not with certainty but a good possibility of it."

"Isn't that type of kindness artificial, arising out of a selfish motive?" asks the pastor.

"Yes, indeed it is," Flap replies. "But kindness is kindness, and few are deceived when it's shallow. The more genuine it was, the better it was for business."

"It was an exercise that often went far beyond the original need for it," Jack adds.

"That's exactly what I'm getting at, Jack," says Flap. "Clerks discovered the joy of serving and pleasing others, and they derived more satisfaction from that than they got from their paychecks—in spite of their education, which told them to expect the opposite."

"I know it well," says Jack. "It started back when people began using money. Those who provided goods and services to others discovered the satisfaction of receiving payment for the proof it afforded them that they had done something that someone else valued more than they did."

"In other words, income was the tangible thanks they got for meeting someone's need. It meant something because those who paid them the asking price gave it by their own choice," says Flap.

"But not all such people are heaven bound, surely," Adam points out. "There are many who cheat and many more who are honest yet give no thought to their need for sanctification."

"You're right about that," replies Jack. "But understand that this was not a school of sanctification. It was a tool we often found useful. We steered many a saint into such employment because it served our purposes."

"Now I'm confused," says the preacher. "I thought this was something that helped prepare people to exercise the unlimited kindness they will need to practice in heaven, not on the earth as it is today."

"So it was," answers Flap. "But we have to see that the soul gets the practice. It's a huge responsibility and often extremely difficult. We found that having the free-market culture available for our use lightened our task in many cases."

"Aren't there other roles in society that are equally valuable training grounds?" Adam asks.

"Servants of any kind are in a position to rise to the level of enjoying the rendering of service: anyone who deals with the general public and not a select clientele, that is. Nevertheless, it must be a position where the person receiving the service has options," says Jack. "Customer service at a financial institution is a good example."

"I suppose that rules out government employees," Alice observes while pouring fresh batter into the skillet.

"Unfortunately." Flap says. "They have no incentive to exercise kindness. A few do it even without the incentive, and for them the training is just as effective."

"You mean it really doesn't matter how they get to the point of showing kindness to everyone—whether incentives and rewards are involved or not?"

"That's right," Jack replies. "But incentive works wonders. The free market was the place where it was the strongest; therefore, it worked for more people. Not everyone, of course. But we trained many that way and saved ourselves a great deal of trouble."

"What about those of us who haven't yet gotten to the place where we know how to be perfectly kind to everyone?" asks Adam. "I'm afraid we will create chaos if we go as we are."

"You'll have to spend time in purgatory, that's all," says Flap.

"Why isn't purgatory mentioned in the Bible?" Adam asks bluntly.

"Oh, it is!" declares Jack. "What do you think the final age is for?"

"The Millennium? I always taught that's when the Lord redeems the earth—civilization, culture, government, religion—making everything be what it was meant to be," says Adam.

"That's true as far as it goes. The more important purpose is to train people to get along for eternity," Flap says.

"I suppose you're going to tell me there will be shopping malls when the kingdom of our Lord is established on earth," Adam says.

"Huge ones! ... Why not?" Jack says.

They sound like capitalists. Who am I talking to?

"I would not have thought any of this would be a good thing for the kingdom of God. What about family life being compromised by shopping trips, enslavement to consumer debt, and Black Friday?"

"None of those things is good, of course, but this just happens to be where we found grace flourishing on earth. We looked everywhere. Genuine kindness was invariably conditional or limited to relatively small circles. In public places, we found only grudging, superficial courtesy for the most part," Flap recalls.

"It's the same in the shopping mall, isn't it?" Adam asks.

The Story

"To some extent, it is," Jack answers. "But we discovered this gem of an exception in some of the sales—no, it's not really sales so much. We would rather say the *shopping* transactions."

Alice comes with a plate of three medium-size pancakes, and the three—What shall we say? Living beings?—each take one.

"I remember one butcher in the supermarket," she says. "Remember Ferdinand, Adam? He was the most helpful, friendly guy. It didn't matter whether or not he was busy or how ridiculous the request was. He was always cheerful and gracious—like he thoroughly enjoyed helping all kinds of people no matter who they were."

"I was thinking of Linda," says Adam. "She radiates cheer—makes each person feel special. She calls me the coconut-water man since that's primarily what I buy at the market."

"Ferdinand and Linda are good examples, indeed. Also, we found that women especially took to the jobs where they helped other women shop for clothing—complete strangers. The patience and kindness that some of them developed were rare virtues—beautiful, wasn't it, Jack?"

"Absolutely, it was," Jack replies. "This phenomenon really shouldn't exist anywhere in this world, but somehow it sprouted up in a commercial setting. So, we used it to our advantage. Can you blame us for that? Why wouldn't it provide us the same advantage in purgatory?"

"Do you mean the purgatory of the Millennial kingdom?" Adam asks.

"Yes. Sorry," says Jack. "I think of them as the same thing—that is, the earthly branch."

"I still don't see how you can be so enthusiastic about this minor aberration in the emporiums of godless materialism," Adam says, mustering a bit of eloquence in defense of his hard-earned world view.

Flap holds up his hand, signaling a time out while he clears his mouth.

"Godless, you say? Nothing is independent of the providence

of our Lord. The consumer markets are a vital link in the life of the world. Without them, there would be no spur for development and no aiming for physical well being. There would be no efficient transportation systems, no high-speed communications, and food production and distribution would not meet the needs of the world's population."

"These economic engines sprang into existence just when needed to feed and clothe the world," Jack declares, holding up a dripping chunk of pancake on his fork. "Do you think this was an accident or according to the wishes of the devil?"

"And don't forget, the same economy, with its communication and transportation technology, evangelized the world," Flap says.

"Now, let me make sure I have this straight," Adam says. "After Christ returns and sets up his kingdom on earth, there will be more automobiles and highways than ever. Is that what you mean?"

"Their equivalent or better," Jack says. "Don't rule out advancement beyond what you know. You can't begin to imagine how much potential your Creator managed to fit into your material universe. It will take most of the thousand years to bring it all out."

"And people will be running here and there, looking for the perfect thing to buy?" Adam presses.

"You're picturing what you know, where people are idolaters," Flap says. "Those will not be allowed to buy or sell, so shopping will not be inflaming sin."

"Curiouser and curiouser," Alice says, delivering another plate of golden cakes to the table. "But I like it."

"It is most peculiar," Adam says. "Isn't it only a small fraction of society that's involved in selling things to the public?"

"Oh, not as small as you think," Jack says. "Leave us a little butter, Flap, will you? It involved everyone at one time. The shoppers often benefited nearly as much as the service people. You see, grace once received is inspiring, and it occasionally fosters like behavior. Furthermore, there is the other side of the

The Story

coin: Being kind to the merchant reaps benefit to the customer. You don't often choose the person representing the item you're interested in, but you need to exercise kindness in order for the experience to be satisfactory."

"An accomplished shopper knows how to bring out the best in a perfect stranger who happens to be the sales person being dealt with. It's a marvelous skill that will serve well in eternity," Flap says.

"If free markets are so good, how did they get started in the devil's world?" Adam asks, still unwilling to give up his ecclesiastical bias.

"Don't think the devil has been for them," Jack says. "They're simply what people do when you leave them alone, and the devil never managed to change mankind that much. What mitigates against free markets is, of course, diabolical: bullying, thievery, and various interventions. These factors have been present and overbearing in most markets throughout the history of the world."

"Truly free markets flourished rather lately," Flap says, "thanks in part to improvements in transportation and even more to the model of a free society implemented on a grand scale in the USA."

"Surely the ideals and practices of true religion have contributed to sanctification. Please don't tell me they haven't," Adam pleads.

"Religion alone was insufficient to overcome the pressure of depraved social conditions," Jack explains. "There were too many disadvantages. Civilization with and without religion was serving Satan primarily—and no surprise, for he dominated most of the rulers of the world."

"The conditions faced by saints and sinners alike were not allowing them to exercise charity save to those within a small circle," Flap adds.

"There were great saints who met the challenge," Jack admits. "But the mass of humanity lived and died without the opportunity to develop unqualified civility."

the Day and the Hour

"Mere survival was task enough for most," Flap says.

"But when the Scriptures finally broke away from the control of the clergy, seeds were scattered, and they began to grow into cultures in which freedom became possible and practicable," Jack says with relish, no doubt remembering the days when this began to happen.

"The devil worked hard to stamp out each one of them; you can be sure of that!" Flap exclaims.

"But he overdid it in one case," Jack says. "Certain persecuted pilgrims were removed from the lion—the British empire, that is—and planted in the New World, and land of milk and honey was the result."

"Out of the brute came something sweet," says Flap.

"That's clever, Flap," says Jack.

"For the first time in the history of the world, social freedoms were established on a large scale," Flap says. "It was exciting to watch the development though it didn't come without bloodshed and the destruction of the lion."

"It was the culture in the USA with its freedoms to compete one with another in a constructive way that fostered civility as never before," Jack says. "I see you're getting the picture, but you still have doubts."

"It's those dark spots that are bugging him," Flap says. "Adam, there were dark spots and failures, for Satan was incensed that such a thing had taken root and gotten out of control."

"In fact, the good that was accomplished for the kingdom of heaven has never been appreciated," Jack says. "I don't blame you for having missed it in this day and hour."

"The USA became the greatest generator of nearly sanctified souls the world has ever seen, believe it or not," Flap says. "The devil worked hard to destroy the system—injecting his corruptions at every opportunity and making the corruptions famous."

"Your rather significant progress in civility went unmeasured and unappreciated and is today virtually unheard of," Jack says.

The Story

"Altogether, it not only aided sanctification, it created more saints than all periods of the world's history combined."

"Their energy and goodness and ingenuity brought the light of the gospel to other nations and wrenched untold numbers of slaves and poorer freemen from the devil's hold," Flap says.

"Now it has been shut down with employment guarantees and welfare payments, so the incentive to treat others kindly has virtually vanished," Jack says. "Mostly, it is large enterprises with teams of lawyers and lobbyists that have survived the regulations, and since the employees are made secure by laws and union contracts, they have no incentive to exercise civility."

"Everything is rapidly degenerating to the stultifying drudgery of the managed economy," Flap says. "Most of the fun in making a living has already been taken back by the devil's operatives."

"Now the White Horse—what you call the Reorganization—will introduce subhuman civility. It's a copy of the infrastructure of hell," says Jack. "In fact, most of the computer code is the same."

"The USA was the jewel of this dispensation," says Flap. "Though not without blemishes, it was far more valuable to the kingdom of heaven than anybody imagines," Flap says.

"Except us," Jack says.

"Right. Except us," Flap agrees. "I said 'any-body.' Are we bodies?"

"That's debatable," Jack says. "But let's not debate it now."

"All right." Flap says. "Sorry, Adam. I know you would be interested. But Jack gets tired of repeating things, and we've done it a million times. That's why it's debatable. He's not supposed to get tired—ever."

"And that was the reason the USA was not able to ward off the attacks from within," Jack says, ignoring Flap's aside. "It became incapable of destroying pathogens precisely because the good people did not believe how good their goodness was. The sweetness that was tasted at first became bitter in the stomach."

"Being undervalued, there was too little will to defend free enterprise. That was Satan's most effective effort: disparaging America to Americans," Flap says.

"As the culture of freedom in the USA died, so did the other useful cultures of the world," Jack says.

"The end has now come," Flap says. "We can make no further use of any of it."

"You mean 'little use,' not 'no use,' Flap. And you know this isn't the reason for the end. The man was asking about signs—whether he had missed a sign."

"There was no sign; he should know that," Flap says.

"But you could have told him that. Instead of spending so much time talking, we could have been eating more," Jack scolds.

"I know. But I wanted to offer these lovely folks something for their hospitality. I thought this was as good a reason for the end of the age as any, if there needs to be a reason," Flap says.

"Anyway, it's all over; that part is true," says Jack. "The Lord will be making sweeping changes starting tomorrow."

Adam opens his mouth to ask for details.

"That's all we're permitted to say," Flap says.

"Would you entertain a question about purgatory?" asks the preacher.

"You're wondering about the dream that came up on Tuesday and how it fits in," says Jack.

"It doesn't *fit* in," says Flap. "It *is* in."

"Now, explain that to them, Flap. And explain it to me too."

"Personally, I liked Lazar's dream. That's all I meant," says Flap. "I thought it was a brilliant heavenly purgatory."

"You don't mean it's really like that?" asks Adam.

"Oh, it is like that. Wouldn't you say it's like that, Jack?"

"Aren't you being a little obscure, Flap?"

"How would *you* explain it?"

"I wouldn't try," says Jack. "I would just say it was a nice dream and leave it at that."

"I've had a little experience with dreams, and they don't always make sense," says Alice.

The Story

"Exactly so!" cries Flap.

"In fact, you're only a sort of thing in the author's dream," says Jack.

"If she were to wake," adds Flap, "you'd go out—bang!—just like a candle."

"I wouldn't!" Alice exclaims indignantly. "Besides, if *I'm* only a sort of thing in her dream, what are *you*, I would like to know."

"Ditto," says Jack.

"Ditto, ditto!" cries Flap.

"Hush! You'll be waking her, I'm afraid, if you make so much noise," says Alice.

"Well, it's no use *your* talking about waking her," says Jack, "when you're only one of the things in her dream. You know very well you're not real."

"I *am* real," says Alice, and begins to cry.

"You won't make yourself a bit realer by crying," Flap remarks. "There's nothing to cry about."

"If I weren't real," Alice says—half laughing through her tears, it all seems so ridiculous—"I wouldn't be able to cry, and ...."

"I hope you don't suppose those are real tears?" Jack interrupts.

"I know we're talking nonsense," Alice says as she brushes her tears away, "and it's foolish to cry about it. But it brought memories back from my childhood."

"There you go!" cries Flap. "That's what Lazar's dream was about."

"Thank you, Alice, for those delicious pancakes," says Jack.

"Thank you, Alice, I'm going to recommend that you get an award for your performance," Flap says.

"Adam, God-speed to you until we met again," says Jack.

"I have one rather selfish request," Adam says. "As long as you two are here, perhaps you could help us out."

"Your request has been granted," says Jack. "For the benefit of the readers, what is it?"

"Thank you. We'll sleep well tonight and be ready for those

the Day and the Hour

baptisms," says Adam as Jack vanishes.

"Oh! Where did he go?" exclaims Alice.

"Now, make sure your alarm clock has a fresh battery," says Flap with a grin, and he too vanishes.

"Are we dreaming?" Alice asks. "Did you see that? He left his grin behind, and it faded slowly."

"No, I didn't. He must have done it for your benefit. They were angels. Angels come and go like that. Generally they leave rather abruptly. I think it's a little awkward for them to be speaking to us at all, and social graces are a little beyond them."

"I thought their sense of humor was interesting."

"I thought they were trying hard to emulate human humor—rather unsuccessfully."

"Could it be that humor in heaven is like that?"

"Among angels, perhaps. But I'm wondering whether we should take any of it seriously. Maybe it was all a joke."

"I don't think so, Adam. Maybe a vision, but not a joke."

"You're right; I shouldn't have said that."

"Their plates are clean, did you notice? Their places look just as they did when I set them."

"Hm—reminds me of the Rapture."

"Do you think it might have been a vision?" Alice asks.

"How could we both be seeing the same thing?"

"The same as if we were both in the author's dream; it would be easy—just like you and so many others heard the same thing a week ago."

"I suppose that could be," he says, "but I do believe we have received information that we have to act on tomorrow morning."

"Oh! It couldn't have been a vision," Alice exclaims. "There are two syrup bottles, and we started with one."

The Story

Chapter 12

Carmen and her untimely date were enjoying soup and sushi and conversation in a corner of the Japanese restaurant. Unfortunately, the dining room afforded none of the privacy of booths and nooks: all tables were in view from the entryway. A fugitive seeking refuge would have wanted a different arrangement.

Their discussion meandered among several light subjects. Carmen was aware that Earl's life included a covert side, which she respected, and she did not seek to understand the circumstances of his present difficulty. Having exhausted their common interests, there was a pause. Carmen had a reasoned premonition about tomorrow, and for something to say, she ventured to bring it up.

"What do you think will happen tomorrow?"

"Nothing."

"No Rapture at all?"

"That's my guess."

"As much as I'd like to, I can't buy that," she declared.

"When did you become a believer?"

"I'm not a believer. I just .... Well, I happen to believe it's going to happen this time."

"Oh, come on. That's for religious fanatics."

"Yes, I agree with that. But I can't see it any other way. There's no better explanation; none even come close."

At that point they were interrupted by Peter who came to inform Earl that a police officer was in the lobby asking about reservations in names including either Kenneth or Clark.

"Randell pretended she could not get reservations up on the screen, and she needed to ask somebody for help. I sent her back to detain the cop as long as she can. Just letting you know. He might want to come in here and look around."

the Day and the Hour

Earl put on the beret.

"That hat will not do it," said Peter, laughing.

"Would it be okay if I play the piano?"

"Can you play good enough so my customers will not leave?"

"I can."

"All right. I will be where you can see me. Thumb up means coast is clear."

"I can't leave Carmen here by herself."

"Come with me, Carmen."

When the police officer looked in, he first scanned the tables for a well-built man with a female companion. He had already checked the sushi bar. He had a photograph on his fuzPad of Earl. Unfortunately, the photo showed him wearing a baseball cap. He became interested in the vacated table for two in the far corner with slices of rolls still on the plates. He was about to go into the kitchen to ask about it when Carmen came out wearing the Japanese-styled uniform worn by the waitresses and began clearing the table.

Earl was at the piano, wearing the beret and playing "I Don't Know Enough About You." From the entryway where the officer was standing, Earl's face could not be seen. The song happened to be a favorite of his, and Earl's rendition was so captivating that he remained there, enjoying it immensely, his eyes riveted to the piano and the beret on the pianist's head. Carmen took notice of this, and concluded that Earl had been caught. But as soon as the last note faded away and enthusiastic applause broke out, the officer turned and was gone.

The thumb-up signal came. Earl acknowledged it but played another jazz piece for good measure while Carmen came out to clear another table. Finally, Earl took a break and went to the restroom, removing the beret on the way.

When he came out, it appeared that he had been in a fight. He ducked into the kitchen and told Carmen they needed to leave immediately. He gave Randell a large bill and told her to keep the change. Carmen took off her costume while Randell called the

The Story

elevator to the lobby. They cautiously and quietly slipped away without being seen by anyone.

Carmen was afraid to ask him what had happened. Not until they were locked in the security of her apartment did she broach the question: "What happened?"

"The cop was waiting in the men's room—in a stall. He came out and tried to arrest me, but I'd seen his hat over the top, and I was ready for him."

"Obviously, he didn't arrest you. What did you tell him?"

"Nothing. I punched him out. Then I stuffed his mouth with toilet paper and handcuffed him to the stall using his own equipment. And look at this. I found these honey-and-nut bars in one of his pockets. He deprived us of half our dinner, so I felt justified in taking them. You can have this one: it has raisins in it."

Carmen wanted to say something, but she was speechless for several reasons: she could not think of words to scold and praise him simultaneously; it was all she could do to keep from laughing; and she was scared enough to scream. She looked up at him and shook her head. Then she noticed what was missing.

"Where is my hat?" she gasped.

the Day and the Hour

Everyone at Detention Suites, except Al Cypher, took part in preparing dinner. Pamela had sent him out with a grocery list and a promise that she would let him have a piece of the pie she intended to make. After he returned, she told him that she needed help, so he opened the suites and allowed the men into the common dining area and into the kitchen, disregarding the "Off Limits" posted on the kitchen door. Then he retired to his office, keeping a watchful eye on the proceedings in the monitors. He kept the audio on, enabling him to hear and see as well as if he had been standing in their midst.

The men hovered about Pamela, begging for jobs. She put Chub to work peeling potatoes, Mule cleaning vegetables, Milt forming hamburgers, Blink cutting fruit for the salad, Red and Buck slicing tomatoes and onions, and Lance making biscuits, while she put the cranberry-cherry pie together. By the time everything was ready, their initial confusion about her had fallen away, and everyone felt that she was his mother.

While things were baking and cooking, she sent them to their rooms to put on what they called the "formal outfits" that hung in their closets. They helped each other with the neckties, and the results were not all perfect, but they all reported for dinner complimenting each other on how fine they looked.

Pamela made up a plate of food for Al Cypher and sent Milt to deliver it to his office.

They sat down around the dining table, and Pamela had Lance give thanks to God. The men said it was the best meal they had ever had, and they kept saying it.

Afterward, they cleared the table, and Pamela brought out the pie. Al Cypher came out of his office to claim his piece.

Pamela had arranged for Al to take her to the Lakeview for the meeting. The hour was late; Cleo would already be well into her lecture. Everyone pitched in again; they hurried with the dishes, and before the prisoners knew it, they were locked back in their rooms.

The Story

*I*n spite of her late resolve to wait for Earl to come back at a time of his own choosing, Leila has succumbed to temptation and decided to make one last contact with the surveillance team. It is no wonder: she has been thinking of him constantly, trying to guess where he is and what he is doing since the last time she checked with them an hour ago.

Perhaps they have located him and forgotten to tell me. If only I could talk to him once more ....

She taps a request on her phone for an immediate voice status report from the FSA surveillance officer in charge.

"This is Lieutenant Watchman. A report has just come in from the city. They've located Clark."

"Can you put me through to the city police officer in charge? Is it still Major Bookings?"

"No, Bookings is off duty. Captain Samuel Clark is handling the case."

"I would like to speak with him directly. Thank you. ...

"Captain Clark, this is Leila Labaki of the FSA under whose requisition you are working to locate Kenneth Clark. I understand that one of your officers has made contact with Mr. Clark."

"*That is correct. There was an attempted arrest at 6:43 PM.*"

"Does that mean Mr. Clark is *not* now in your custody?"

"*Affirmative. The arrest was not successful.*"

"Was anyone injured?"

"*The officer has bruises on his face.*"

"Please give me the details."

"*I have the report in front of me, and I'll send it to you immediately if you like.*"

"That's fine. However, go ahead and read it."

> 5:37 PM: Request for information submitted to Traffic Surveillance.
>
> 5:55 PM: TS reports a matching vehicle entering the parking garage of the Vineyard Building at 5:07 PM.
>
> 6:15 PM: Officers stationed at all entrances to the building.
>
> At approximately 6:30 PM, Lieutenant Headworthy entered

the Day and the Hour

Peter's, one of the three restaurants in the building, and asked to see the guest list. He was told that the computer was malfunctioning, and the attendant went for help. After he waited several minutes, she reappeared, saying that someone would be out shortly to help her with the computer. She engaged the officer in conversation, and finally, after several more minutes, she was called away. When she reappeared, she said the computer server had been rebooted. She then allowed Headworthy to examine the guest list. There was a Kenneth Johnson but no Clark. He then asked to see Peter, the owner, who informed him that he did not meet guests personally but would take him to the dining room entryway for a discreet look.

Approximately thirty-five diners were present in addition to the staff and the piano player. No one fitting the description of Kenneth Clark was observed. However, it was difficult to see every face in the crowded, dimly lit room. Officer Headworthy believed that if Clark was in any publicly accessible place within the building, it would be that particular restaurant because it was the best and most popular. Having no warrant to remain in the premises, he decided to go into the men's restroom where he could wait for a chance encounter without drawing attention to himself.

At approximately 6:50, a man entered the restroom whom Headworthy recognized as matching the photo of Mr. Clark. He stepped out and asked him his name. The suspect admitted that he was Kenneth Clark, and the officer announced that he was under arrest and approached him with handcuffs. At that point Clark struck the officer on the face and knocked him unconscious.

6:59 PM: The restaurant called to report a policeman in the men's room lying on the floor, gagged and handcuffed to a stall. His mouth was stuffed with paper, and his equipment was in the toilet.

Leila lowers the phone and slaps a hand over her mouth to muffle a giggle.

"Ms. Labaki? ... Yes, I know. And Headworthy is not easy to restrain—he's a lion of a man."

The Story

"Then, is Clark still at large?" she asks after regaining her composure.

"We believe he is somewhere in the Vineyard Building. A hat was found in the restroom that is believed to be the one worn by the piano player. Officer Headworthy does not remember Clark coming in wearing it. If it was Mr. Clark who was playing the piano, the hat would explain why Headworthy did not recognize him in the dining room. I happen to know that Earl Clark plays the piano."

"Yes, that's right. He does."

"A name was found in the hat—which apparently does not belong to Earl. There is some question as to whether the hat was left by him."

"I happen to know that the hat he was wearing earlier today is at the bottom of the lake, and he left here without a hat, so I would not be surprised if he had been wearing a borrowed one. What was the name in it?"

"C. Hayrab. It's a women's beret. We have determined that a Carmen Hayrab resides in the building, and we are in the process of generating a search warrant. We checked her phone's location history and determined that it was in the restaurant between 6:03 and 6:53 PM, and it's now in her apartment. It is too late to get a warrant tonight without an urgent requisition, and that will be at your discretion."

Leila's phone is wet with tears. *He already had a girlfriend.*

"I want you to call the search off permanently," she says quietly.

"I can't do that. He has assaulted an officer. And I thought you were acting on behalf of the FBI."

"You're right. I can't call it off either. Forgive me for suggesting that he could be set free."

"There won't be much risk of his escaping during the night. We have personnel nearby, and we're monitoring the hallway cameras."

"Excuse me, Captain Clark. ... If I may—I'm just curious. How did you know that Earl plays the piano?"

"I paid for his piano lessons. I'm his father."

the Day and the Hour

The Story

Chapter 13

At the moment when Al Cypher came in with Pamela, Clio was away from the podium, having taken a break after speaking at length on the adventures of the patriarchs Isaac and Jacob. Two young children, who had been looking forward to another lesson with Pamela, left their parents and went with her to a separate room. Al took a seat with his back to the door, facing the dining room turned lecture hall. He sat with his arms folded and his hat pulled down, shading his eyes.

Four days ago this body of believers materialized out of thin air, so to speak. They had no pastor. Their nightly meetings consisted of a free supper, courtesy of the Lakeview's owner, followed by a lecture featuring some portion of the Bible. They received a fine introduction to the Christian faith on Tuesday in a talk by a local physician, Dr. Luke Martin, who drew his material from the book of Acts. On Wednesday, Pamela presented First Corinthians chapter fifteen, an essential chapter of the Bible.

Clio was the first convert and original member of the church. Being enthusiastic about history, she convinced Pamela to let her tell the story starting from the beginning. To be more precise, it was the children's insistence that Pamela be their teacher which gave Clio her opportunity.

Having returned to the podium, Clio opened her large notebook to the place where she had stopped. Then she began turning pages, sadly, for she had run out of time. She had decided to leave Genesis and not go any further. She wanted to tell her favorite story instead, the story of Samson and Delilah. There remained just enough time for it.

> We must skip ahead some seven hundred years to a time when the children of Israel had multiplied and become a nation numbering in the millions. They were living in Palestine, the promised land, after hundreds of years of slavery in Egypt. Although they had nominally conquered and subdued the

the Day and the Hour

former inhabitants of Palestine, things were not going well because they had failed to purge the land of evil. They had spared portions of the pagan culture, which turned around and bit them, infecting them with the poison of idol worship and its attendant evil practices. God had told them what they must do, and they obeyed only up to a point. Consequently, they found themselves in a weakened and defensive position with respect to the pagans.

As yet, the Israelites had not taken the yoke of a formal government upon themselves. They relied on leaders whom God raised up from time to time to meet certain needs and challenges—arbiters and champions they called *judges*. Later, they would seek the security and endure the burden of a formal monarchy. In the meantime, there were some memorable judges whose achievements and exploits are recorded in Holy Scripture.

The most celebrated of the judges is Samson, who came from the tribe of Dan. The territory originally allotted to Dan lay west and a little north of Jerusalem, including twenty miles or so of the Mediterranean coastline. Much of this area, and southward to Gerar and beyond, was controlled by the Philistines. Samson was born when his people had suffered forty years under Philistine oppression.

His birth had the miraculous about it. The angel of the Lord appeared to his mother, who had been barren, announcing his coming. Samson's mission would be to restrain the Philistines, and it would require a champion of unusual physical strength. Emphasis was placed on his diet. His mother was instructed by the angel that he was to be kept from drinking wine and eating anything from the vine. Additionally, his hair was to remain uncut. These rules characterized the Nazirite vow, and set him apart from others for this special purpose.

"A man of God came to me," she told her husband. "I think he was an angel—very awesome—so I didn't ask him his name or where he was from. He said, 'Behold, you shall conceive and bear a son. Drink no wine or strong drink, and eat nothing unclean, for the child shall be a Nazirite to God from your

The Story

womb to the day of his death.'"

Her husband, a wise and devout man, believed her report and immediately prayed, "O Lord, teach us what we are to do with the child." The Lord answered his prayer and came again to the woman as she sat in the field. She ran to tell her husband, and he followed her back and addressed the visitor:

"When the child is born, what is to be the manner of his life?"

"Take care and do all that I've already told your wife," the angel said. "She also is not to eat anything from the vine; neither let her drink wine nor eat any unclean thing."

"What is your name, so that when your words come true we can honor you?" he asked.

"Why do you ask my name, seeing I'm not an earthly being? My name is too wonderful to tell."

This seemed to call for worship and a sacrifice. He took a young goat along with some grain and offered them on his rock altar to the Lord who works wonders. When the flame of the offering went up, the angel ascended in it. Seeing that, they fell on their faces, worshiping the Lord.

"We shall surely die, for we have seen God," the man said to his wife.

"If the Lord had meant to kill us, he would not have accepted the offering or shown us all these things," she reasoned.

As the Lord predicted, she did bear a son, and she called him Samson, a name meaning "serves," implying "one who serves God," or "of the sun," implying "one who is radiant and mighty."

When Samson had become a young man, the Spirit of the Lord began to stir him. While he was at Timnah, a Philistine-occupied city to the west of his home, he noticed a particular girl who—what shall we say? In Samson's eyes, if ever there were a girl perfect for him, it was she. Or so he thought: he had fallen in love with her. When he returned home, he told his father and mother that he wanted her for his wife. Of course, they were not in favor of his marrying the daughter of a pagan.

the Day and the Hour

But Samson's heart was set on her.

He took his parents to Timnah to meet her, and while they were encamped outside the city, he went looking for food, leaving his father and mother in the tent. Hunger drove him into a wild vineyard where he was tempted to break the Nazirite vow. He put his hand out to pick a cluster of grapes, and just then a young lion attacked him. I think the Lord sent that lion because as soon as Samson dropped the grapes, the Spirit of the Lord rushed upon him, and he killed the lion, tearing it to pieces with his bare hands. He took care to clean his messy hands in a brook on the way back, and he did not tell his parents about the incident because he did not want them to know that he'd been in the vineyard.

The next day, they went into the city. He located the home of the girl, and they talked her father into letting him marry her. Then he and his parents returned to their home in Zorah where he prepared a place for her in his father's house.

After some time, they returned to make wedding arrangements, and while they were camped outside the city, Samson went to see what was left of the lion. The carcass was there, and bees were flying around it. Opening it with a stick, he discovered a sizable quantity of honey, and he withdrew the honeycomb, being careful not to touch the dead flesh. Then he returned to camp, ignoring the bees buzzing about him, and eating honey as he went. He shared what was left with his folks, but he did not tell them where he got it.

As they were arranging for the wedding feast, a magistrate came with a number of young men, informing Samson that the groom must have companions, that these fellows would be his attendants, and that they would expect to receive linen garments for their service. It was typical of the customary tests designed to prove whether the husband would be resourceful. But Samson did not like their terms, so he proposed an alternative that they would not turn down. Though it was in the form of the customary riddle, it had a purpose beyond what they knew.

"If you can answer my riddle during the seven days of the

The Story

feast, I will give you the garments you asked for plus another set of clothes for each of you. But if you cannot give me the answer, then you must give me the same number of linen garments along with extra sets of clothes."

"What is the riddle?" they asked.

Out of the eater came something to eat;
Out of the brute came something sweet.

They reasoned: how could they all, thinking hard for seven days, fail to hit upon the answer? So they took his challenge, and the wedding feast began.

Samson informed his bride about the foxy deal he had made, and they both laughed about it, for it would make a nice dowry. But he was wise enough not to reveal the answer to her.

For three days the young men strained their brains trying to answer the riddle, using every clue in what was known about him. They even enlisted the help of older men in the city. None of them came up with anything that worked. Their leader—let us call him Ali—convinced the others to let him handle the matter. He was supposed to be Samson's best man, but I suspect (my reason we shall see in a moment) that he hated Samson for taking the girl *he* wanted. I think she had convinced her father to turn Ali down before Samson came along.

On the fourth day, Ali approached Samson's bride with a threat couched in a deceitful accusation:

"Have you brought that Israelite here to impoverish us? Entice him to give you the answer; then tell it to me. If you don't, we'll set fire to your father's house and blame it on Samson."

She feared Ali and didn't know what else to do, so she went to Samson in tears: "You hate me; you don't love me: you haven't told me the answer to our riddle."

"I haven't even told my father or my mother, so why should I tell you?" he replied.

It made no difference. She did nothing but weep and carry on for the remainder of the feast. Finally, on the last day, Samson broke down and told her, and she let the secret out to

the Day and the Hour

Ali.

The young men came to Samson, chanting:

*What is sweeter than **honey**?*
*What is stronger than a **lion**?*

"If you had not plowed with my heifer, you would not have found out my riddle!" Samson replied.

He was furious, and the Spirit of the Lord rushed upon him to do some great deed. He didn't want to upset his wife, so he went a respectful distance away, down to the city of Ashkelon over on the coast to the southwest, and struck down enough of the enemies of Israel to collect the garments he needed. He brought the clothes back and threw them at the Philistine cheaters. Then, still hot with anger, he left and went home, back to his father's house. And Ali took his wife.

Later, at the time of the wheat harvest, Samson went to get his wife, taking a young goat as a gift for the family and expecting to spend the night with her. But her father stopped him.

"I thought you hated her," he said. "So I gave her to Ali."

He didn't like the way Samson was looking at him. He had heard what happened in Ashkelon. "Take her younger sister," he said. "She's prettier, isn't she? What do you say?"

"This time you really have it coming," Samson said.

He went out and captured young foxes—ten times as many as there were young men in his wedding party—and tied them in pairs by their tails, attaching a torch to each, so when he lit the torches they ran around like crazy, setting fire to everything. Exactly how he accomplished that, I don't know. Obviously, Samson was an ingenious man. The grain in the fields, the stacks of wheat, and even the olive orchards were damaged by the fire.

When the farmers discovered who had done it, they were afraid to confront Samson directly. Instead, they sent a mob to burn down his in-laws' household. The fire killed both his wife and her father.

"If this is the way you're going to be, I'll be avenged of you once and for all," said Samson. He went through the city,

The Story

disabling the men by putting their thighs out of joint. Then he retired into the hill country south of Bethlehem in the territory of Judah, to a place called Etam. It was a secure spot, essentially a cleft in the rock.

So Samson became a headache for the Philistines. He was unstoppable when the Spirit of the Lord came upon him, and there was no predicting what he would do next. Ali saw to it that he became the most wanted man in Palestine, and his apprehension became top priority. He had to be captured and imprisoned.

Since Samson was a Danite lodging in Judah, Ali came up with a scheme to get the sons of Judah to expel him and turn him over to the Philistines. They staged a surprise raid on Lehi, a Judean town between Zorah and Etam.

"Why have you come up against us?" the citizens of Lehi demanded.

"Why do you think?" answered Ali. "It's because you're harboring our most wanted criminal."

"If you mean Samson, we can't help you. He's our judge. People are going down there all the time to get his advice and have him adjudicate their disputes."

"Let's put it this way: you need a new judge. If you don't turn Samson over to us, you can expect more trouble like this. Whether he's your judge or not, he has engaged in wanton acts of violence against our people, and they're demanding justice. Why should you risk the lives and property of the families of Judah? He belongs in Dan. They're the ones who should be taking responsibility for him."

"Give us some time, and we'll see what we can do," they replied.

The men of Lehi enlisted help from neighboring towns, and a large delegation went down to Etam and confronted Samson with their problem.

"Don't you know that the Philistines are in control here? They're all up in arms now because of what you've done."

"They had it coming," Samson replied. "As they did to me, so I did to them."

the Day and the Hour

"We understand that. But you have made yourself very unpopular in Judah. Please don't force us to fight you. Why kill your own countrymen? You can't overpower us and tie our tails together as if we were so many foxes. Take a look out there: we are ten times as many as there were foxes. We've come to bind you and take you back to the Philistines. Please don't resist us. After we deliver you to them, you can do whatever you like."

"All right—if you swear not to attack me yourselves."

They agreed. They tied his hands, arms, and legs securely with new ropes, lifted him up, and marched him back to Lehi where his enemies were waiting.

When the Philistines saw him bound with ropes, they rushed at him, shouting vengeance and waving their short, curved swords. Then the Spirit of the Lord came upon Samson. He broke the ropes around his arms and legs as if they were charred candle wicks, and the cords binding his hands literally melted away. He picked up a jawbone of a donkey that was lying on the ground and began swinging it, striking down three and four of his attackers in one swipe as wave after wave of them came at him. He stepped over the fallen bodies and met them with mighty swings of the big bone. Finally, they turned and ran, but Samson pursued them, leaving his countrymen behind to pile up the dead. Few Philistines escaped that day. At the end of it, Samson sang out:

With a donkey's jaw made I heaps upon heaps;
A thousand I struck with a donkey's jaw.

After such exertion, he was thirsty, as you can well imagine. He tossed the jawbone aside and looked around for some water. But it was a dry land, and there was no sign of it. So he called upon God:

"O Lord, you have granted this great salvation by the hand of your servant. Now shall I die of thirst, and we all fall back into the hands of the ungodly?"

The Lord answered by splitting open an artesian aquifer. Water gushed forth, and Samson drank; his spirit returned, and he revived. They named it "the spring of him who called."

The Philistines left him alone for a while after that. It was rumored that his superman strength came from the Spirit of God, which left them little hope. He moved freely about the country; nevertheless, Ali never forgot to watch for an opportunity to capture him.

One day when Samson was down in Gaza, a certain prostitute attracted his attention, and he went in to her. The Gazites, realizing they had him in a vulnerable way—no doubt estranged from the Spirit of the Lord—planned to ambush him at the city gate in the morning. But Samson surprised them: He rose at midnight when the gate was closed. He pulled it up, bar and all, and carried it away on his shoulders to the top of a hill.

On a certain farm in the valley of the Sorek there lived a woman whose name was Delilah. She was a delicate thing, and Samson loved her and often went to see her. What was it about these Philistine women?

The Philistines had been maintaining their surveillance team to monitor Samson's movements, hoping to discover some weakness they could exploit to contain him. Ever since the episode at Gaza, they doubted that he was still in good standing with the God of Jacob who, they understood, did not approve of the sort of thing he had done. Being devout pagans, their understanding was limited: They did not know the God of Israel. They refused to recognize that the children of Israel had a legitimate claim to Palestine, which blinded them to the purposes of God. They thought the alleged promise to Jacob was something his descendants had fabricated. Moreover, the theory that made the God of Jacob out to be the supreme deity of the universe had been discredited by the fact that Dan and much of Judah had fallen under Philistine dominion. It was inconceivable to them that his love for Israel was unconditional and everlasting. It would not have occurred to them that while Israel was reaping punishment for disobedience sown, God would not permit another nation to oppress her beyond certain limits. That Samson's being called a judge was a badge of his divinely appointed office meant nothing to them. It would have been ludicrous to their way of thinking that his strength was a manifestation of the Spirit of God designed specifically to limit

the Day and the Hour

Philistine strength. They would hatch their plan to exploit Samson's vulnerability without the slightest fear that it would be turned around and used against them.

Someone on the anti-Samson team remembered how his wife had weaseled out of him the answer to his wedding riddle. Of course, it was Ali. Who in all of Palestine was more motivated to get rid of him? Evidently, Ali had a taste for women that mirrored Samson's, and it would not be surprising if he had his eye on Delilah.

In any event, Samson's history was known, and the fact that a woman once made him give up his secret was no secret. They saw an opportunity to exploit this weakness again.

These officials were well equipped. They had manpower and money. It was expected that obtaining the information they wanted would involve bribery, and putting the intelligence to use would require muscle. In addition to these physical assets, Ali was well equipped with jealousy and vengeance. He went to Delilah with the following proposition:

"My dear, we happen to know that Samson has a weakness for women such as yourself; you can make him do anything you like. Now, listen to me. He is an exceptional man, as everyone knows, and he thinks he's invincible. It would be a good thing for you and for him and for everyone if we could humble him just a little. So, here is our plan: 1) You seduce him. Then you will own his heart, and he'll tell you anything you want to know. 2) You coax him to tell you the secret of his strength. 3) You tell us the secret, and we overpower him briefly—just to show him that he's not everyone's master. Oh yes; we'll each give you a bag of silver."

Delilah had no appetite for intrigue, and she despised Ali, for Samson had told her about him. However, she did like his suggestion about winning Samson's heart. She was not one to get involved in conflicts, but on the other hand she was afraid to resist Ali and his men. She suspected that he wanted her for himself, and she knew he had a way of getting what he wanted. It was a risky bargain, but she believed Samson would protect her if she won his heart. And the longer she could mollify Ali

The Story

the better. It never occurred to her that any of them could do Samson any real harm.

So Delilah seduced Samson and captured his heart. She was not aware that she already had it: Samson was hesitant to fall under the influence of a woman after what had happened with his former wife, so he had been reluctant to let her know how much he loved her.

"I have to ask you this," Delilah said. "Do you have any vulnerability where an enemy might subdue your great strength?"

Samson was indeed fearless, and he took it in good humor, making up a silly thing they both knew was in fun.

"If they bind me with seven fresh bowstrings, then I'll be weak like any other man."

The Philistines were a highly superstitious people and thought it might be true. They went back and reported it to Ali. He had them take her seven fresh bowstrings, which she tied around him. Husky henchmen lay in wait, ready to pounce on him.

"The Philistines are upon you, Samson!" she said. She couldn't keep from laughing, for it was a game now. She and Samson were making fools of the Philistines. He snapped the bowstrings as if they were the proverbial charred candle wicks.

"You have mocked me and told me lies!" she exclaimed for the sake of the spies who were listening. They must not be given reason to suspect that she betrayed them. But between her and Samson it was make believe, and they were grinning at each other.

"Now, please tell me how you may be bound, so I can turn you over to the Philistines. They just want to talk to you, that's all. They're afraid to approach you unless you're bound."

"If you bind me with new ropes, then I'll be weak like any other man," Samson declared.

That was a little more reasonable, and Ali was willing to give it a try, so they supplied Delilah with new ropes. The next time she and Samson were together, she brought out the ropes.

"Okay, so now I want to find out if you were telling me the

the Day and the Hour

truth!"

She wound the ropes around him and tied knots that made him laugh. When she had finished, she sang out, "The Philistines are upon you, Samson!"

He could easily have shaken out the knots, but he didn't bother with that. He simply snapped the ropes like threads.

"Until now, you have mocked me and told me lies!" she shrieked for the benefit of the spies and with a wink for Samson. "Now, tell me *truly* how you can be bound."

"If you weave the seven locks of my head with a web and fasten it with a pin, then I'll be weak like any other man."

That was delightful, and she couldn't wait to do it. But she feared that the Philistines would catch on to their game. So, after they were gone, she told Samson everything. He thought it was a jolly good joke on Ali to be leading him on this way, and they conspired about what to do to keep him from becoming suspicious.

She invited the spies back, and while Samson pretended to be napping, Delilah lovingly took the seven locks of his head and wove them with a web, making it tight with a pin.

"The Philistines are upon you, Samson!"

He pretended to wake from sleep. He moaned and groaned, sat up, and calmly undid his hair, letting the seven locks fall free.

The spies were wise to Samson and Delilah now, and they were tired of the game. Ali was furious when they reported back to him, and he vowed not to let Delilah mock him again and get away with it. So he had them tell her that they would give her one more chance, and she had better deliver, or else ....

Al Cypher stood up and left the room, but no one paid him any attention; they all were eager to hear the conclusion of the story.

Delilah was scared now. She did not doubt that Ali and his gang would carry through with the threat. However, she had every confidence that whatever they did to Samson would not permanently harm him. She knew his strength was in the Lord. Everyone knew about the time he broke the ropes and overcame a thousand foes. She believed that her lover would

The Story

come out of it unscathed and would keep her from harm as well. So she went ahead and tried to appease his enemies.

"How can you say that you love me when your heart is far from me?" she asked Samson in their hearing. "You have mocked me these three times: you have not told me where your great strength lies."

Samson had had enough of the game, and he ignored her entreaty. Poor Delilah was between a rock and a hard place as we say. She pressed him with her plea day after day, vexing his soul. Finally, he told her.

"I have been a Nazirite to God from my mother's womb. If my head be shaved, my strength will be gone, and I'll be weak like any other man."

Delilah knew he had revealed his secret. She notified the spies and had them take a message to Ali:

Tell them to come out again. He has told me all his heart this time. No fooling!

When the officials arrived, they showed her the bags of money. Delilah had to deliver this time. It was a scary place to be, but she believed they would not be able to subdue Samson entirely, no matter what. Surely the Lord would not leave him at a time like this.

She made love to him and got him to sleep upon her knees and then called in a servant who was waiting outside with a razor. Her eyes filled with tears when the first lock fell; and by the time the seventh one dropped to the floor, she was wishing she had not done this. It would have been better to die. But now that the evil deed was done, she desperately hoped he would lose *some* of his strength to prove that she had done her best. She did not believe he would lose all his might simply by having a haircut.

Then, to show them she was not really defending Samson, she began tormenting him with words meant to rouse his spirit. He didn't resist. He went back to sleep.

Delilah was horrified. She had pushed him too far. If the Spirit had left him, so would he have lost his strength.

"You've done it this time," whispered one of the spies as he

the Day and the Hour

slipped cuffs around Samson's wrists. "Now, wake him up."

"The Philistines are upon you, Samson." She said it with trembling and covered her face.

Samson stirred and woke from his sleep. Discovering the handcuffs, he tried to break them. They held because the Spirit had left him.

The henchmen came in, and they blinded him. Ali came in as they were fastening heavy bronze shackles around his wrists. He hauled him off to Gaza and put him in prison where he was forced to grind grain like an ox at the prison mill.

Pamela and the children reappeared with Al Cypher following behind them. Everyone turned to look, and Clio interrupted her narrative.

Cypher went to stand against the post by the door. Amber dropped Pamela's hand and went to her mother, who was scooting her chair back to make room for the little girl on her lap since there was no vacant seat next to her. Skyler was reluctant to let go of Pamela's hand and allow her to go back to jail, so she took him to his mother who captured him with an arm and a hug. Everyone's eyes followed the long, flaming-red hair to the door. Just before disappearing, she turned and waved goodbye with a kiss for them all.

The room remained silent for a moment; then heads turned back to Clio, and she continued:

But his hair began to grow.

After some time, the Philistine priests and leaders in Gaza announced a major gathering at the temple of Dagon to offer a sacrifice to their god, for they believed that an idol had given Samson into their hands. The common people from all around came too, and when they saw Samson with their own eyes, blinded and in captivity, the air rang with shouts of praise to the devilish deity who they believed had done it.

An immense crowd had materialized, and they made an orgy of it as usual. When their heads had become dizzy and their hearts had gone wild, a chant rose up demanding that Samson entertain them. So he was brought from the prison,

The Story

and as he passed between the pillars of the temple, he said to the young man who led him, "Let me feel the pillars on which the building rests, so that I may steady myself against them."

The place was crammed full of people. The Philistine officials and priests were all there, and the roof barely held the men and women who had piled onto it—ten times as many as the number of fiery foxes Samson had sent into their fields. Samson had slaughtered a thousand Philistines with a quick eye and a strong arm; now he had neither, but he would destroy these enemies too. He called on the Lord:

"O Lord God, remember me and strengthen me only this once, so that I may be avenged for my two eyes."

He felt for the pillars, and he pushed against them, his right hand on the one and his left on the other. "Let me die with the Philistines," he said.

He pushed for all he was worth; the pillars buckled, and the overloaded building collapsed, crushing Samson and those inside and dashing the ones on the roof to the ground. Thus he killed more enemies of Israel in his death than he had during his life.

Samson's family came down to Gaza, and they took him home and laid him in the tomb of his father. He had judged Israel twenty years.

Delilah was never heard from again. I suppose that she ran away to escape the clutches of Ali, leaving the sacks of money behind. She must have known, from listening to Samson, that he had been set apart to defeat the enemies of Israel—even should it require his life. She would have turned it over and over in her mind and come to understand that God had used her too, as frightful as that was. We would not expect her to be thankful for her role: that would be too hard. However, she did have something to be thankful for: she had come to know the God of Israel for herself. If he loved the people of Israel as he did, he would love anyone, even Delilah.

That Samson had died to save Israel was not so important to Delilah after a while. More and more she thought of him as her savior. She understood that in his dying, God had proven

the Day and the Hour

something to her. And I suppose she never forgot the lesson, but kept it alive in her heart for the rest of her life and was ever thankful that she had the privilege of knowing him.

The Story

Chapter 14

The two children had been quiet as they left the dining room, holding tightly to Pamela's hands with Al Cypher towering behind them. As soon as the door of their makeshift classroom was closed, they wanted to know why the policeman was there.

"He brought me here because I was in jail. When you're in jail you can't go anywhere by yourself."

"Why were you in jail?" Skyler asked. "Did you do something wrong?"

"No, she didn't!" Amber exclaimed.

"I wanted to help some men who are in the jail—to help them find their way home."

"Don't they know where they live?" Amber asked.

"They don't have homes."

"Where do they sleep?" she persisted.

"Wherever they can. Sometimes in the woods."

"Like the deer?"

"Just like that."

"Don't they get cold?"

"Yes, they do sometimes."

"Why are they in jail?" Skyler asked.

"Just to hold them until they're ready to be taken somewhere else."

"Where are they being taken?" Amber asked.

"To heaven, tomorrow, if they want to," Pamela replied.

"My mom says Jesus is going to ask, 'Who wants to go to heaven?' and if you want to go, then he will take you, and if you don't, then he won't," Amber reported.

"If they're homeless, does it mean heaven is where their home is?" Skyler asked.

"Yes, it could be."

"Do they know it?" Amber asked.

"Not yet. I need to tell them."

the Day and the Hour

"If she doesn't tell them, they won't know to say 'yes' when Jesus asks them," Skyler explained.

"I know that!" Amber declared, putting her hands to her waist.

"How did they get homes just in heaven and not here?" Skyler asked.

"Everyone has one there, but some don't know it."

"So, if they don't know it, they say 'no' when they need to say 'yes,'" Amber reasoned.

"That's right. Someone could have told them there is no heaven, and they believed the lie," said Pamela.

"Who lied?" Amber asked.

"It could have been someone's father."

"My daddy used to say there's no heaven. But Mr. Felix made him change his mind," Amber said.

"Do you believe there's a heaven, Amber?"

"Yes."

"Why?"

"Because .... I just know there is."

"I think you have to grow up before you can imagine there isn't a heaven," Pamela said. "It's hard to imagine a nothing. It takes a lot of training."

"Maybe they forgot about it when they grew up," Skyler proposed.

"Yes, I think so. When people stop thinking about it, they forget," said Pamela.

"Somebody needs to remind them," suggested Skyler.

"That's what I'm going to do."

"What if they still say there's no heaven, like my daddy used to?" Amber asked.

"They need someone to show them, not just tell them," Pamela said.

"How can you show them heaven?" Amber asked. "I don't see heaven."

"I'll have to show them something that came from heaven."

"What?" Amber asked.

The Story

"Jesus."

"I know Jesus came from heaven, but he's *in* heaven now, isn't he?"

"His Spirit is also in us."

"I know. But nobody can see his Spirit inside of us," she insisted.

"We have to show them that he's in us by doing what he does."

"What does he do?"

"He loves people."

"I know. He loves everybody. Does he love dogs too? My mom said to ask you."

"Not the same way."

"I love Agnes more than I love anybody," Amber declared.

"Do you know what Jesus does to show us he loves us?"

"No."

"He does something for us that no one else would do."

"Like what?"

"It depends what you need. Some people need to be able to see heaven. So he shows them what it looks like. Then they can recognize it. For example, what if you did everything your father asked you to do without complaining and without waiting, and you did it just the way he wanted it done? Wouldn't he think he was seeing an angel from heaven?"

"But I'm not like that."

"Jesus can make us do things we wouldn't be able to do without him."

"How?"

"Just try it. Say, 'I'm going to let Jesus live in me and do things the way he wants, not the way I want.' Just try it when you get home tonight and see what happens."

"Are we going to heaven tomorrow?"

"That's where our real homes are. I'm eager to go. Aren't you?" Pamela asked.

"Will Agnes go too?"

"I can't say for sure. We'll have to leave a lot of things behind

173

because they're not good enough for heaven."

"But I'm *sure* Agnes is good enough. She's just as good as *I* am."

"Remember, heaven is where you can see Jesus and be with him."

"Will he like Agnes too?

"He will like *you* the most. He can't wait to see you. Do you know how I know that?

"Because it's in the Bible?"

"Well, it's because he had something that was very precious to him, and he gave it away so he could have you instead. In fact, you are like a precious pearl to him. He went without something that was very valuable so he could have you. I think if you and Agnes went to heaven together, he would only be looking at you because *you* are the one he's been waiting for."

"What did he give away for her?" Skyler asked.

"He gave away his good reputation. The devil said,

>Amber and Skyler can't come to heaven because they once disobeyed their parents."

"More than once don't you mean?" Amber said.

"As many times as it really was. The devil says,

>Amber can't come to heaven because she isn't perfect. She was disobedient all those times.

"And Jesus says,

>I know. But I love her so much I'm going to make a way for her to come anyway. How many times did she disobey?

"And the devil tells him. Then Jesus says,

>Then erase that from her report and put it on mine: put it down that I've been that many times disobedient. Then take my obedience and put it down for her. Now, there! She's perfect.

"Then the devil says,

>Yeah, but now you're the sinner!

"But Jesus says,

>Not so fast. Remember that day you killed me by nailing me to the cross, and my blood poured out? What did I do to

The Story

deserve that?

"The devil admits that Jesus did not deserve to die. So Jesus says,

> Then take my innocent blood and blot out that sin you transferred to my record. See? I already paid for it. It's all taken care of. Now Amber and I are both blameless, and I'm going to make sure she has a home that's ten times better than what she had before. And if Amber wants Agnes now that she's perfect, all she has to do is ask me!"

"What about Skyler?" Amber asked.

"Skyler, what do you think? Does that make sense to you?"

"It's more complicated than I thought," he said.

"Well, when the devil gets involved he makes it complicated. But God had it worked out from the beginning."

"If he wants me too, like he does Amber and everyone else, how can he be meeting all of us at once?"

"Girls get to go first!" declared Amber.

"No, they don't. That's only the way it used to be," Skyler returned.

"But heaven *is* the way it used to be because God is old," Amber pointed out.

"Heaven has lots more time than we have here," said Pamela. "It's not a problem at all: you don't have to wait a long time to see Jesus; God has that all worked out too."

"I think it's scary," said Skyler.

"I do too," said Amber.

"If you were older, I would be concerned for you. But you both still belong to God; he hasn't let you be on your own yet. And that's a good thing because now you will never be homeless like those men at the jail."

"I'm not really scared," said Skyler.

"I am," said Amber.

"That's 'cause you're a girl."

"Boys get scared too, even more than girls do."

"I never heard that before," Skyler maintained.

the Day and the Hour

"Ms. Pamela wasn't scared to go to jail."

"But you were scared of the policeman."

"That's different."

"Will you help me pray for those homeless men? We need to pray for them because they might never see heaven on their own, and then they'll be homeless forever."

"They would always have to sleep in the woods," declared Amber.

"When they miss out on heaven, they don't even have the woods to sleep in," Pamela explained.

"Then where do they sleep?"

"They never do sleep. When you miss out on heaven, you miss out on everything."

"Don't they have anything to eat?" Amber asked.

"All they have is themselves. And it's always dark."

"I thought people die if they don't eat," said Skyler.

"People never really die. They just go to live in a different sort of body."

"In heaven will we have a different sort of body?" Amber asked.

"Yes, a very good one, I'm sure."

"Could somebody have one like a dog?"

"Would you like to be a dog?"

"If I didn't have to eat what Agnes eats."

"I'm sure you'll be very happy with your body in heaven. It will be just right for you."

"Don't forget we're just kids," said Skyler.

"Yeah. Do we have to be short in heaven?" Amber asked.

"Would you rather be grown up?"

"Grownups never get to play," said Amber.

"They always have to be taking care of their kids," said Skyler.

"I'm sure God won't make you into a grownup until you're ready."

"Will you teach us like this in heaven?" Amber asked.

"Maybe."

The Story

"We're all going together tomorrow morning. Will you go with us?" asked Skyler.

"I have to go back to jail. But in heaven I'll find you."

"Heaven sounds like fun," said Skyler.

"It does to me too," admitted Amber.

"Those homeless men don't know what they'll be missing. What would you tell them if you could?" Pamela asked.

"I would say, 'Wouldn't it be nice to be in heaven instead of in jail?'" said Amber.

"Um. What would you say, Skyler? I need to have something to tell them."

"What do they like?"

"They don't like anything, really."

"Then I guess there's nothing in heaven for them, and it wouldn't do any good to tell them about it."

"Don't you think there are things in heaven they would like if they saw them?"

"Like what?" Amber asked.

"Like someone who loves them."

"Just tell them that, then," said Amber.

"They don't believe in Jesus, right?" Skyler said.

"It seems so."

"Then they wouldn't believe he loves them," he reasoned.

"She loves them. That's why she went to jail with them," Amber pointed out.

"Do they know that?" Skyler asked.

"Do they know that?" Amber echoed. "You could tell them if they don't."

"I *will* tell them. I hope they will believe me. I'll tell them that going to jail for someone you don't even know is not what people do. Then why did I do it? Because Jesus did something that is not what people do, and it's Jesus living in me that made me do it."

"Then what? Will they want to go to heaven?" Amber asked.

"I don't know. That's why we need to pray for them."

"Why do we need to pray for them if God already wants them

to be in heaven. Can't he do it anyway?" Skyler asked.

"I'm afraid he can't."

"Yes he can! God can do anything," Amber declared.

"God obeys his own rules. One of his rules is not to steal. Those homeless men belong to someone else, not to him."

"Who do they belong to?" Amber asked.

"The devil," stated Skyler.

"They can't belong to the devil! Everything belongs to God," declared Amber.

"Some things got spoiled, like an apple when it gets soft and inside it's all brown," said Pamela. "What good is an apple like that?"

"Yuk. Throw it away," said Amber.

"First it was the devil that got spoiled," Pamela explained.

"Is God going to throw the devil away?" Amber asked.

"Yes," Pamela said.

"Why didn't he do it already?" Skyler wondered.

"Because the devil has some people God wants back, and he doesn't want *them* to be thrown away."

"Does the devil have everyone who's in jail?" Amber asked.

"Not only them, he has the whole world."

"The whole world is the devil's?" Amber asked, wonderingly.

"He has a right to everyone who disobeys God."

"Even us?" Amber asked.

"If you were older and separated from God, the devil would own you too—until Jesus took away your sins. But now we belong to God, not the devil. Nevertheless, we still live in the devil's world. While we're here we can help God reach into the world and make things happen that even God can't do by himself."

"That's why the devil hates us," reasoned Skyler.

"You're right," said Pamela.

"I hate him too," said Amber.

"We don't need to hate the devil. But we do hate what he does. And we can work to undo the bad things he does. If we ask God to blot out someone's sins, it's not the same as him just doing it. If

The Story

he did it by himself, he would be stealing what belongs to the devil. If we ask him to do it, he has an invitation from inside the devil's world, and it's okay."

"Why can't we just ask for him to blot out everyone's sins?" Skyler asked.

"Because that would be just words. It wouldn't mean anything. 'Everyone' is just an empty word with nobody in particular in it. God doesn't understand words like that. They have to be real because he is real. If we ask him to blot out the sins of those homeless men in the jail, it gives him something to work with. But it might not be enough. That's why he sent me there. I'll be able to pray for each one even while I'm looking at him. The best thing you can do is ask God to keep me from being hindered by the devil."

"What does *hindered* mean?" Amber asked.

"It means the devil will stop me from doing exactly what God wants me to do if I'm not careful. So, let's ask God right now to fill me up with so much light that the devil will not be able to stop them from seeing and believing that Jesus sent me there to bring them his love."

"Dear Jesus, please make Miss Pamela really bright. And make her say something to the homeless people that they will want to hear," prayed Amber.

"Dear God, please protect Miss Pamela and help us find her in heaven. And make all those homeless men want to go with her too," prayed Skyler.

"Thank you."

"What about the policeman? Does he want to go to heaven?" Skyler asked.

"I don't think so!" declared Amber.

"I don't think he believes in heaven either," confirmed Pamela. "Shall we pray for him too?"

There was a loud knock on the door. It opened, and Al Cypher looked in.

"Time's up! We gotta go," he said.

the Day and the Hour

"It did cross my mind, I must admit, when I heard the name Samuel Clark. Do you have a little time right now? I would love to talk with you about your son. You see, he is ... well, he is—or was—my special friend."

"I'm sorry."

"That you don't have time, or that he's my friend?"

"I'm sorry for you, my dear. We had great hopes for Earl—not that that has anything to do with you. What I mean is he was—or we thought he was—specially blessed by God. You see, his mother had a vision of an angel telling her to keep herself from wine and strong drink for the sake of the child. This was even before she had conceived. We thought we would be childless, but she was convinced it was a message from God. And sure enough, she became pregnant that spring and gave birth to Earl on February 29th."

"How old is he?"

"We used to joke about that, telling him he had a birthday only once in four years; so he wasn't very old at all. Have you noticed that he acts like a ten-year-old sometimes?"

"Today he did."

"Well, you can reason it out and come pretty close. ... Another thing his mother was told in that vision was that he also must not eat or drink anything from the grapevine. She followed through with that—I would assume he follows it to this day."

"Have you always been in law enforcement?"

"It's been my career. You're probably wondering why Earl has an aversion to the police. I don't know why. He frequently got into mischief but seldom had to pay the price. Somehow, he always managed to escape the consequences. He liked to wear hats, as you know; and he always said as long as he had a hat on he felt stronger and everything went fine, but whenever he lost his hat he felt vulnerable. There may have been something to it."

"Do you suppose he was wearing that beret when he encountered Officer Headworthy?"

"I reckon if he didn't have it on when he went into the restroom, he put it on before he punched him out. If he carried it in his hand

The Story

initially—as apparently he did because Headworthy doesn't remember seeing it—he would have needed both hands free and would have been more likely to put it on than toss it aside.

"He was always losing hats. If he came home with some injury from having been in a scrape, it would be without his hat, and he would blame it on that. The only time the hat didn't protect him was when he set the barn on fire. He had to pay for that one."

"I must admit I'm curious."

"It was when he was in high school. He liked this girl in a neighboring town, and he called to ask her father if he could take her to the Independence Day parade. For some reason, her father didn't like Earl and told him she was going with a local guy, which was not quite correct. When Earl found out the truth, he decided to take revenge.

"On the night of the parade, when the girl and her family were away from home, he went to their house, which was out in the country. The man had a pair of hounds, and he kept them in a kennel in his barn when he was away. Earl's plan was to surprise them with a little prank. When he saw the headlights of their car returning from the parade, he slipped a pair of Chinese finger traps over the tails of the two dogs with a sparkler tied between them and let them loose. They ran around the yard, yelping, with the sparkler sparkling, while Earl took off and ran away across the field. The dogs went back into the barn and set some straw on fire. The fire quickly spread and burned the building to the ground."

"Do you think there is any hope for him?"

"I'm not sure what you mean."

"Do you believe in the Rapture tomorrow morning?"

"Oh, yes. I've served the Lord nearly all my life, and I've been expecting this. But I'm disappointed in Earl that he hasn't followed in my footsteps. His mother has no fear of him being left behind—because of that angel vision before he was born. She is usually right, but this time I have to disagree with her."

"I'm glad you told me that about his mother."

the Day and the Hour

The Story

Chapter 15

On returning Pamela to Detention Suites, Al Cypher announced that he was leaving for the night and that he would be locking her in her rooms. She had been hoping he would leave the door unlocked, allowing her free access to the corridor from which she could speak to the inmates. She did not yet know about the conferencing capability of the entertainment system, which would allow her to visit the others with virtually the presence of being in the same room with them.

After the door clicked shut, she sat down and waited for an inspiration.

"Hey, Pamela!" It was the voice of Milt yelling from the suite next door. "Turn on yer entertainment system an' press the Meet'n button."

She could not help laughing at what she saw: the seven men were in a cave, sitting in high-backed armchairs hewed out of huge logs.

"What's funny?" Milt asked.

"Oh! You can hear me?"

"We can see ya too. Ya look jist like one o' the gang," said Blink.

"I don't know about that. But I think we'll keep her, just the same. Whadya say?" said Buck.

"Ya got my vote, honey," said Red.

"But I'm sitting in an easy chair, not a log!" Pamela protested.

"So are we!" exclaimed several at once.

"What sort of chair would you like?" asked Lance.

"Give'r the board room," said Milt.

"Okay, but she's going to be the chairwoman," said Lance.

The scene switched to a polished boardroom table with the jailbirds sitting at it. Pamela saw them lined up on two sides of the table, all turned toward her.

"I liked the cave better," she said.

the Day and the Hour

"Maybe she likes bikes," suggested Chub.

The picture switched to seven motorcycles parked in a semicircle with the riders in various poses.

"Can ya put'r on back of mine, Lance?" Red asked.

"Try the beach," said Mule.

The picture switched to a sandy beach on a sunny seashore. Their seven heads were perched upon necks protruding from the sand, bodies apparently buried beneath the surface. Everyone had a good laugh. It must have been comical.

"I still like the cave best," said Pamela.

"How about this?" said Lance.

The scene switched to the quaint interior of an old church building. The seven men were sitting in two front pews, facing her as though she were the preacher.

"What do I look like?" she asked.

"You're in the pulpit, honey. Best lookin' preacher I ever seen." said Red.

When the idea first came to Pamela—to join the men in the jail in order to present Christ to them—she had pictures in her mind of talking to them one on one or being with them all in one room. The setting she had imagined would be relaxed and informal. As much as the pews and pulpit suggested her purpose and though the men seemed to accept the setting, she did not feel that it was ideal.

"The church is good. There is nothing wrong with it. Is there anything else at all?" she asked.

They were all silent, looking up at her expectantly from the pews. They thought she was starting a sermon and were waiting for her to deliver the next sentence.

"I mean, is there any other sort of picture we can be in?"

"There's this," said Lance.

The scene switched to a Christmas tree with everyone sitting on the floor cross legged, each having a present wrapped in colorful paper on his lap.

"I like this one," Pamela said.

The Story

"There's some kinda light 'round ya," said Milt. "Did ya jist turn on a light?

"No, I haven't done anything."

"It's her halo," said Chub.

"I don't see no halo; it's somethin' like fire," said Buck.

"Does yer head feel warm?" asked Red.

"Must be somethin' wrong with the equipment," quipped Mule.

"Does it make me look spooky?"

"No, I like it," said Chub.

"Kinda gives her a ho-ly look," said Buck.

"She looks like an angel," said Chub.

"Maybe we should go back to one of the other settings," Pamela suggested.

"No, we like this one," said Red.

"I like it because it reminds me of being a child," said Pamela. "Did any of you look forward to Christmas when you were a little kid?"

All either raised his hand or nodded.

"As adults, we forget what it was like to be a child. Let's try to imagine we're children receiving a gift. Are you thinking, 'How am I going to pay this back?'"

"No," said several.

"No way; it's a present," said Chub.

"Is your present a reward for being good?"

"Not really," volunteered Buck. "My folks said it was—to try to get a little good behavior out of us."

"I always knew I'd git somethin' even when we was too poor to have much," said Blink.

"Did you have to understand why you were getting your gift?"

"Ya mean did I hafta b'lieve in Santa Claus?" asked Chub.

"Did anyone demand that you believe in Santa Claus before they would give you a Christmas gift?"

"Prob'ly not," said Milt.

"Not that I know of," said Blink.

the Day and the Hour

"They say there is an art in gift giving. We always try to make the gift be a surprise. The perfect gift is one you get without any reason for it. Art is like that. You don't have to understand how or why you receive what you receive from it.

"Were any of you born into a family with plenty of money?"

"Lance was, wasn't ya, Lance?" said Red.

"You could say that," he replied.

"Was that something Lance earned?" Pamela asked. "Well, that's a silly question. Of course he couldn't have worked for it when he wasn't even born yet. It was a gift.

"Take a guy who was a born singer. He turned out to have a voice that made him rich. Did he make those vocal cords himself? Of course not. It was a gift.

"When you were born, did you have to do anything?"

"Not that I remember," said Mule.

"Life's a gift," said Red.

"Where did *I* come from? Why am I here?" Pamela asked.

"Beats me," said Mule.

"Were you surprised when I came?"

"I never heard o' such a thing," said Milt.

"Did you ask for me?"

"Baby, we's jist as well ask fer the moon," said Red.

"You didn't ask for me to be here. You didn't expect me to be here. You didn't even want me to be here. Yet here I am! Not just anybody would give you a gift. If someone does give you a gift with no strings attached—I mean a real gift—what does that say about the person?"

"They're nuts!" said Mule.

"Hey, watch out. She's give'n us a gift, an' she ain't nuts!" said Chub.

"If she ain't, then why's she in here?" Mule retorted.

"Cuz she's preachin' at us, stupid," said Buck.

"Well, she's no preacher. How come she's the one in here instead of a preacher?" Mule demanded.

"Preaches ain't allowed in jails." said Milt.

The Story

"You guys are gettin' awful close to sayin' somethin' as ain't nice about her," said Chub. "She don't deserve nothin' but respect from us fer what she's done already. So let 'er have 'er say, an' don't be criticizin' 'er. If ya ask me, she's been sent by the good Lord above. I agree: she *is* our gift. Like they say, the Lord loves everybody, an' I'm startin' ta believe it."

"She come in here on her own free will, an' she gets locked up with us on purpose. I'd say she's better'n all them preachers put together," said Red.

"Let's shut up an' let 'er have 'er say," said Milt. "I don't think she come in here to listen to us analyze her. She knows why she's here; we don't hafta tell her. I think she'll tell us if we shut up an' listen."

"I would like to tell you why I'm here, but I'm not sure you would believe me," said Pamela.

"Go ahead; I'll believe you, Ms. Evans," said Chub.

"It's the same reason anybody gives you a gift. It's because I love you."

There were no replies.

"Yes. Because I love you," Pamela repeated. "Every one of you. How do you know I love you?"

"Cuz you're here." said Chub.

"Blink, do you wonder why I love you?"

"Yeah."

"Buck?"

"Yup."

"Milt?"

"Do ya really?"

"I really do. I just—I just do."

"Red? Do you know why I love you?

"No, ma'm."

"Mule?"

"No, ma'm."

"I wonder too! I don't know why. But I do love you. You see, it's a gift I received! Maybe I could have said, 'No, I don't want

the Day and the Hour

this gift, and I don't want to go spend time with those men in the jail.' But I don't think I could have said 'no.' This love I have for you guys is the real thing, a real gift that was given to me. It was a surprise to me. But I liked it! I wanted to come to you in your prison. ... Does that make me someone special?

"Shore does," said Milt.

"Not really. I'm just a regular person like you. I'm not really much of a gift."

"You're shore perty ta look at," said Red.

"My looks aren't worth much; my looks can't help you; my looks aren't your gift. I'll tell you what I am: I'm the wrapping on a much better gift that someone wants to give you. You haven't opened your real gift yet. Did you think I came on my own? No! I didn't make up this love. As I said, this love just showed up. Someone gave it to me, and he told me to share it with you. So I'm here to give you the big gift that's wrapped in my love. Maybe you thought nobody would ever love you. Now you know differently. Why? Because here I am! I came to join you in your prison, which proves it.

"Maybe you thought you'd never love anyone. Do you love me?"

"Yes," came a chorus.

"Why?"

"We all want to say it's because you're a good-looking woman," said Lance. "But that's not the real reason. We just don't want to admit it. It's because you first loved us."

"We ain't never seen nothin' like this before," said Red.

"I haven't either," said Pamela. "Love isn't something you can come up with on your own. Love is the most precious thing in the world. It's worth more than all the gold that ever was in this hill. You can't get a gold nugget just by thinking *gold nugget*, right? You have to find it. That's the way it is with love. There is someone who has a fortune in love that he wants to give you as a present. And he sent me to tell you about it."

"Is he gonna get us out of here?" asked Blink.

The Story

"Yes, if you want him to. He has offered to do that."

"Why does *he* care 'bout us?" asked Mule.

"It's that love. I can't explain it. You can't understand it. You just have to accept it. It's your gift."

"Why don't he come 'round, then? I take it you can't get us out o' here cuz you're locked in yourself. But this here friend o' yours can?" asked Milt.

"Why didn't he come himself?" Buck asked.

"He's prob'ly too busy," said Mule.

"No, he's not too busy at all. It's because he's in hiding. You all know what *that's* like! He's hiding from the world. They're out to get him because he's been critical of the way they run things. He can't just come around in plain sight anymore. The last time he did that, they tried to kill him. You have all heard of him—everyone has—but what you have heard is not true. The world hates him because his ways are not the ways of the world, and they spread lies about him. And because they can't get their hands on him, they say he's just a myth. But I'm here to tell you he's for real. He has several names, and you have heard some of them. You even use some of his names without knowing you're really crying for him in your heart. He has heard you, and he understands your need better than I do. When you say 'Jesus' you don't know what you're saying. But he knows. When you curse using his name, you don't know why you do it, but he knows. And he sent me to tell you that he heard you and he loves you. He had to send somebody, and he happened to pick me.

"Now, this gift he wants to give you is a wonderful thing. Inside of the package it's much bigger than the outside. You can't get a grasp of it by looking at me. It's bigger than the whole universe. It's as big as God himself. In fact, it is God himself."

"God gave himself to us," said Lance. "It's the last thing we would expect. Who in his right mind would even think of it?"

"This is a perfect gift because it's a complete surprise," continued Pamela. "You weren't prepared for this. Nobody was.

"You have heard about heaven and hell. It so happens that

the Day and the Hour

God is the boss of both."

"Everybody knows that," said Blink.

"He made everything else too, and if you have a complaint about anything, your complaint actually is against him. You would think that he would throw all the complainers into hell. Some say he'll do that, but it's a lie. I'm here to tell you that he is going to rescue you from hell if you let him—no matter how much you have complained, no matter how much you cursed his name, no matter how much hell you raised in your life.

"Now, I don't understand much myself, but here's how I think of it: Jesus, who is the part of God called the Son, went to the part of God called the Father and asked for each of you by name. And the Father gave every one of you to him!

"Why did Jesus want you in his own family? You know—that's a good question. He knew every one of you was headed for hell. Jesus wanted you because he loves you. And if you don't believe that, look what he had to do to keep you from going to hell. Here is what he did: He went right into your prison like I came in here. I mean, not a prison like this one with walls and locks. I'm talking about the prison that kept you from being happy and prosperous and fruitful all your life. Not only that, he had to get you out legally. He is not someone who breaks the law. I'm talking about the big law that's above every law, and it says that anyone who disrespects God and God's laws goes to hell.

"There was only one way he could get you out, and that was to pay your penalty himself. And do you think he doesn't love you?

"He figured if he did that, you would believe that he loves you, and you would love him back—because that's all he ever wanted in the first place! All God ever wanted from anyone was that they love him! It's so easy once you know! You love him, and you love to obey him!

"You say it isn't easy to love. Well, that's what the gift is! When you open this gift, you find out it just simply makes it easy to love. And love is from God because God is love. And Jesus is from God because he is God. And he served your sentence—the death

The Story

sentence, by the way; that's how serious the big law is. He died to pay your penalty to prove that he loves you. Then he overcame death to prove that he is God. And when God says your sentence is paid, let me tell you, *it is paid!*"

"Sounds good to me," said Chub. "Count me in, Ms. Evans. How do I open my present?"

"Just tell God you understand that Jesus died for your sins and you accept his gift of freedom from hell and his promise of life forever. You can say it out loud or say it in your heart. If you mean it, I guarantee he will hear you."

"Milt, what do you think?" asked Buck.

"Do you think I'm stupid? I wouldn't pass this up."

"I reckon I won't either."

"Red, Blink, Mule?" Pamela asked.

"I believe you," said Blink.

"I'm waitin' fer Mule," said Red. "I ain't goin' without him."

"When did you start bein' so lovey dovey?" asked Mule.

"Jist now. Dang if I can help it. I'm stickin' with ya, Mule. Ya give me a place to hang out when I come here, remember?"

"So what? You never thought it was such a big deal before."

"Well, maybe it ain't. But I'm still hangin' with ya. If ya insist on goin' to hell, I'm goin' with ya."

"Oh, shut up. I know she's right. With you tuggin' on one side and the Lord's tuggin' on the other, I ain't got a prayer."

"Look, buddy, we both gotta start prayin'. The rest o' the gang's all gettin' saved."

the Day and the Hour

Leila has eaten nothing since her apple at noontime. That was between the baseball game and the sailing lesson. It seems days ago now. But she is not hungry for anything so easy to obtain as physical food.

She is praying again, kneeling at her bedside with her Bible open in Ephesians:

> In love he predestined us for adoption as sons through Jesus Christ, according to his plan.

Hopefully, it includes daughters too.

She has come to accept that Earl will not be joining the Rapture. Whether she perceived this during prayer or whether she reasoned it out makes no difference. She is not sure herself how she became so certain of it.

This is not how stories should end. She is disappointed not only with her life but with the whole thing. She imagines that he will become a believer as soon as he finds that she and the Murphys and so many others are missing. How could he not?

He might not. How could he not believe now, after the events of this week? It will be terrible for him when he finds that he has been badly mistaken. What will he believe then? She thinks of asking God to let her stay with him. The thought elicits a sick feeling; it would be the worst thing she could do, rejecting the gift of life in heaven—rejecting her Lord, actually. Pastor Adam told her that the reason she was brought to faith now in the nick of time is that Jesus is anxious to have her with him. But isn't he with her now through the Spirit? If so, why does it hurt so much? And what will life in heaven be for her? Will she be as alone there as she has been here? Jesus cannot be present with everyone at all times; she will still be without a real family.

Leila never experienced much real fellowship although people were part and parcel of her professional life. Her time with them was consumed with management issues: examining and judging performance; correcting misunderstandings; guiding the application of regulations so as to avoid doing irreparable harm; arbitrating turf wars; allocating resources that inevitably fell

The Story

short. During most of her career, she lacked peers who were immune to being intimidated and dominated by her brilliance. This excluded her from friendships. The lonely desk was her companion, and the quiet apartment was her only solace until Earl came into her life and opened for her a vibrant new dimension. Now that door has slammed shut; she may never see him again. And should they meet in some distant turn of events—what of the intervening times?

She understands about risks and that she lost her bid for love. Earl was not for her; it was a mistake; he had other women. Her aim was too high; her error was not settling for an ordinary man. If she had it to do over, would she take another man? No. It is inconceivable. She loves him.

She asks her Lord to have mercy on him, not for her sake but for his. She comes as close as she dares to telling God she would die for Earl if she could.

An answer comes to her: he is sustaining her even now. She turns the page to chapter three and reads the promise again:

> He is able to do far more abundantly than all that we ask or think, according to the power that is at work within us. To him be glory
> ....

He is able to give me the joy he deserves from me instead of these tears. I will ask him to give me joy. I will not withhold my praise because I am sad. I will trust him.

She closes her Bible and crawls into bed with wet eyes, strangely at peace yet longing to be close to one who loves her, one she can love and hold.

She takes up the Book again, and it opens to the Song of Songs where she was reading this morning. She left the ribbon marker there. Her eyes fall on the words:

> I will rise now and go to the city and search the streets.
> I will seek him whom my soul loves.
> I sought him but found him not.
> The watchmen that patrol the city found me.
> I asked them, "Have you seen him whom my soul loves?"
> A little while later I found him whom my soul loves!
> I held him and would not let him go

the Day and the Hour

> until I had brought him into my mother's house
> and into the chamber of her who conceived me.

Good for her.

Leila turns off the light, and sleep comes quickly to the call of her exhaustion.

The Story

*A*dam Murphy operates on the principle that faith is strengthened and even proven by deed as much as by word. Now that the last day is nearing its end, he is looking back at what he did to demonstrate his trust in the communication he received a week ago.

It would be impossible to doubt that the week was extremely unusual. Nonetheless, nothing is comparable to the event that he has been saying will take place at eight o'clock tomorrow morning. It is utterly unprecedented. The disappearance of a person—the translation of an individual from one point to another—is on record, but the world has yet to see a mass disappearance—let alone a mass resurrection. Frankly, it stretches one's faith nearly to breaking when one thinks about it in those terms.

Is there any further deed he can do to strengthen his faith before retiring for the night?

He begins enumerating the steps he and Alice have taken: 1) They used up the food. What else? 2) They decided to leave the bank account to the bank—that counts for nothing. 2) The credit-card balance has been paid—no credit there. *I could close out the account.*

He calls customer service.

"This is Janette. How may I help you?"

"I would like to close this account."

"All right, Mr. Murphy. I can do that for you. I see your balance is zero. You have a lot of points, which will be lost if you close the account. Are you sure you want to go ahead and close it?"

"I think it's a little late to be doing anything with points."

"There is a Great City promotion going on right now. You have enough points for a two-week vacation for two, including travel and hotel."

"I don't think we would be interested in that. You may go ahead and close the account."

"How about if I send you cash?"

"Can you do that?"

the Day and the Hour

"I can do anything. Just ask me."

"I'm not sure I could use the cash myself. Can you send it to someone else?"

"Of course. I'd be glad to. Who would you like to give it to?"

"There's a man, a good friend of mine—I could give you his address."

"What is his name?"

"Earl Clark."

"I'm looking to see whether he has an account with us. I'm assuming he lives in the same town."

"Yes."

"There is no Earl Clark. I'm showing a Kenneth E. Clark."

"That's him."

"That's odd: it looks as though he has had some big hospital bills. I rarely see that anymore."

"That's exactly why I was wanting to send the money to him. He paid for emergency treatment of a homeless man who was not in the system. I promised Earl I would contribute something toward it and then forgot to do it."

"Wonderful! I love it when things come together like this. Do you want to transfer the points to his account, or just the cash? The points are actually worth more."

"The cash would be fine."

"Cash is good, isn't it? That's what I think too, especially with these hospital charges."

"You said you can do anything. Did you mean that?"

She laughs.

"I'll certainly try. What do you have in mind?"

"Could you take the balance from my checking account and transfer that to Earl's account too?"

"If you authorize me to withdraw a certain amount, I can do that. Then I can transfer it. How much would you like it to be?"

"I don't remember the amount exactly. I would have to log into my account. Just a minute."

"When you're in there, why don't you make a payment to this account? I think that would be the easiest way. I'll undo the

The Story

closing."

"You can do that?"

"I can do anything, remember?"

"Okay, if you will bear with me."

"Of course."

"Do you see that anything has come in?"

"... There it is! Now, I'm assuming you want your entire balance, including your points in cash, to be transferred to the account of Kenneth E. Clark, and then close your account. Is that correct?"

"That's correct."

"All right. Just give me a moment. ... Your account is now closed, Mr. Murphy. Is there anything else I can do for you?"

"Would it be possible to send him a message, so he doesn't wonder where the money came from?"

"I think I can do that. What would you like to say?"

"Come to think of it, I should be sending this to someone else. Would you check to see if by chance you have Karen Martin in your system?"

"I have a Karen Martin on Beach House Road. She must be a neighbor of Mr. Clark's."

"That's the one. I hate to put you to the trouble of changing everything. But could you move the money to her account instead?"

"I'd be glad to. It's no trouble, really. So you want the entire amount from your points as well as the transfer you made from your checking account to go to Karen Martin?"

"That's correct."

"All right, just give me a moment. ... Would you like to send Karen a message?"

"Yes, please."

"What would you like to say?"

"Say, 'Adam Murphy has transferred funds to your account for you to hold for Earl Clark. In the event he becomes unavailable, please donate the full amount to the hospital to help offset the expenses of Franky's care.'"

"I will do that. ... How is Franky?"

the Day and the Hour

"He died Friday morning."

"I'm sorry to hear that. Was he a good friend of yours?"

"He was an acquaintance. We tried to help him from time to time—when he would let us."

"I will fold my hands and remember Franky."

"Thank you, Janette."

"It has been my pleasure, Mr. Murphy."

"Are you—are you, um, looking forward to tomorrow morning?"

"Not really. I'm not working tomorrow, which always makes for a long day. Housework, you know. The house never thanks me."

"I was wondering because I'm pretty sure I'll be going in the Rapture. I thought you might have been looking forward to the same thing."

"A lot of people mentioned that to me this week. Earlier in the week, I was bringing up the subject too. But it usually ended on a sour note, so I stopped talking about it. Actually, it's against company policy to discuss it with customers now."

"I see. Well, it's not easy for me to ignore since I'm one who experienced the dream a week ago."

"Oh, you must be a pastor. Shall I call you Pastor Murphy?"

"That would be fine. Or just *Adam* works too."

"Pastor Murphy, ... you know, the Rapture wouldn't work for me. There would be nothing for me to do up there. It's a funny thing: I took this job out of desperation because I needed the money. It was about the last thing I wanted to do. But now I love it. I can't wait to get to work each day and help people with their problems."

"Don't you find that a lot of customers are calling in because they're unhappy about something?"

"Most of them are. But I've learned to make them into friends. It's the most wonderful experience you can imagine. I wouldn't think of doing anything else. I'm afraid I'd be unhappy in heaven."

"You may not believe this, but my wife and I were visited by a pair of angels this evening, and they gave us a glimpse of what is ahead in the kingdom of God. This is true, Janette; I'm not making this up. They told us there will be commerce with people

The Story

doing customer service just as it is now only more and better. You will be able to continue what you're doing. I must warn you: in the meantime, things will become extremely difficult on earth, and many will die because of the hardships. I would most definitely recommend the Rapture."

"That's fascinating, Pastor Murphy. Did they look like angels—wings and everything?"

"No. There were no wings. But they certainly seemed to have superhuman knowledge."

"Did they have names?"

"Yes. They used nicknames though."

"You mean like Mike for Michael?"

"Uh, ... no. Their names were Flap and Jack."

She laughs.

"You're a wonderful storyteller! Is there anything else I can do for you?"

"That's all. Thank you."

Adam was yawning during the latter part of the conversation. Sleep is about to overcome him. He remembers the request he made of the angels. The house has become unusually quiet. He goes into the bedroom and lowers the bed from the wall and then to the den where he left Alice. She has fallen asleep in her reclining chair. He gently lifts her, expecting that she will wake up, but she does not. He carries her into the bedroom, lays her on the bed, and covers her with a blanket. He is too sleepy to undress himself or even to brush his teeth. He lies down beside her and falls asleep without remembering to set his alarm clock.

the Day and the Hour

The Story

Chapter 16

Philip Evans had finished doing everything that needed doing. On a normal day, that would have been immensely satisfying and the precursor of a good night's sleep. But this evening he was having trouble settling down. Without the company of his wife to consider, there were too many options. However, without her company, he had little interest in any of them.

After feeding himself the chowder that she had prepared this morning and left for him in the refrigerator and after washing the bowl and the pan, he considered going back to the store.

Letting go of the hardware store was at odds with Philip's makeup. It had been his life: keeping the business profitable had been a never ending challenge. It was a formidable testimony to the man's faith that he even attempted to throw that ingrained concern to the winds. Therefore, we must forgive him for allowing it to infringe on his solitude during the final hours of his life on earth.

More than anything, Philip needed something to relieve him from thinking about the absurdity of Pamela being in jail with vagrants. It was true that he had agreed to the scheme in advance. At the time he did not notice the other side; he saw it only as a generous gift to the spiritually needy. Now the time had come to taste the sacrifice and feel the bereavement.

Of course, he was curious about what might have transpired at the store after he left it this afternoon. The doors were left unlocked, and anyone could have come in and taken whatever he liked. Might the shelves have been stripped bare by now?

He told himself that if he were staying awake all night, he might as well be at the store: he would be more likely to find the company of another night owl prowling about there than at home. It was a good-enough excuse. He got into his car and drove down to Evans Hardware store once more.

the Day and the Hour

The lights were on, and the door was stuck in the open position when he arrived. It appeared that there had been no wholesale assault on the stock. He walked the aisles, checking for damage. Someone had carried all the flashlight batteries away, and most of the camping equipment was gone. Otherwise, it appeared that there was roughly double the attrition that would be expected on a typical Saturday.

He climbed the stairs and found the upper room just as he had left it. He went downstairs and walked the aisles again. He could almost hear the shelves talking to him. He had designed and redesigned, arranged and rearranged every detail over the years. This was his work of art, his contribution to the world.

He did not want to speculate about what might become of the store, but it was inevitable. Perhaps Russell Tarr would find a way to take it over. He had refused to sign the paper that Russell had handed him this morning, for he thought it would be an incentive for that vacillator to attempt to leave himself behind.

Thus we find Philip strolling the aisles, stopping occasionally to correct a mislocated item. In the lawn-and-garden section are certain ornaments that have become popular: statues of St. Francis standing on shiny, colored balls the size of bowling balls. There is also a five-foot replica of the Eiffel tower. He stands looking at them for a minute, shakes his head, and moves on. A stack of sacks, newly delivered, is partly blocking the aisle. They contain blue gravel that people have been spreading on paths in their gardens.

What compels him to continue roaming the aisles is the need not only to keep from thinking about Pamela in jail but also about what might lie ahead. In spite of all the talk this past week, certain questions have received no certain answers, and much of it seems impossible. Philip is not the type of man to indulge in philosophical or theological speculation, and this is not something to be discovered by taking abstract thought. It is now a well known fact that the so-called Rapture, seen at close range, is a preposterous thing. It is no wonder that people who have little or no faith in Biblical revelation are unwilling to allow it to invade their sanity. It occurs to him that without reference to the acts of the Creator, belief in the Rapture would be a form of insanity. Indeed, it now strikes him as being an insane idea in spite of his respect for the prehistorical record.

He decides to turn off most of the lights and sit down to rest. Evidently, no one is out to rob the store by night when it can easily be robbed at any hour of the day.

Ah, ... I don't know. Maybe I should go home.

No, that would only present him with acute reminders that Pamela is not with him—not now and perhaps never will be again. He has faced the fact that there is no guarantee backing up the common sentiment about meeting every person one may wish to meet in heaven.

Better stay here in the store. Perhaps someone will come in yet.

Even a robber would be welcome company. Already, he is missing his home on earth. He knows well that he is supposed to be a glad citizen of heaven. But how can an ordinary man be expected to feel fond of a place he has never seen?

Nevertheless, the roots of his faith are deep, and he trusts that the reward of being with the Lord will be to have everything set right. It is only a melancholy mood precipitated by Pamela's absence that troubles him.

Philip takes one of the folding lawn chairs from the display rack, unfolds it, and sits down to rest his back. Although he cannot see the door from here between the aisles, if anyone comes in, he will hear the door open.

It has been a demanding day. His body is tired; his eyelids are heavy—and drooping.

If I'm going to fall asleep, why not get a little more comfortable?

He remembers that one camp cot was left. He rises from the chair with a groan, goes to the outdoor-equipment aisle, finds the cot, takes it out of its box and sets it up, unrolls a foam pad onto it, and lies down, pulling a tarp over himself to provide a little warmth in case he should sleep for long. Weariness is dulling his senses, and the worries about Pamela and tomorrow are mercifully fading. Philip falls asleep.

A noise gets his attention, and he sits up to listen. It is a sound like that of many footsteps outside. He goes to the door to investigate. The morning light reveals a street full of people going this way and that, apparently on important errands. He opens the door and steps outside, amazed at the size of the crowd out so early. Then it dawns on him: The street is all wrong; this is not home. It appears to be a large city. He must be in heaven!

Philip stops a man going by and asks him: "Excuse me. I'm new here. Is there somewhere newcomers can go for directions?"

"You need to go see the Father."

"Is he a priest?"

"No, he's God. You will find him in the tower at the center of the city. You can't miss it. All the straight streets go that way like spokes on a wheel. Look, there it is; it's that tall thing."

Philip sees the tower. It is several blocks—or perhaps miles—away. The man he questioned went his way before he thought of asking about the distance. It must be extremely tall, for its top is enshrouded in a cloud. A bluish glow is being emitted from the center of the cloud, apparently from a blue light at the top of the tower.

No vehicles are in sight though some people are somehow being conveyed along rapidly. Some are walking on sidewalks, but the ones moving so quickly are in the street, standing on balls—like those lawn ornaments. But these balls are rolling, and the riders appear to be balancing on them effortlessly. Little platforms for their feet cover the tops of the balls and seemingly house part of the mechanism that makes them work. Philip is curious about how this is accomplished, but right now his main concern is to report to the Father in the tower as directly as possible.

He sets out on a sidewalk, walking briskly, and covers a few

The Story

blocks without reaching his goal. The tower is still a mile or more away. He has been watching the ball riders and has noticed that when they stop and disembark at the sidewalk, they simply abandon the thing in the gutter. Then someone else comes along, steps onto it, and goes rolling away. The curb makes the stepping on and off easy, or so it appears. Somehow, the platforms always remain upright. These clever devices seem to constitute the public transportation system. Philip decides to try one.

Several riderless balls lie along the curb where he is walking. He chooses one and puts a foot on it. It feels solid, with no tendency to tip. He senses minute pulses in response to the shifting of his weight as the mechanism keeps the platform upright. Evidently, some magnetic interaction with the street is taking place also; otherwise, the ball would not be able to remain stationary. Seeing that the platform has the ability to stay upright without his weight having to be perfectly centered, Philip boldly steps aboard with both feet. It still feels solid. Now, how does one travel? Do these people carry some control device in their hands?

It must be something like that. I'd better get on my way and not mess around with this till I find out more about it.

As he turns to step off, he gets a clear view of someone stepping onto a nearby ball and scooting away from the curb. It appeared that she simply pressed down with her toes. He turns to face the middle of the street, waits for a gap in the traffic, and presses down with his toes, leaning forward slightly as he does so. The ball rolls away from the curb and then comes to a stop because he instinctively leaned back to balance himself.

Traffic goes whizzing by.

Philip pivots himself on the platform so that his expected direction of travel is aligned with the traffic flow and not across it. Again, he presses his toes forward, and again he reacts, causing it to come to a halt after advancing only a short distance. Once more he tries, determined to trust the thing to keep him from falling. And it does. He concludes that the ball will do whatever it needs to do in order to keep him in balance. All he has to do is lean

the Day and the Hour

toward the direction in which he wants to accelerate.

It works beautifully. The more he leans the faster it goes. He is moving along now, and having gained a bit of confidence, he is ready to consider collisions. He has not noticed any mishaps among the other riders, in spite of their weaving in and out as freely as if they were on roller skates. He is not yet confident enough to go near the middle of the street where the speeds are greater, so he is cruising along perhaps too near the curb for his speed. Presently, a ball with a little girl on it darts out from the curb directly in front of him, making a collision inevitable. His ball suddenly shoots forward toward her, while still keeping in contact with his feet, and stops abruptly, skidding slightly and making a sound like a jackhammer as it chatters to a stop. The angle at which it left his body when it moved ahead was just enough to transfer the energy of his motion to the ball, and he finds himself standing upright and motionless a few inches from the youngster. She looks up at him, laughs, turns around, and rolls back to the curb.

Being thoroughly impressed with the capabilities of the ball board and trusting that it will neither allow him to come to harm nor harm another, he boldly accelerates toward the tower and goes whizzing along with the fast traffic, leaning into the wind, zipping around the turnabouts at intersections, and performing remarkably like a teenager on a snowboard.

The tower at the center of the city is looming ever larger, and presently he gets a clear view of its lower parts. He thought of the Eiffel Tower when he first saw it, and now it appears to be exactly that.

As he approaches the plaza beneath the huge arches, he becomes concerned about what his next step will be. There are no signs providing information and no waiting lines that would indicate where people are registering. But there are people about. The street ends abruptly, and the ball brings him to a gradual stop. As he steps off onto the plaza pavement, he notices a man standing nearby looking intently at him. He walks over to make

The Story

an inquiry, but before he can get a word out, the other speaks:

"Are you Philip Evans?"

"Yes, sir."

"Harold Foster is waiting for you. He's having breakfast in the Jules Verne restaurant on the second platform. Take the elevator there on your right."

The elevator takes him nonstop to the second platform. He steps out, and the vast city is in view on the right and on the left. Straight ahead is the Jules Verne restaurant, a rather small place, and through the open door he sees Harold seated at a table with another man whom he does not recognize.

The table is set for four. Harold introduces Philip to Jim, and Philip knows immediately who he is—the Jim who has been on his prayer list for years, a colleague of Harold's. A breakfast of steaming coffee, eggs, and toast is waiting for him. It perfectly suits his appetite, and he sits down with the two men.

After a short while another man approaches. Harold and Jim stand up, so Philip does likewise.

"Welcome to my Father's garden," says the newcomer. "Please sit down. It's good to have you all here. I've been waiting for this day forever, so take your time; finish your breakfasts. Then I'll take you up to the Father. Jim, I think you have guessed who I am. I know you well, but you are still new to my ways. By the end of this day we will all understand one another and be getting along together very nicely indeed."

Philip finds himself immediately at ease with Jesus, as do the others according to what he reads on their faces. It is as though he has met an old friend. The fact that his friend happens to be the Creator of the universe does not seem relevant at the moment. Philip is the first to speak, being eager to satisfy his curiosity about a few things.

"Can people come and go here as they please?"

"Yes, but only this far. To go higher, they need me. I am the key to the only elevator. It opens when it recognizes me and no one else."

"Where are we?" is his next question.

"Paris. Paris of the future. Or what Paris will be in the future, if you like."

"I expected you would be in Jerusalem," Philip replies in surprise.

"This is a receiving point for the Rapture—an outpost in the wilderness, really."

"The city seems to have been rearranged quite a lot," says Jim. "I don't remember the Eiffel Tower being at its center."

"The old city was destroyed during the Tribulation."

"Are we in the Millennium now?" Harold asks excitedly.

"Yes—temporarily at this point."

"Did you guys ever suspect this?" Jim asks, looking at Harold. "You never mentioned that the Translation might be in time, not space—or not simply to another place on earth, anyway."

"I never thought of it or heard of it," Harold replies. "But I don't know why we didn't think of it. I guess we were all hung up on the idea that everyone would arrive at the same place in our own time frame."

"It works out quite conveniently this way," says their host. "It makes little strain on the facilities when you're all spread out over a thousand years."

"How is that fair to those who get here near the end?" asks Jim.

"Oh, there is much that's better than this to look forward to. Why not say those who were received *earlier* in the age were not treated fairly?"

"Is it like in your parable where all the laborers were paid the same for different amounts of work?" Philip asks.

"Not at all. Let me explain. You are here in Paris, halfway into the age, for the duration of one week, a week of orientation and training. Then it will be back to the start for all of you. You are fortunate to have leapfrogged over the Tribulation; that's the real blessing in all of this. I have jobs for everyone. You can't imagine how much work it took to renovate and rebuild the world—or I

The Story

should say that it *will* take, for you will be taking part in doing it."

"I see," Philip says excitedly. "Then, will we be working to renovate things back home?"

"Precisely, Philip. It's the place you know best. The three of you will be working with nine others of my disciples as the leadership team rebuilding your town. James is the only outsider, and he jumped at the chance to work with you guys when I offered it to him."

"So our town was destroyed too?" Philip asks.

"I'm afraid so."

"It was badly in need of renovation anyway," Philip remarks. "I have another question," he adds. "I hope I'm not out of line asking this. Will Pamela be there too?"

"Yes, of course. She was—or I should say, 'will be'—part of the early support team. We have the men's and women's roles properly sorted out, of course."

"Is she here now?"

"No, the women came last week. Men and women are kept apart during the transition. Until all the babies are delivered, some will not have their glorified bodies."

"Are all the women kept waiting until that happens?"

"No, Pamela's preparations are only a week long, like yours."

"So is she already back home?"

"Yes, and so are you, if you understand what I mean. But don't try too hard to understand it. We'll work on that later."

Philip, noticing that the others are ahead of him, concentrates on finishing his breakfast.

There is a lull in the conversation.

Harold, who once visited Paris with Jim on business, looks around to see whether he can identify buildings that may have been rebuilt to resemble the originals, as this tower obviously was.

"It appears that the city was completely redesigned," he says.

"Indeed it was. This tower and a few other buildings you can't see from here are the only reminders of the former city. There was much more to be forgotten than there was to memorialize."

"I always liked the Eiffel tower," says Jim. "I'm not sure why—something about the shape. It was inspiring, somehow, but I never understood it."

"We don't call it the Eiffel Tower anymore. It's the Koechlin Tower. Maurice Koechlin saw this tower when he made the first drawings. The one that Eiffel built was smaller, but the shape was accurate. We rebuilt it larger, as you can see, following the same design."

"I'm confused about which one was the original," says Jim.

"You can't separate them that way," the host replies.

Philip sees that Jim has a blank look on his face, and since he is hesitating, not following up with another question, Philip asks, "Is our town going to be completely redesigned also?"

"Yes. The design was done in the beginning."

"Were the women in on it, then?" Philip asks again.

"No. The beginning of time. Before anything existed."

Harold, seeing that Philip also has a blank look on his face, says, "I guess all the buildings we had were wrong because we didn't have access to your design."

"The pioneers could have had access to it—some of them did."

"What about my store? Was that all wrong?" Philip asks.

"Well, the building you just left was not too far different from what I have in mind. It will be larger, and the upper level will be finished."

"Then will we build that new one, doing it properly?"

"That's your assignment, Philip. But don't get ahead of me. We have a lot to cover in this week's training before you are ready to do any real planning."

Philip drains the last of his coffee as the others stand up. Apparently, the meals are on the house, for the waiter shows no alarm when they walk out without paying.

The elevator door opens as they approach, and the four men step in. No buttons or controls are in the car. It accelerates rapidly, and they reach the top of the tower without anyone

The Story

having spoken.

The door opens into thick fog. There is no way to judge the size of the platform: no walls, no railings, no edges are in sight. What dominates the scene is a huge blue flame seeming to rise from the platform although the base of the fire is indistinct in the fog.

"Follow me," their Master says and walks directly toward the pillar of fire.

Philip is expecting to feel heat as they approach what looks like the flame of a gigantic propane torch. However, as they draw near, there is no heat and no sound.

Their leader walks into the fire and disappears. Harold is next, and he disappears; then Jim. Philip steps in after Jim and finds himself in another world.

It is a garden, a lush, semitropical place, the extent of which cannot be determined, for the colorful trees and glistening plants go on as far as one can see in every direction. They are standing on a path of blue gravel that is coming from somewhere and going somewhere. There is no evidence of the flame and nothing that looks as if it could be the portal through which they entered. This is truly a separate world.

The path is wide enough for two abreast. Jesus has an arm over Jim's shoulder, and the two of them have started off. Harold and Philip follow.

At intervals, off on side trails, are benches for seating, some of which are occupied. Philip believes he recognizes a man sitting on one of them. He is a nice-looking gentleman with a Bible open on his lap. Sitting next to him is a muscular fellow who is pointing to something on one of the pages. After passing them and rounding a bend, Philip remarks to Harold:

"Did you see McGee back there?"

"I thought that too. There was a resemblance, definitely. Who do you suppose that strong man was?"

"The way he was dressed, I don't think he's anyone we would know."

the Day and the Hour

"That was Samson," says Jesus. "He's explaining Judges sixteen to John Vernon."

The trail breasts the top of a knoll, revealing a building ahead. It reminds Philip of his store. In fact, it looks exactly like it, and the path leads directly to it. Jesus and Jim go in through the open door and climb the stairs to the upper room. Philip and Harold follow close behind them.

The other nine are there. Philip knows them all. Ken Martin is coming to greet him with clear eyes and a wide smile. Lonnie is standing, grinning. Jeremy gets up from the yard chair with the broken armrest. Carl jumps up from the spool of rope. Francis swings his leg over the air compressor and joins the others in welcoming Philip and Harold. Harold introduces Jim to them. Apparently, they all are acquainted with Jesus, who no doubt told them what to expect. And there is Geoffrey the plumber and Archie the architect, and Leonard and Stan from Grace Bible Church.

"I thought you fellows might feel more at home in a place like this than under the trees in the garden," says Jesus. "I asked Archie what he thought of the idea, and he was all for it. Did we get it right, Phil?"

"Just about perfect. Only, it was the left arm of that chair that was broken, not the right one."

"We did that to see if you would notice," Lonnie says with an even bigger grin.

"You have been chosen to carry out that renovation you always said your town so desperately needed," Jesus continues. "You twelve will form the backbone of the crew. Conditions are different from the way it was when you left. Much of civilization had to be restarted after the Tribulation. It took some time to rebuild infrastructure and clean things up. Some, but not all, of that will have been done when you arrive.

"I know you're all curious about the plan for this week. In order for you to accomplish in a year what took a hundred years before, you will have to come up to speed with your basic knowledge. Here is the outline of the course:

"Today—this is Sunday—you will be going through orientation together as a group. Then I will meet with each of you individually for counseling in order to separate light from darkness, which heretofore have been mingled in your minds. This will expand your mental powers. At that time you can put before me any special requests you may have. That takes care of today. You will spend the night here in the store. I took enough camping equipment from the old store to provide you with mats to sleep on and cots for you senior fellows in case you think you need them.

"Monday, you begin exercising your newly empowered minds. In the morning you get intense sessions in math and physics. For lunch you will find plenty of nourishing and tasty fruit out in the garden. Don't worry about inadvertently picking fruit from the tree of the knowledge of good and evil. That one I cut down and burned. But the tree of life you will not be able to avoid; all the varieties of trees out there are its descendants. Just be careful to stay on the blue trails, or you will get into another time thread and not find your way back.

"On Monday afternoon you get chemistry, engineering principles, electronics, and information science. You will be amazed at how easy it is for you to learn when these subjects are presented in all correctness. You will not need to take notes, and you will not have books. Information in the form in which you will receive it cannot be written down. You will remember everything.

"Your education this week encompasses more knowledge than you will need at first. During the course of the age, you will be involved in other projects where you will need to know these things.

"Tuesday morning, you start with materials science and then earth science and oceanography. In the afternoon comes biophysics, botany, and agriculture.

"Wednesday, you get a break and will not be taking in so much. You will learn the origins and meaning of the universe in the morning. In the afternoon you master atmospheric science, aeronautics, solar science, nuclear engineering, and rocket science.

"On Thursday you will plunge into marine biology, aerobiology, naval architecture, and aeronautical engineering.

"Friday is reserved for animal biology, zoology, human biology, nutrition, psychology, sociology, and medicine.

"On the seventh day you learn correct worship disciplines and rituals.

"Are there any questions?"

"Who will be our teacher?" asks Archie.

"The Trinity. We are in the Father, the pillar of fire; he is in us, and all knowledge is in him. I am his Son, your Rabbi, and our Spirit within you leads you into all truth."

"Will there be other people involved in our restoration project?" Philip asks.

"More and more as time goes on. At first there will be only the twelve of you. Then, after transportation is established and the housing capacity begins to increase, we will be bringing more in."

"Will everyone from the past who lived in our town come back?" asks Ken.

"Not the resurrected saints; they stay in heaven. By virtue of your translation, you are able to reside in both places. The old timers would have too much of an adjustment to make, anyway."

"Will anyone survive the Tribulation?" asks Stan.

"From your town? Yes, many did, but they all were taken away. Some have come back—or from your point of view, some *will* come back. You are fortunate not to have them there when you start your work since most of them are permanently unregenerate. In other places, management of the beast-marked populace is the biggest task and takes most of the raptured personnel that I have available. They are unable to buy or sell while the devil is banished since they have the mark of the beast. They have to be cared for as slaves. Gradually, as the population of the earth-dwellers multiplies, more of them will be moving in from other places. In addition, you will be hosting tourists from

The Story

all over the world after things get well established."

"What about those who didn't survive?" asks Leonard.

"The Tribulation martyrs stay in heaven with the other martyrs. They have blessed duties there. The saved join the resurrected saints in heaven. Those who died in their sins are resurrected with the lost at the final judgment."

"You will have access to most of the materials and equipment needed for the project, so you will not have to make everything from scratch. Some of you will start out from the city with trucks and equipment. The bridge on 321 where it crosses Sorek Creek is down, and the bridge on Mountain Highway between Herne and Crossroads is missing its middle span. There is a lot of earthquake damage on 321 to the north, and the farm road has a bad washout. Since your town is isolated, you will have to build a temporary bridge at Sorek Creek in order to bring the equipment in. The runway at the airport was not badly damaged, and Harold will get the rest of you in by plane. Hike to Crossroads, and you will find motorcycles and four wheelers at Don's Cycle—enough to get you around to other places. Motorcycles will go where other vehicles won't until the debris are cleared from the streets. Don't worry about taking what isn't yours. I own it all, and I'm giving you permission to use whatever machines and fuel you find. There is no power, so the electric vehicles and equipment won't be of any use until we bring in generators. It will take a month or so before electric power and communications are restored.

"Here, let's look at the plan."

The Master produces a rolled-up plan from somewhere and spreads it out on the floor. They all kneel around it. Philip notices that nothing hurts; his joints are delightfully supple, and his eyesight is sharp enough to see minute details on the far side of the plan.

"As you can see, Ken, the church building has been restored to its original location on the crest of the hill. That's one building your ancestors got right. The old Good Samaritan hospital has been restored there too. A hotel stands in place of your Fitness

the Day and the Hour

Center, and a museum is located over the ruins of the Federal Building. Administration offices for my government are on the upper floors above the museum."

"I see that the Beach House is included in the plan. It looks just like the old one," Philip says.

"It *is* the old one. It's the only building east of the hill that wasn't destroyed. It will be your headquarters initially."

A vision of being at the Beach House comes before Philip's mind's eye, and the voices around him fade.

"Is the jeep still there?" asks Harold.

"Earl left it on the road to .... One of you will take a motorcycle up there and .... It will come in handy, especially before the equipment .... "

It was during that exceptionally cold winter, the first year he lived there, before he met Pamela; it is early morning; the fire has gone out, and he is cold waking up.

The Story

Chapter 17

Sometime during the night, Leila dreamed a dream: She is seated in the first-class section of an airliner, which has landed safely and come to a halt at its destination. The other passengers who were seated nearby, some of whom she knew, have gotten up and filed out. Across the aisle were Alice and Adam Murphy. She noticed the Foster family as they went by: Harold, Harrietta, and their two daughters. The seat next to her was empty.

Only the captain remains, standing in the passageway from the flight deck.

She is confused. What happened to the Rapture? Could this be it?

It must be!

Suddenly, realizing the impropriety of her solitary presence, she rises to leave. As she passes by the pilot, she looks him in the eye to thank him for the flight as is her custom.

He is Earl.

She reaches for the bulkhead to steady herself.

"Let me escort you off the plane, Leila."

He takes her arm, and they walk side by side down the narrow corridor to the terminal. She steals a sideways glance. He looks magnificent in his uniform. All she wants to do now and forever is live in this moment—never, never ask why he is here or whether he will stay. They step out into the busy concourse.

People are everywhere, hurrying at the direction of signs:

FATHER CLAIM →

← MOTHER CLAIM

SISTER CLAIM →

← BROTHER CLAIM

Leila wonders where she should be going, whether there is a

the Day and the Hour

sign somewhere for her; she has no relatives to claim. However, she will not feel orphaned as long as Earl is with her. They walk along the gold-paved concourse, arm in arm, going on and on, the crowd becoming thinner and thinner, until they have left the claim signs far behind and people are nowhere to be seen.

They have come to a large rotunda under a high, arching ceiling, which appears to be the terminus of the corridor. The expansive floor is richly inlaid in some pattern that she does not understand. Around the perimeter are what appear to be tall hanging draperies, alternating white and crimson. Leila, ever responsible, always thinking of her duty, is remembering what she has been taught. She knows that Earl is not supposed to be here. Finally, determining to be obedient, she musters the ultimate of her mettle—contrary to all her feelings—and says, "You must be going. I'm supposed to meet Jesus."

"I am Jesus."

Shocked and incredulous that he would say such a thing, she turns to face him.

He is no longer wearing the uniform. But he *is* Earl—no, only *like* Earl. There is a radiance about him, and he is nobler yet somehow humbler than Earl had been. He raises his right forearm, letting her see his wrist where the ancient scar still shows. A heaviness descends upon her, and her knees give out. She sinks to his feet and curls her arms around his bare ankles. Scars are there too, beginning now to be bathed with tears.

He bends down and places a hand on her head. She does not want to release his feet: it is fitting and feels good to be embracing him thus. Nevertheless, the weight that pressed her down is lifted, and she floats to her feet.

"Dear one, you knew me long before you met Earl, and what you loved about Earl you loved because it reminded you of me. You can call me Earl, if you like, when we're together alone; it will be our secret. I have known you forever and have been looking forward to this day since before the world began—to be close to you in sight and sound. But you had become separated from me.

The Story

It was Earl's love for you that brought us together. And he is satisfied."

He places a circlet of gold on her head.

"You are altogether beautiful, my love; there is no flaw in you. Come with me from Lebanon, my bride."

She opens her arms to receive his embrace. Strength and courage and understanding flow into her. Her mind clears: everything is vivid, replete with significance, and pregnant with potential. She feels taller. She stands before him and sees him in his fullness—because she has become like him.

All around the rotunda, emerging from behind the draperies, are maidens dressed in flowing, pastel-colored robes. They are chanting something in a tongue she does not understand.

"Are they angels?"

"Yes. They are The Daughters of Jerusalem. ... Listen."

Their words are now clear and meaningful to Leila's ears. They are addressing her:

> What is thy beloved more than another beloved, O thou fairest
> among women?

Her new spirit rises to meet this challenge. She takes a step back and looks at him. She wants to sing. She feels that she has it in her to sing but remembers that she never could sing.

Dare I try? ... Oh, I must!

She looks into his eyes. Music of pipes and strings fills the room. He smiles, and a song springs from her lips:

> Among ten thousand you'll know him:
> > handsome, strong, all aglow.
>
> Behold, his head is noble,
> > surpassing the finest gold.
>
> His locks, black as ravens, are
> > wavy, glossy, and full.
>
> His eyes, shining with wisdom,
> > in pools milky white,
>
> Like doves both mild and quick,
> > are making my soul delight.
>
> His beard is a garden of spices,
> > sweet smelling, round and neat.

> His lips—oh delicate flowers—are
>   dripping with myrrh to heal.
> His arms are strong and golden,
>   each wearing a band of jewels.
> His tunic's of polished ivory,
>   overlaid with gems of blue.
> His legs are pillars of marble
>   carved, set in bases of gold.
> The words of his mouth are sweet,
>   true when all has been told.
> He's the choicest cedar in Lebanon,
>   a man to desire and hold.
> O Daughters of Jerusalem, this is my beloved, and this is my friend.

The music ends, and they curtsy to her, for they were the players of the instruments.

Leila was surprised that she was able to sing, and the words that came to her were surprising yet familiar too. She called him her beloved friend, and he is obviously happy that she did so. She wonders how all this could be. He looks more like Earl now; he is Earl, somehow.

The Daughters of Jerusalem resume their playing: quicker music, a tune for tapping one's foot, yes, a cadence that calls forth dance. Leila has not danced since childhood, and she believes that dancing is best left to others. Her partner knows otherwise. He takes her hand, and they begin with easy movements. As long as she keeps her eyes on him, she knows exactly what to do; her feet obey as if trained by much practice. He guides her through arm motions, and they flow together in harmony, whirling across the floor. All her attention is on him; only by the feel of the flowing air does she know how quickly they move. She thrills when he makes her twirl, and in those moments she catches glimpses of the angel band. She learns to relax when he lifts her, and she loves falling into his strong arms.

The music slows and stops. How long they danced, she is not certain; it might have been an hour or a few minutes. She is not tired; she is ready to face whatever comes next.

"Will I stay here?" she asks her Lord and friend—her new and

The Story

old and forever Earl. "Will you go now to meet with others?"

"I am meeting them now. I am not limited by time and place. However, I will not always be fully tangible to you as I am at this moment. There are many things I want you to do for me. I will be with you always—very close indeed—but not exactly as I am now."

"Will I be alone, then?—I mean, I've no relatives here. Everyone seemed to be meeting mothers and fathers and other family members. I have none."

"No one here has relatives such as you are thinking of. The signs we passed in the concourse were there to comfort them because that's what they expected. They will indeed meet loved ones from their former lives. But here we adopt.

"You have no children, and you have wept about that. Those tears, though recent and few, had great value. I collected them and spent them on something you will like: you and I now have three adopted children. I have told them about you, and they're anxiously waiting to meet you. One of them is very young, and she needs you now. She will be a joy to you and to many. There were others who wanted her, but my bid won her for us."

He takes her arm and sings:
> Lo, the winter is past;
>> the cold and the fierce winds are gone.
>
> Lilies are blooming on earth;
>> the time for singing has come.
>
> Bright are the tips of the fir trees;
>> the vines are in flower again.
>
> Come, my love, my fair one;
> I'll show you our new home.

As he sang, they walked toward one side of the great hall where another corridor leads away. There is a sign over it:

ADOPTIONS

Passing under the sign and entering the avenue, Leila notices more signs: doors on both sides of the street have names inscribed on them. They stop at one bearing a golden plaque:

the Day and the Hour

> Leila Lolomi
> Predestined for Adoption
> In Love

He opens the door for her, and they enter a spacious room. It reminds Leila of the great room at Lolomi Lodge in the mountain valley; only this one is larger, and some of the outdoors has come inside. Instead of the few stunted plants confined to pots, here is a veritable garden of vines growing from beds arranged about the perimeter of the room and climbing to the rough-hewed beams above. Where there were small windows in the earthly image, the heavenly house has its walls open to the fresh and fragrant mountain air. What walls there are are made of logs; the floor is of boards and colorful rugs. A great stone fireplace over on the left is just where it was on earth. The view too is similar: The opposite side of the valley is a mountain wall green and gray and streaked with slender silver falls. Seen from here in the lodge, it rises beyond the tops of the windows.

"This is your reward," he says.

Coming into view on the right is a girl leading a horse.

"That's Flo! And Baxter!" Leila exclaims.

"Yes, and here come your father and mother."

While she was watching Flo, catching her eye and waving, a man and a woman came through the gate. The woman is holding a baby. They are on the path leading to the porch, and they remind Leila of Adam and Evelyn.

And so they are.

Leila wants to run out and greet them all, but she stays close beside her soul's mate. She will not make that mistake again. Adam and Evelyn step onto the porch and come through the open doorway.

"It was Evelyn who first asked me if she could adopt you," says Jesus. "I told her it was a good choice and suggested that Adam would make you a good father. I knew he wanted to ask me but was uncertain about the propriety of it. Adam and Eve, you know.

The Story

They do fit the part, don't you think? He thought it would be intruding on sacred ground belonging to your first parents. There are many Adams and Eves.

"That is her granddaughter Eve is holding. She is ours, and she is yours, my dear."

"Oh, but I was never taught to care for a baby! Changing diapers and all—will they teach me?"

Evelyn laughs, a melodious sound that makes everyone feel a tingle of joy.

"There are no diapers here," she says. "Though we resemble earthly bodies, it's the outward appearance only. The inner workings are of a superior principle."

"And I'm happy to tell you that Murphy's law has been repealed," Adam adds, with a smile nearly as bright as Eve's.

Again, Evelyn laughs. It seems that she is unable to contain her mirth. The baby tries to imitate her, but the best she can do is flail her little limbs. Evelyn gives her to Leila.

"What is her name?" asks Leila.

"We were waiting to see what you would call her," says Jesus. "She was not wanted in the old world, and they did not have a name for her."

"She will be our little Rose of Sharon," says Leila. "We shall call her Sharon. She is beautiful."

They all stand looking at the baby, who seems to be pleased with her name and is adoring her new mother.

No doubt, Leila would have been overwhelmed by this abundance of family had she not herself become a glorified creature. Even so, she is speechless. Her adopted father, having quietly left the room, is descending the stairs with two young children hanging on his arms. Leila looks up at the sound of their approach. Both children, a girl and a boy, are gazing at her with wide, dark eyes.

"This is Shada and here is Salim," announces Adam. "Here is your mother, children."

Leila gives Sharon back to Evelyn and goes to the children,

crouching down to meet them at their level.

"You are perfectly wonderful children. I like you both very much already."

They stare at her shyly.

"Salim, you will be safe with me. Shada, you are a sweet-smelling flower."

"I think they couldn't imagine that their mother would want them," says Evelyn. "We told them it would be so, but now they see you face to face, and they know it is true."

"Grandma, I believed you," says Shada. "So did I," says Salim. "She's exactly the mother I wanted."

It occurs to Leila that Jesus has been silent and that they have been ignoring him. Still crouching by the children, she turns to look for him. He is there, obviously enjoying himself. At the invitation of her look, he comes over and kneels beside her, putting his strong arms around them all. "Daddy, thank you for Mommy," says Salim.

"Thank you for Grandma and Grandpa, too," says Leila, laying her head on Jesus' shoulder.

Suddenly, a question forces its way into her thoughts, and it stuns her for a moment. She looks over her shoulder toward Adam and Evelyn who are standing there, beaming over the new family. Jesus, knowing her mind, loosens his embrace and allows her to stand. He faces her and answers the question before she can ask it.

"There is only one marriage here, and that is between me and you and all those for whom I have lived and died and now live for. All of you are my new creation; there is no procreation here. Envy and strife are unknown. Your common bond to me ensures that. You will find no difficulties in your families and no mistrust or jealousy between yours and others, for we are really one. Your question is about Alice. She and Adam are sister and brother. They have adopted each other. Adam and Evelyn are brother and sister. Alice and Evelyn are sisters. Alice is with her son, Andrew. Perhaps you and Andrew would like to be sister and brother, but I

The Story

will leave it for you to decide. You will meet him soon. By the way, Flo is without family yet. She might like to be your sister.

"There is no lack here, no compromise, no sacrifice of love for another, only fullness and overflowing. All we who have come out of the curse and through the vale of tears will soon be free even of the echoes of those old conflicts. For now, rest and enjoy one another my beautiful children and my bride. In a little while you will be called to begin your preparations for the future and for the feast, for we will be celebrating our marriage. After that will begin the day when the old earth is renewed—my enemies having been subdued for a time—and it will freely enjoy our presence.

"By the authority of the Creator of heaven and earth, there shall be no more delay! There is about to be born a new age on the earth, and the mystery that my prophets wrote about will be fulfilled. The birth pangs are even now beginning. The judgment of the Antichrists has been set, and there will be great tribulation for those who were left behind as they witness the unfolding of the Scriptures that they disparaged. After our wedding supper, we shall proceed to establish the long-awaited peace and prosperity that men have dreamed of and have attempted to bring about—and have suffered for because of their misguided designs and personal failings.

"The time is near, and we must be ready. I will need you all to help me govern the world. Leila, you have been prepared for a special role in my administration. Never fear, your children will remain with you; they will always be a joy and a help to you, and their grandparents will never be far away. This house is your retreat, and you will come here often."

The two children held Leila's hands as the Master spoke. He bends down and lifts them both up. They know him well. Their faces light up, and they wrap their arms around his neck.

"Listen to everything your mother tells you. I must go now, and while I am away she will help you with everything." He kisses them and lowers them back to the floor.

"Adam and Eve, you will come with me now."

the Day and the Hour

Evelyn reluctantly gives Sharon back to Leila.

"Leila, stay here with the children until Andrew comes. He will be here soon. Flo will show you around and help you with the nursery."

"Thank you for the sunset."

"You have captivated my heart, my sister, my bride."

As he leaves, an old feeling returns, the feeling of not having the one she loves nearby and not knowing where he is. She remembers that she must be watching for him. It will not do to have her eyes closed. She must try to wake up and watch for him.

The Story

The day had defeated hatless, fugitive Clark. He lay on Carmen's couch, staring at a streak of light on the dark ceiling from a gap in the curtains where a sliver of nighttime illumination from the courtyard came in. The whirlwind day had allowed little opportunity to look back; it was almost as though nothing had existed prior to each moment. It was a day of mounting difficulties—more even than could be remembered. What was to be done about the city police? He closed his eyes, and the solution came as he drifted off to sleep:

Let it go until tomorrow.

Rather than drawing the curtain closed on the day, this advice smote his conscience and jarred him awake, for procrastination was contrary to his nature. A semblance of his troubles rose up, challenging the wisdom of leaving everything for later. Earl opened his eyes and tried to think. *I need a plan and the sooner the better.*

Unfortunately, his condition was not conducive to clear thinking and realistic planning, and he knew it.

It need not be the best possible plan ... but some plan, some starting point at least, ... a head start for tomorrow, ... an idea of where to begin. ... Begin with what? What was beginning?

Exhaustion was overcoming him, and it gained a partial victory: A hypnotic half sleep took hold, and out of it came the voice of Evelyn telling him that his inability to make a plan was caused by something other than fatigue, something rising out of the past. Indeed, something had crept in, and it had obliterated his troubles: no longer was he concerned about the police; he was not in the least afraid of the feds; he had not given the resistance a thought in days; the maddening party that drove him from his home was but a misty memory.

The part of him that knew he was under a spell tried to release him from the grip of it. In his stupor he groped in the darkness, straining to make contact with the real world.

Carmen is in her bedroom—what is she doing there? No

matter: that problem will be solved. What is the problem? Is it to make the plan? No, there is another problem, a serious problem.

It was not to be denied: a dam had broken; a fortress had fallen. Someone—who was it? Someone, somewhere, had been invaded and overpowered by something in his past. He refused to believe that he himself was that one, that he was the one who had suffered the defeat.

She grasped the tiller with both her hands, forcing the lee rail down, and the boat boiled over the billows. Pure joy was on her face. ... It was too much for him. His defenses would not bear the strain. She put her arms around him—those dark eyes sparking from the heart he had awakened. ... He was in love with her!

Earl, you were always in love with her. You pretended it was not so when she first came to your gym, and what did you do? You loved her anew, and again you made it to be not so.

But she was dangerous! She could slay his independence. He would never allow another woman to bind him.

She did it quite suddenly. She found a fault in your strategy: you had ignored the affinity of your soul for hers—yes, too terrible for you to admit. But you were unable to keep her from proving it.

He preferred her on a cool, rational basis. He admired her in a well controlled, disconnected way. That was good: it worked well for him; he kept his soul's secret—until now. Now the jig is up for that poor man!

Yes, she broke in and came to claim her place, laying her head on your soul's bosom—the real woman, not the one you expected: not the demanding boss; not the coy manipulator; not one of the inconsistent, contradictory, inscrutable creatures made to torment men; not the whining, nagging wife; not the fearful child who wore mittens in winter and picked flowers in summer. Those were only possibilities, and she rejected them for you.

I see her now: she stands before him, defiant, having torn up and cast the flimsy things away. What can he do?

You were the first man she ever loved, and she loved you as no woman could. She was in a class by herself, a creature made for you.

The Story

Yet you were stern with her. You wounded her as you could not bear to hurt another. You left her, turned away, and went away. ...

Stop! It is me! Please, leave the dreadful score uncounted.

She will not count it.

Only let me think of her. The thought of her is enough for now; I care for nothing else. I'm lovestruck. ... No, it is not enough; I will go ... go back to her—must find her. Must leave and go back immediately. Get up and get dressed. ... Sleep a little first. ... Sleep ... and then ... go back.

the Day and the Hour

The Story

Chapter 18

Leila woke to the great disappointment of being in her bedroom. It was early; she closed her eyes and tried to drift back into the dream. Parts of it were still vivid at first as she lay between sleeping and waking, but as the hour of her normal rising approached, even those scenes faded, leaving her alone with the noisy birds working hard to sing up the sun and the faint light of the autumn morning filtering through the curtains.

With nowhere to go and no desire to partake of breakfast, she is uncertain about whether to get up and dress or stay in bed. She decides on the former for no particular reason, makes the bed, showers, and puts on clothes as though she were going to the office.

This doesn't feel right. I wonder what they wear in heaven.

She changes into the clothes she was wearing when she sailed with Earl yesterday.

She opens the bedroom curtains, revealing through the glass door the lawn, green and damp with dew, and the garden of shrubs with its pathways. Beyond it dark evergreens tower above the nearer trees whose fall-colored leaves of red, yellow, and amber are pale in the early light.

Leila goes wandering about the apartment, entering each room. In the living room, she stands for a minute before each of the paintings on the wall. One in particular holds her gaze longer than the others and brings a tear to her eye. These pictures are reminders of that momentous time when unexpected circumstances kept her at Lolomi Lodge in the mountain valley—kept her much longer than she had planned to stay. It became a turning point in her career, causing her to leave the national headquarters and step down to manage the administration in this small town. She chose these mountain scenes to be reminders, but none of them had ever made her cry before. Is she sorrowful because she will be leaving this painting behind?

It was in the dream! That very mountain.

In the kitchen she finds Earl's hat, the one he left there on Wednesday. She picks it up and puts it on. It is too large. She takes it off and holds it to her bosom, carrying it with her as she goes from room to room, looking for something to put in place or straighten up.

Her thoughts have returned to Earl, if ever they left him, and she decides it will do no harm to get an update. Returning to the bedroom, she picks up her phone and checks the mail. Hourly reports from her local surveillance team are there, but they are informative only in that Earl's location is still presumed to be in the city. They are reporting no new information from the city police.

It is still possible that he might escape and come back just in time. If he were to get to his car, he would be hard to catch. Their rubber bullets and short-range patrol cars would not stop him. Maybe that Carmen woman isn't truly his girlfriend. He won't be able to stay with her long without being arrested, anyway. Good thing I'm dressed. If he comes, it will be in a roundabout way. He might leave his car behind Pastor Adam's church and take the trail. ...

She stops herself, realizing that she is engaging in wishful thinking. She remembers that she has already decided that the question is settled: he will not be joining her. She is not tempted to go back and review the reasoning on which she based that conclusion, for she is not sure there is a reason she can articulate. But neither does she want to believe that her conclusion cannot be wrong: hope never dies completely—not permanently.

Even if his spiritual condition won't allow him to go with me, he might come to say goodbye. ... No, I'm dreaming again.

She is suspended between despair and some unearthly hope seeming to have emerged from last night's dream. She tries once more to reconstruct it. She danced—or something like it. Then there was another scene.

The Story

That's it! He was there. We were in a wonderful lodge in the mountains, like Lolomi but more .... I know he loved that place too, even though it was only in his imagination. We talked about it Wednesday night when he was here. ... But the one in the dream was open to the fresh air. ... And I had children—and a baby.

She goes to the dining room and sits where she was sitting when he was there for dinner, when they talked about the ranch resembling the one in a book they both had read. The memory of other things from that evening and the rift that ensued brings on a wave of regret and a feeling of disappointment.

It just didn't work out. ... But he was there in the dream.

Leila gasps. "Flo! Flo, how could I forget you?"

In her preoccupation with Earl, she forgot to find out whether Flo was prepared for the Rapture. Florence is here in town because of Leila. She found her the job at the flower shop after Lolomi was shut down and the valley turned into a wilderness nature reserve. It was Florence's parents who owned the lodge and Florence who had lent her the book that captured her imagination and led her to look for a place to live in the West.

Leila spreads her arms on the table, bows her head, and pleads with her Lord on behalf of Flo; and the Spirit comforts her, letting her know that Flo is ready. They will meet again as they did at Lolomi.

It is now close to the promised hour. During the past two days —since her rebirth in Christ—she often tried to imagine what it would be like when this hour drew near. She would be praying constantly, perhaps seeing visions of heaven, excited as never before in her life. It is not that way at all: she is still attached to earth and hurting for Earl more now than ever, in spite of her repeated resolutions to let him go. To offset this, she determines to spend the last few minutes with her Bible.

Hebrews, she learned somewhere, is an important book, but it is not one with which she is familiar. She finds it. The eleventh chapter is where it happens to open, and her eyes fall on *Samson*.

the Day and the Hour

She was unaware that he had a place in the New Testament. It fascinates her. He is listed along with other heroes of the faith: Abel, who offered the proper sacrifice; Enoch, who was translated before the flood; Noah, Abraham, Sarah, Isaac, Jacob, Joseph, Moses ....

"Rahab, the prostitute?"

> She did not perish with those who were disobedient because she had given friendly welcome to the Hebrew spies.

"I'm going to ask her about that! ... Gideon, Barak, ... Samson! ... Jephthah, David, Samuel ... who through faith conquered kingdoms, ... stopped the mouths of lions, ... of whom the world was not worthy, ... and apart from us they should not be made worthy."

The world was not worthy of them, yet they needed to be made worthy. ... By us?

"There's a mystery here."

While the fragmentary similarities between Earl and Samson of the Bible were intriguing, she never before regarded them as being seriously significant. If anything, it warned her to be on guard against becoming a Delilah herself. She recognized the potential and saw the danger long before becoming actively involved in detaining Earl for his captors. Looking back, she sees the plot unfolding, casting her in the role she had wanted to avoid. Yet hadn't she deliberately written the play to cast herself as Delilah and him as Samson? What made her decide to retell that story? At that time the answer seemed simple: it was a great story, and great stories needed to be told and retold over and over again. Could it be that all of life's experiences are based on stories being retold? How often it has been observed in history! Are there eternal scripts being replayed with variations on themes? If so, why? Because patterns are the very stuff of life? If so, the future might be read in the past: the resemblance between Earl and Samson could be significant.

"Who am I to make him worthy? He needs to believe the Scriptures! I'll leave the book open and the door unlocked."

The Story

*P*hilip woke with an aching neck from sleeping on the cot without a pillow. He tossed the tarp aside, stood up with a groan, and walked to the front of the store. Outside, the street was in dim daylight and deserted. He looked at the time; it was seven o'clock. He recalled coming to the store last night but could not remember exactly why he had done it. It now seemed rather foolish. He went back, put the cot away, left the hardware store, and drove home.

As soon as he arrived, he called Pamela. She told him about the responses of the men last night, and he thanked the Lord for letting him suffer a little in support of what she did.

"How was your night? Were you able to sleep?"

"I did sleep. But I had a crazy dream."

"Was it about heaven?"

"I'm not sure what to make of it. How would I know if it was true?"

"I suppose it doesn't matter much now. We have only a few minutes to wait, and we'll know."

"Has Al Cypher come in yet?"

"No. He said not to expect him very early on Sunday morning. These are not his normal working hours. There are some eggs left, in case you want to have breakfast."

"I'm not hungry at all. I feel like I had breakfast already."

"The refrigerators in these suites are stocked with fruit and milk and yogurt, and there is cereal on the shelf—in case the prisoners need midnight snacks. But I'm not hungry either. I was praying when you called. I wish you were here and we could go together."

"Yeah, me too."

"Well, we'll soon be together in heaven. ... Phil? Are your still there?"

"I'm here. That dream is bothering me. It might be more complicated than we ever thought it would be. I'm sure there will be time for us; I'm just not sure it will be immediately."

the Day and the Hour

Earl is awake but not dressed—awake enough to be brewing a pot of coffee. He is standing in Carmen's kitchen, wearing only his underwear. He slept in—slept much later than is his habit—and is groggy for it. The night's sleep was not refreshing.

Carmen's bedroom door is still closed. He misses her—misses sleeping with her, which is why he is not dressed. He checks the clock again. Ten minutes to go. Then he will knock on her door, go in, and comfort her. He knows she will want him then.

She was always eager to give herself to him from their first date. He was determined not to get involved, but her invitation was hard to resist. He still considered himself fully independent of her, nevertheless. It was not that she was unqualified. She was a fine specimen of a woman in every way: mentally, physically, emotionally. Nonetheless, he had his principles, and no woman would be his captor.

Carmen was not essentially promiscuous. She was strongly attracted to Earl for his talents and kindness as well as his manly aspect. She wanted to bear a child by him, a baby who would be a superchild and change the course of the universe. Someday, she had believed, nature would not be denied, and he would give in. Meanwhile, she lived for weekends, working during the week in her dental practice.

This routine ended abruptly several weeks ago when Earl called to say he had made a commitment to perform in a play, and the Saturday rehearsals would make it difficult for him to continue seeing her regularly. She was relieved, in a way. The drive to make him her mate—a mandate she had believed was in the stars—had taken a turn, which she had to accept. Mating with Earl then lost its urgency and inevitability. She decided to begin looking elsewhere.

So, when Earl came knocking on her door yesterday afternoon after this long absence, it was a complete surprise. She had to make up her mind quickly. Had he called and directly asked her for a date, she would have turned him down. But she could not

The Story

refuse his plea for shelter. She decided that she would have dinner with him but not invite him to spend the night in her apartment. However, after she helped him elude the police and he needed a hiding place, she gave in. It caused a terrible struggle within herself to make him sleep alone.

Earl believes he will yet be in bed with her this morning, for such was his reasoned expectation when he lay down on the couch last night. He knew she believed in the Rapture, for they had talked about it. That is why, he thought, she had held out on him.

Regardless, it seems to him highly unlikely that she will be taken on any basis. In just a few minutes that will be made clear.

Last night when Carmen asked Earl what he believed about the Rapture, she would have agreed with his skeptical stance, but she could not. She was not a student of the Bible and had no theological basis for believing that it was what Christian believers said it was; she believed it simply because she saw no other way to understand how so many prophets could be in agreement: it was altogether beyond human nature. When Earl scoffed at her, she did not take offense, for she scoffed at herself too. It was not like her to believe something having to do with religion. Whether it made sense or not would not have been an issue: she would not have stepped beyond the security of her agnosticism long enough to ask that question.

Indeed, something had undermined her agnostic fortress. A sympathy lurked within her that made her susceptible to considering the evidence on its own merit. Where could that have come from? The only thing she could put her finger on was that she had never disliked real Christians. She could always tell when she had one in her dental chair, and she loved having them.

As Earl drinks his coffee and waits to go in to her, he remembers that he is in a precarious position with respect to the law. He decides to get dressed in case there comes that unwelcome and inevitable knock on the door sooner than what he originally expected. Leaving the hat behind last night was a big mistake.

the Day and the Hour

Carmen thought her name was in it. If there's any competence on the squad at all, they'll have my location pinpointed. I wonder if Dad knows about my predicament. It won't be any surprise to him if he does.

Earl hurriedly puts on his shirt, pants, and shoes; then he goes to stand at the patio door.

The courtyard is one floor below. There are various small structures in the area, one of which must be the entrance to an emergency stairway. As he sips his coffee, he studies the layout and determines that a particular housing near the middle is the most likely candidate. In fact, there is a small *Exit* sign on it. But how would he get down to the courtyard level from here?

†

Carmen has been in and out of sleep for hours, sometimes dreaming of the numbers on the clock, sometimes waking and watching the minutes go by. What if she should be taken along with the Christians? She would be painfully out of place. No way would she be worthy to join them in heaven.

They're not perfect either, but they have peace. They have been forgiven and made perfect in God's eyes by means of the blood shed by Jesus on the cross—so they tell me. Apparently, it works for them.

It had never meant anything to her before.

Little time is left. She hears Earl in the kitchen. She does not want to get out of bed and have to face him. She wishes she were sound asleep.

What ever possessed me to believe in this fantasy? ... If it works for them, might it work for me too? I know there is a God. ... Is this me? I'm supposed to be agnostic!

Shedding his blood for sinners is what only an extremely loving God would do. If there is a God, why would he be that way? ... Of course! He would have to be that way! If his love were not that far above human love, he would not be God!

Who can remain unmoved by that?

I can't. If he bought me with his blood, who am I to resist?

The Story

You would be throwing it back at him!

How awful! Never, never would I do that. ... How could anyone?

She reaches to her nightstand and takes up a pad of notepaper. She will leave a note for Earl, just in case. One minute to go. It had better be a quick note.

†

As the coffee brought on more awareness, Earl began to realize that his escapade had hit a brick wall. The way he used to feel about using Carmen was gone. In its place was a sensation that he was in the wrong place—not just that he was not in his proper place; that much was obviously true. It was as though he had gone down a road using the wrong map, and he did not know what road he was on. Something had gone wrong with the way he felt about being there. He stretched, swung his arms, and took another gulp of coffee.

Every few seconds, he checked the clock. He had thought it would be easy to pass the time while the world waited with bated breath. But he found himself disoriented, nervous, and perspiring.

A new light was dawning, and a new mind was coming to Earl Clark. He had forgotten what had gotten him here. Who was Carmen that he should be in her apartment? Everything was wrong about it. The wrongness had nothing to do with the imminent danger of his being arrested: it was worse than that. He felt he had omitted something, and whatever it was, it was more important even than his freedom.

Earl looks into his empty coffee mug.

Was there something in there besides coffee?

He sets it down on the counter and peers out through the glass door. The sun is not high enough to cast direct rays into the courtyard, which is surrounded by the towers of the building, but enough light is coming directly from the sky overhead to make it morning in the garden. It reminds him of the garden behind Leila's apartment building, and the answer comes to him in a still

the Day and the Hour

small voice that seems to be Evelyn's: *She was in your thoughts last night, and she will never leave you.*

Grabbing up his mug again, he takes a step toward the coffee pot and remembers: it was not a dream! He had resolved to return to her immediately but fell asleep.

There is a bump; the coffeemaker skips on the counter, and the floor sways. He looks at the kitchen clock:

8:00

The Story

Chapter 19

An earthquake! That's what it was, an earthquake! They got warned of an earthquake, bless them!

Earl goes to Carmen's bedroom door and knocks. There is no answer.

"Are you all right?" he shouts.

No answer.

He opens the door. She is not in the room.

"Oops. ... It was more than an earthquake."

No, she wouldn't have been taken. She must have gone out for a walk while I was sleeping—probably didn't want to be here when the cops came. Why didn't I think of that?

The bedclothes are thrown aside, indicating that she got up in a hurry. There is a note on the floor; it could be for him.

The doorbell rings. He snatches up the note and tiptoes to the entryway. The hallway monitor is showing two husky police officers at the door. One of them has a key card in his hand, undoubtedly programmed to unlock the door. The other holds a large handgun.

Rushing back to the kitchen, he slides the glass door open and steps out onto the patio balcony. *Bam! Bam! Bam!* Loud knocks assail the apartment door. It is perhaps twelve feet down to the garden level. There is no fire escape: no way down.

"Oh, yes there is!"

Rolled up and bound by a scarlet thread is a fire-escape ladder. Apparently, Carmen put it there. He snaps the ties, and it flops down, unrolling an array of rungs. Swinging over the railing, he scrambles down the ladder and takes off, running for the emergency exit in the middle of the courtyard.

Scarcely has he started across the garden when the cops emerge from the apartment onto the balcony. They take a stand there and aim the gun at him.

"Stop! Clark! Stop, in the name of the law!"

the Day and the Hour

He keeps running. Gunshots tell him he should be feeling the sting of bullets. Instead, there comes a buzzing, humming chorus, and several large bees attack him.

It's a bee-bee gun.

Robotic bees are darting, diving, and attempting to land on him. One of them alights on the back of his neck. He plucks it off and smashes it to the ground. Others are clutching his clothing, trying to poke their needles through to his skin. He brushes them off—the ones he can feel—while striving to maintain his stride. The door to the exit stairway is on the opposite side of the small structure, and as he slows to round the corner, two of the bees attack one side of his head simultaneously. He knocks them off, and they swoop back almost immediately. Another is clinging to his shirt in back where he cannot reach it, extending its needle into his flesh. He backs against the wall with a twist, crushing the mechanism. It drops to the concrete. The booted feet of his pursuers are pounding on the garden path, their echoes clattering in the courtyard.

Clark's hand is on the exit door, pulling it open. He feels another needle in his back. He must either let go of the door, allowing it to slam shut, or permit the bee to inject him with sedative. He tries to fling it wide, but it is stiff, and his usual strength has waned. It opens partway and springs back immediately, but he scrapes through and in doing so dislodges the bee. The door slams shut behind him.

Down the stairway he plunges. Only one bee has remained with him. He takes a swipe at it and knocks it out of the air, damaging its wings. As he leaps to the first landing, he hears the door opening above.

"Stop! Clark! You're under arrest!"

Bang! Bang!—rubber bullets this time; one has hit him in the back. It stings badly. Rounding the switchback at the landing, he goes leaping down, taking three steps at a time. The heavy boots come pounding after him, resounding in the narrow stairwell. Another landing and another go by. He is far enough

The Story

ahead that they are unable to take another shot at him. He is leaving them behind. If he can get down to the garage level and to his car before they emerge from the stairwell, he might have a chance.

Flight after flight, the floor numbers go by. He started at **18** and is now passing **10**, but he is out of breath and taking only two steps at a time. He is ahead of them by three or four floors, but he must increase his lead. Apparently, they are slowing; they sound farther away. Even so, once down and into the garage he will have only a few seconds to reach his car, and he is not sure where it is relative to this stairwell.

Reaching the **P1** level, he bursts through the door into the underground garage. Thinking it will increase his chance of escaping if he can find a way to barricade the door, he looks around for something to serve the purpose. He finds nothing. It wastes a few precious seconds.

Now, where is the T-bird? ... There!

Fortunately, the car is nearby, not fifty feet away. As he dashes toward it, the sound of the boots in the stairwell increases. He is about to unlock his car door when he notices a heavy chain lying on the concrete floor. The car has been shackled to a pillar.

The stairway door flies open.

"Stop! Hands up—we'll shoot!"

Clark crouches behind the car for shelter. He sees the exit that he would be driving through, but there is no possibility of removing the chain. Adjacent to the vehicle doors is a pedestrian exit. The only possibility remaining is to get to it—while still alive.

A determined spirit has come upon Earl Clark. His mind is clear now. He remembers the dawning that came to him last night; the full awareness of it has rushed upon him. His life is worth nothing if he cannot reach Leila. He must make it very clear that he loves her. He must reach her before the authorities capture him. After that they can do whatever they will with him. But she will know what has been a mystery to her.

Unless she's gone.

the Day and the Hour

Half running, half crawling, trying to stay out of their sight, he steals to the next car and the next.

Even if it was the Rapture, ...

This method of movement is working; the noise of their footsteps has ceased. He dashes across an aisle, exposed briefly to their sight. There is a shot and its echo, but it misses.

... she might not have been taken.

They will have to be careful to avoid shooting the cars, which gives him an idea: he is almost as safe in front of a car as he is behind one—unless they send the bees again. Perhaps they used them all.

He must move fast now because they know his location, and they are coming after him on the run. He takes off, heading straight for the exit door.

If she's still there, I'll get to her. ...

He knows they are unable to shoot while they run; he also knows they will stop and fire at him before he gets to the door. He goes for it anyway.

Somehow, I'll get to her.

A spray of shot stings his back as he reaches the door. He plows into it, and it swings open into daylight as another shot peppers him with stinging beads.

If she isn't, ...

Whether he is losing blood or not, he cannot tell. He suspects that he is, but he is not taking time to find out and does not care. The door swings shut behind him, providing a few seconds of shelter from the bullets.

God forgive me.

Up the ramp he runs, panting heavily as he reaches the street level.

Now what?

A police car is there to greet him.

It looks as though he has lost his desperate attempt to get home. Truly, there was little possibility of it even had he left last night; no doubt his car would have been chained to the pillar even

The Story

then.

He has not the wind to go running down the street. *What good would that do anyway?*

Earl decides there is nothing left to do but allow himself to be taken into custody. His pursuers are charging up the ramp.

He steps toward the car with his hands up, letting them know he is surrendering. There is a reflection on the windshield; he is unable to see the officer inside. As he comes to the side of the car, the truth is revealed through the side window: no one is in it. The engine is running—a gasoline engine. He tries the door; it opens. His pursuers, having seen him with his hands up and believing they have him surrounded, have stopped a short distance away.

In a flash, Earl is in the driver's seat, slamming the door shut, and squealing away from the ramp. Finding the siren and light controls, he blasts a path through traffic, sending vehicles scurrying to the curb. With sirens wailing and warbling, he goes speeding down streets and careening around corners.

Having attained the main arterial heading east, it is now a straight shot to the freeway. Traffic lights are cooperating, holding the cross traffic and allowing him to travel at high speed.

While weaving among the city blocks, he had a close follower, an electric car whose ability to accelerate to high speeds in short distances more than matched that of his vehicle. But the heavy drain on its battery caused it to drop out of the race. Now another one is on his tail; in the rear-view mirror he sees its array of bobbling lights not far behind.

Nearing the freeway entrance, he slows for cone-bounded curves and other obstacles in the vicinity of a construction project. His pursuer draws nearer, being in a smaller, lighter car, and is bearing down on him. Rounding the last curve, Earl hits the brakes. A barricade is blocking the road: a makeshift gate constructed especially for him. Police cars are stationed on both sides of it, their lights dancing in seeming delight. They have placed a bar through the loops at the tops of two tall, weighted traffic tubes, preventing him from going ahead and leaving no room to maneuver. They have him trapped.

These guys are good.

Earl comes to a full stop at the bar. They will be adding the theft of the cruiser to the counts against him. An officer walks toward him as the loudspeaker on one of the cars blares, "Shut off the engine, and get out of the car. You are under arrest!"

In answer, Earl presses the accelerator. The tires squeal; the hood of his car contacts the bar, and it slides back to the windshield. He surges forward, dragging the heavy tubes, but he knows he will not be able to go far in this condition, especially considering the incline immediately ahead.

The car that was pursuing him is still on his tail. With the pedal to the floor and the engine roaring in low gear, Earl is nearly to the crest of the hill when he cranks the steering wheel hard, sending his car into a spin and flinging the bar with its orange-and-white tubes back down the incline. Completing a full circle, he twirls the wheel back, arresting the spin, floors the accelerator, and peels away, leaving behind a cloud of smoke and burnt rubber on the pavement. The car that was chasing him turns sharply in order to avoid the tumbling bar and lanky tubes; it runs off the road and disappears over the embankment.

Earl never turned off his dazzling lights, and he presses the siren button once more. The traffic gives way as he charges into the freeway stream and speeds ahead, changing lanes frequently to zip past unresponsive vehicles. The pedal is on the floor, and he is passing moving traffic as if it were standing still. He zooms by a highway patrol car, which seemingly ignores him—but only briefly. The officer inside, who failed to heed an announcement about the chase, quickly becomes informed of the maniac in the stolen patrol car heading east. She turns everything on and goes after him, but Earl continues to draw ahead of her with his daring driving. The miles slip by.

Three lanes peel off to the south, and the former freeway becomes a two-lane highway. Ahead is a long backup of cars and trucks nearly at a standstill. Slowing a little, Earl takes to the oncoming lane with screaming siren and alarming lights warding off the approaching traffic.

He is into the farming country of the Sorek valley where he has in mind to leave the highway and follow a route on which there will be little chance of meeting another roadblock. Turning left onto an unmarked dirt road, he douses the siren and lights and speeds over the uneven terrain as fast as possible without losing control of the car, disappearing over a hill and vanishing from view of the highway. After some miles the road makes a ninety-degree turn, taking him eastward once more.

The intense effort of the past half hour kept him from thinking much beyond each moment. Now, on this isolated stretch of the rural road, there is time to take stock of the situation and consider the prospects ahead. What bothered him earlier returns to mind as a strong sense of destiny stemming from the breakthrough last night when he realized he had been denying Leila her right to know the place she always held in his heart. There was no valid reason for the denial: it had less to do with her than with the painful experience of his former wife's having left him to marry her church's minister. There were other complications too, but he now disdains them all.

Earl fell in love with Leila the first time he saw her, over a year ago, when she was presenting a paper at a security conference in Boise. He told himself then that it was only her professional competence that he admired. Had he admitted to himself that she held a much wider attraction for him, it would have made no difference, for he would not have followed her to Washington DC, and any plan aimed at bringing her to him would have been a long shot indeed.

So he did not speak to her at that time, but he did speak to Kevin Martin, who worked at the hotel where the event was being held. Kevin then recommended the Lolomi Lodge to her. After the conference, Earl went home and uncovered corruption involving both the former mayor and the former FSA chief. They were removed from office, and Leila came to fill the vacancy at the FSA, stepping down from her CEO position at the national level.

It was not a scheme that he thought would succeed. It was only a series of steps with their own benefits. He saw Leila as one who was trapped in a maze of bureaucratic pettiness that took itself to be the real world. He thought she deserved a little fresh air, which a side trip to the lodge would provide in some small measure. He knew Kevin Martin, Ken Martin's son, and was confident that their little conspiracy would work. But he saw her stepping down and coming West only in a pipe dream. After she did come and began attending the Fitness Center in order to meet him—his long shot having hit its mark—he raised his guard. *He was the mark*, and he had never considered what it would mean to be hit; hence, he still did not acknowledge that he loved her; he kept it a mystery even to himself.

The mystery finally ended last night as he lay on Carmen's couch. With a nudge from Evelyn, the secret broke free: Leila was the pearl of great price; he had found the pearl and had brought it home without possessing it.

Is it too late?

It occurs to him that this extended escapade with its batch of new crimes might keep him closer to her if she can convince the FBI to let him serve a jail term at home before being taken away. Even in the worst case—if it turns out that they are separated by the Rapture—there will be a time for them.

There's a time for everything.

The road makes a left turn, now heading north. It will take him behind the Sorek Valley airstrip. He knows where it comes out, at Highway 321 almost opposite of where Deer Drive meets the highway.

If they're waiting for me, chances are it will be at Hill Street, Crossroads, and Market Street, not here.

Earl has forgotten that, unlike his T-bird, this vehicle is equipped with devices allowing it to be tracked even when off the road. He is soon to be reminded of the fact. As the primitive road turns right to skirt the north end of the airport, he is greeted by a

The Story

dazzling array of lights on two patrol cars parked a quarter of a mile ahead at the highway juncture.

The only thing to do now is go back. He backs the car around the corner, hoping they did not see him. The startling sounds of the latest siren hit tunes tell him that they did see him and that he has little time in which to react. The beacon tower is located at this corner of the airport; and being familiar with the service road, a narrow gravel driveway overgrown with weeds, he pulls into it far enough to be out of sight behind bushes.

The siren-and-light show comes jostling around the corner without them noticing exactly where he turned off. He gives them five seconds and then backs out and proceeds to the end of the road. There, he makes the short jog on highway 321 and heads up the hill on Deer Drive. He knows that the police are at that moment looking for a place to turn around, if they have not done so already, and are watching his movements on their map displays.

I've got to ditch this car.

Having sped up Deer Drive without incident, he takes the corner to Creek Street without stopping. As he flies by Grace Bible Church, he glances toward it. Several cars are there, and people are out front on the sidewalk.

Even though he had concluded that the Rapture turned out to be nothing more than an earthquake, this confirming evidence dispels lingering doubts, and he is more hopeful than ever of finding Leila waiting for him at her apartment. She would have been there at eight o'clock, he is sure of that, and there is no reason why she would have gone anywhere else on a Sunday morning.

At the foot of Creek Street, he turns into the Lakeview parking lot and swings into the only vacant parking spot. He expects that they will waste some time searching for him in the restaurant.

A trail from here at the end of Lake Way leads down to the small beach park at the mouth of Gold Creek. He walks briskly to the trailhead and then breaks into a run. Coming to the junction

the Day and the Hour

with the Gold Creek trail, he turns onto it. This trail parallels the creek and will take him back to the end of Deer Drive where Leila's apartment building is located. All he has to do now is watch for the bench with S+D carved into its back. The branch trail leading up to her place comes right after that.

The Story

Chapter 20

Adam and Alice Murphy arrived at the Beach House baptistery a little early. (We can call it that because nothing else happened there since yesterday's ceremony.)

As it turned out, they had no need of the alarm clock. Alice woke up at six and found it impossible to be still and wait. After prayers and dressing she needed to be doing something—anything—to keep nervous energy from building. She grabbed all the bath towels in the house, threw them into the back of her car, grabbed her husband, and drove him to the Beach House. It was a little after seven.

No response came to Adam's knocking on Earl's back door. The pastor was concerned about the timing. He would not be comfortable doing the baptizing without Earl's permission to use the beach, let alone the house and its bathrooms. Although Earl had never turned down his requests in the past, Adam wanted to give him the opportunity to say "no." Perhaps to someone else, that would not seem necessary. But a long friendship develops certain aspects that are not readily apparent to outsiders.

He tried the door. It was unlocked. Footprints on the floor leading to the bathroom appeared to be from yesterday. He tried calling Earl's phone. It was unavailable. He knew what that meant. It meant that he was on a secret mission.

Adam and Alice walked to the water's edge and stood by the dock, intending to wait there. The sky was clear, pale in the early light. Beyond the mountains a halo of yellow marked where the first rays of the sun would break over the darkly silhouetted peaks and ridges. Not a ripple was on the surface of the water. The world was silent. A poet might say nature was holding her breath. A falling maple leaf made an audible landing. The only sound was that of their own breathing, from which thin puffs of vapor ascended in the cool air.

the Day and the Hour

"How many did they say were coming?" Alice asked—not because she had forgotten but just for something to say.

"Forty-nine, wasn't it?"

Alice shivered.

"Our towels won't go very far," she said. "But some will benefit from having an extra one in this chilly air even if the wait is only a few minutes. I'll go up to the car and get them." Adam wanted to tell her they should wait for Earl's permission, but he let her go.

As Alice walked back up the hill to her car, putting a distance between herself and her husband, the fact of the fateful moment being only minutes away swelled up and became a frightful monstrosity. The sky was about to split, and an unseen force would snatch her away. It might as well be that the earth was going to open and swallow her; it came to the same thing: every tangible element of her life that she had known and loved and trusted herself to was soon to be taken from her.

Opening the car door, she retrieved the towels from the cargo area and stacked them neatly on the seat.

She loved what her Maker had made and the place where he had placed her. This was the end of it all. It was profoundly saddening.

She lifted the stack of towels and pushed the door shut with her foot.

She knew something was wrong. She knew she should be glad to be going to her heavenly home, to be seeing her Maker face to face. But this was a difficult way to go. People had always said it would be a blessed privilege to bypass death in this manner. She had said so herself. (It was tricky descending the steps from the driveway because she could not see ahead over the towels.) But it had turned out to be a trial. Abandoning her familiar home was a sacrifice of everything: a death, really. Yes, a death is what it was. (Having reached the walkway, she managed to stay on it by looking down to the side, following the edge of the bricks.) It was easier to think of it as death. She knew that believers died every day rather than give up their trust in the goodness of God, and

The Story

she had considered what she would do if that test should ever come to her. She had decided that she would die, or try to die, with praise on her lips. Now the time had come. It was time to die for him who had died for her. But he suffered unimaginable pain. For her it would be painless as far as anyone knew. (She heard footsteps: Adam was coming to meet her.) She kept that thought firmly in mind and was glad.

†

The plan had been to do the dunking just before the appointed hour, thus avoiding the need to change out of wet clothes. The pastor had not gotten far enough in his thinking about it to consider that it might be disrespectful to arrive in heaven dripping wet, but the thought now crossed his mind. He chuckled.

Foolish thought.

Was it? Would it not be more fitting if you were dressed in your best clothes, waiting quietly in prayer?

Well, a case could be made for that, certainly.

But it was much too late to make such arrangements.

It's almost too late for anything.

It was not too late for another heavy feeling of responsibility to be descending upon Adam Murphy. Nearly a week ago, he had discussed the Rapture's timing with Earl. Their meeting took place in the shop not fifty feet from where he now stood. That and the fantastic week that followed seemed to have made no difference: Earl had maintained his determination not to escape the coming troubles. Had he sufficiently impressed on his friend what that meant?

Technically, it was not too late. But very soon it would be—unless .... The doubt was there again: Nothing could be more normal than this peaceful morning. To a man who knew not the day and the hour, there would be no reason to suspect that this morning would be radically different from the millions of mornings preceding it. There was no necessity for this to be the Day—other than the dream. Although it had happened merely a week ago, that seemed a long time ago now. The impression it had made was worn, and its hold on his mind had weakened. Every other prophecy known to man had multiple interpretations. Why not this one? Earl's stand was not without precedent. If his disregard turned out to be appropriate, he would be glad for Earl. But what about the church?

Many, many others over the years had been deceived by mistaken hopes and had waited like this with unwavering expectation only to have their faith cruelly shattered.

The day always passed the same as every day since the world began.

And with what result?

They got marginalized and sometimes branded heretical.

The doubt would be profoundly distressing if given a chance to take root. It was tempting, but Adam rejected it.

It had to come sometime, and this is it. Earl has chosen to stay behind and suffer.

Still, Earl could change his mind.

What if he appears in the nick of time to forbid the use of the beach?

It wouldn't be unreasonable if he turned us out after what happened here yesterday.

Alice was coming down the hill with a tall armload of towels. She could not see over it, yet somehow she was negotiating the walkway. Adam shook off his brooding and went to help her, lifting several off the top of the stack and allowing her to see over the rest.

The lights and the warning whine of an electric vehicle announced the first arrival of Felix's converts.

This would be the first time in Murphy's career that he would baptize without having spoken at some length to each candidate. People had so many mistaken ideas about what it meant. Most had to be talked out of the idea that it secured them some privilege. A few had to be coaxed and coached into accepting what they perceived to be humiliation. It should be humbling, he would tell them. If humiliating, it was as death is humiliating, for it was

The Story

the symbol of ultimate death to the proud, self-serving old nature. Even more, though, it declared resurrection to the ultimate gift of glory. All this was symbol, hope, and expectation, not an immediate experience.

There will be little time to explain things. Some of it doesn't apply now, anyway.

It was a good thing, a beautiful thing, that these new believers wanted to be baptized. But what had Felix told them? Were they true believers or superficially swayed by one man's enthusiasm?

What a disappointment it will be if someone is left standing here alone.

The balance of these thoughts was not helping him overcome the ever present temptation to hedge his hopes.

Making their way down the hill were the couple from the car. They appeared to be about his own age. Meanwhile, a van had come down the driveway, and it appeared that a whole family was emerging from it.

Two, ... no, three, ... no, four children. I should have asked how many of the forty-nine were children.

The youngsters were full of energy, almost falling over one another coming down the steps. Alice had gone up to meet the first couple. Adam knew he should be going to meet them too. But he was holding out for a final word from Earl.

Why did I ever consent to do this for Felix? He's a crazy man. What will they say if Earl calls it off? Worse, when the hour passes and we're still here, dripping wet, how will I explain that?

The doubt was never far away, and it would keep nagging when given the slightest chance.

He left it to Alice to greet the arrivals, turned his back to them, and walked to the water's edge. He knelt down on the sand beside the dock, bowing his head in a distinct attitude of prayer. This would keep him safe for a few minutes, relieving him from having to face these credulous souls who were trusting him.

He remembered Moses with his staff, the man of God who put

his faith on the line at the edge of the sea.

I'm not Moses. Moses was acting on a command from above. There was no one telling me to be here doing this other than those pancake eaters. And they wouldn't come right out and admit that the Rapture was for real! ... What is for real?

He took a peek at the time: twenty minutes to go.

Only twenty minutes left of being a respectable preacher.

If his faith was still intact, his enthusiasm was at its lowest ebb. The sounds told him that more people were arriving. He marveled at their casual behavior on the brink of the cataclysm about to occur. Did they have any idea what this meant? Seen from this perspective, he could easily forget his reputation and believe it was a mistake. He yearned for a return to normal. If the prospect of departing his earthly homeland had made him more fond of it yesterday, the sensation was ten times worse now. He had an impulse to grab the dock and hang on for dear life.

How ridiculous.

Why so?

It has to be. All of it is ridiculous! It's fantastic, the work of imagination without any basis in experience. It's only an hypothesis.

What were the chances of this hypothetical mass translation out of one space-time into another being real? The sand at his knees, the crystal water, the crisp autumn air—these things were real.

It was an untested theory at best.

This is a nightmare. I'm about to join the ranks of the crackpots. How did I get into this?

He picked up a handful of sand and let it sift through his fingers.

This is real.

The preacher's whole professional life had dealt with the hypothetical. It now occurred to him that his profession took itself far too seriously.

It's easy when nothing can be proven one way or the other.

The Story

That's where I belong. I should never have stepped out of it and bought into this. I'm not constituted for it.

How could anyone be? No training, no lab experiments, no prototypes—just straight from tentative hypothesis to full-blown, life-or-death deployment. Everything lined up: they had a theory that seemed to fit the Scriptures. But no miracle comparable to this had taken place since creation.

Seventeen minutes to go.

Indeed, it was outrageous; it *was* absurd; it was preposterous in the light of natural history. The entire vocabulary of the world had nothing to describe it.

How could I have dared to interpret things this way and been so sure of myself?

Behind him were more voices—happy voices, laughter, joy.

What am I among these? They have nothing to lose. They can afford to be happy. They will have had a fun time. No risk of disgrace. They're all waiting for me as if I could perform the miracle.

Where is your faith, Adam?

Fools believe this. There is no basis for it in reality.

Faith is holding tight to what you hope for, being sure of what you have never seen. God commended the men of old for it.

"My God, I know you can do all things; no purpose of yours can fail; I have uttered what I did not understand."

"Adam!" It was Alice's voice. "There are a lot of people here. You had better get started."

The pastor placed his hands on the dock and raised himself up, his legs tingling and shaky. He turned around. About thirty people had gathered.

He looked at his watch. Fifteen minutes to go—only thirty seconds to baptize each one.

The crowd fell silent when they saw him rise. He scanned the faces, looking for Earl. Earl was not among them. He must now assume that Earl would not be stopping him from going ahead. It felt good to have that decided at least.

the Day and the Hour

"Greetings, everyone, in the name of Jesus Christ our living Savior. Today you are declaring that the Lord Jesus is your own personal Savior, and you are trusting him with your life and eternal destiny. If you agree with that, say Amen."

"Amen!"

"All right, I'm going out, ... out into the water, ... like this."

He was wading out without removing even his shoes.

"I want you to come one by one. If you have a towel, leave it with Alice. As soon as you get up to your waist in the water, I'll put my hand on your back. Then, hold your breath and close your eyes, crouch down a bit and lean back. I will lower you gently into the water. All right. We have to hurry. Who will be first? As soon as you have been baptized, go right back and get your towel from Alice and then go stand on the dock."

The children were eager. One of the boys came splashing out, obviously enjoying getting his clothes wet.

"I baptize you, my brother in Christ, in the name of the Father, the Son, and the Holy Spirit."

Down he went, holding his nose, and up he came, spluttering and wiping water from his face.

"Okay, keep coming; we have very little time."

One by one they came—down under the water of death, up into new life in the Spirit.

More were coming down the walkway, but Felix had not yet arrived.

"Quick, quick, we're running out of time! I baptize you in the name of the Father, the Son, and the Holy Spirit. Amen."

"Here comes Felix!" someone shouted, and a cheer went up from the congregation.

Eight minutes were left.

Several were now in the water at once, coming to him and wading back. He was baptizing one every ten seconds. The dock was crowded with dripping, shivering, hopeful believers. They were huddling together, trying to keep warm. The talking and laughing had ceased altogether. Everyone was aware of the critical

The Story

timing. They were lined up now in an orderly queue on the beach.

Felix was helping an elderly woman down the walkway. So many cars were jammed into the driveway and on the road above that she had had a long walk. Adam lost count of the number he had done.

"They're all here, every last one!" Felix shouted.

One minute was left. There would not be enough time. Felix was at the end of the line. There was a limit to how quickly a person could be safely submerged and brought back up. Footing and hand placement had to be sure. It would not do to have an accident now. He was baptizing them as fast as possible. He had shortened the words to the bare minimum. Four were in the water, wading toward him.

Felix was still on the beach with several in the line ahead of him. Someone on the dock who had a watch started a countdown.

"Ten."

"In the name of the Father …"

"Nine!"

"Son, and the Holy …"

"**Eight!**" (The others had joined in.)

"Amen."

"**Seven!**"

…

"**Six!**"

"… the name of the Father …"

"**Five!**"

"… the Son, and the …"

"**Four!**"

"… Spirit. Amen!"

"**Three!!**"

…

"**Two!!**"

"In the name of the Father, …"

"**One!!**"

"… and the Holy Spirit …"

the Day and the Hour

"Zer ...."

The Story

Chapter 21

Earl Clark is on the Gold Creek trail, fleeing his pursuers and running toward his goal, his only goal, the one thing remaining in life that he cares anything about. In spite of certain signs to the contrary, he has set aside the possibility that the Rapture occurred. Even if it did occur, apparently not all Christians were taken. The one thing that matters to him is convincing Leila that he loves her above all others and that she would be his perfect bride. He knows that he must bear the penalty for opposing the works of the enemy, but after that there will be time for them.

The trail through the woods follows the curving course of Gold Creek. So far he has encountered no one, but he expects it will not be long before the police will be combing the area. Deer Drive and Leila's apartment are a short hike up the hill, branching to the left on a path off the main trail. It should be coming up soon.

A siren goes by on Creek Street above, going in the opposite direction. Evidently, they have found the car. They will soon be on the trail behind him.

Two benches have gone by. The next one should be the one that comes just before his turnoff. ... There it is, fifty yards ahead —if it bears the initials **S+D** carved into its backrest.

That's it!

Earl sprints up the hill, breathing hard. The dead end of Deer Drive comes into view; her apartment building is on the left. He turns aside into the garden behind the building in order to avoid being seen on the street. In a casual manner he saunters toward her door, steps onto the deck, and taps the glass. The curtains have been drawn open, and he can see her bed. Her Bible lies open on it, and next to it rests his hat. Her personal phone is on the nightstand. Another siren goes by on Creek Street, but it barely registers in his consciousness because what he is seeing is telling him that she is gone.

the Day and the Hour

He taps on the glass again and tries sliding it open. It yields. Closing it behind him, he calls her name, but the evidence tells him not to expect an answer. He picks up his hat and puts it on, grabs the Bible, steps out, slides the door closed again, and walks stiffly back to the woods. He wants to find a place to hide, to mourn, and to die.

Earl Clark tramps back down the hill and carelessly approaches the main trail. No one is in sight, and there are no sounds of approach. If he is to put any distance between himself and the main trail, a side path would be preferable—quieter and easier than plunging through the wild wood with its thickets, mossy windfalls, and uneven ground. Suddenly, it occurs to him that they will be using dogs. Realistically, there are no practical means of escape.

He must face what is coming.

Earl returns to the bench bearing the S+D and sits down to await the inevitable. As you know by now, this is contrary to his nature. He needs to be doing something—but what? A stupefying lethargy is pinning him in place. Forcing himself to think, he begins talking:

"She wasn't there. ... She couldn't be there. ... She's no longer anywhere."

The evidence strongly suggested it, and now his gut assures him that the Rapture took place, and it took Leila. How could he have been so mistaken? He remembers that Carmen's note is in his pocket, and he takes it out.

> *Earl - If I'm gone, I'm gone*
> *and you're wrong.*
> *Sorry. Hope they*
> *don't get you. - C.*

He crumples it and puts it back in his pocket.

Earl opens the Bible at the ribbon, the page where Leila left it open, and *Samson* arrests his eye. It surprises him, for this is the

The Story

New Testament, near the end of the book. He reads:

> And what more shall I say? For time would fail me to tell of Gideon, Barak, Samson, ... who through faith enforced justice, ... were strong out of weakness ... refusing to accept release so they might rise again to a better life ....

He flips through the pages and notices notes done by her hand. He begins reading what she underlined.

The sound of a dog's panting brings on a rush of energy and pulls him back to the present. He cannot see them yet, but they must be close, coming up the trail on the right. Actions at once come to mind: he could avoid being seen either by bolting back up the path to Deer Drive or by charging down into the woods toward the creek. Neither option would erase his scent, and neither would be silent. In any case, the instinct to escape is dead without the desire to carry it out, and his desire to escape disappeared with her.

Earl closes the Bible and folds his arms across it, pressing it tightly to his chest as if to absorb some solace from it or protect it from the enemy.

A German Shepherd on a leash followed by an officer from the local police department is coming around the bend. Earl recognizes them both. The officer is reporting his discovery by radio:

"Dispatch, Fillmore. ... Clark is on the Gold Creek trail near Deer Drive. Over."

"Is he in flight? Over."

"Negative. He's sitting on a bench, the one with the S+D carved on it. Over."

"I'll have the FSA send a car to Deer Drive."

"Roger. Fillmore out."

Earl sits still with his head bowed. The dog is straining at the leash and whining with Fillmore trotting behind. The Shepherd comes to Earl's feet and lies down, putting a paw on his shoe.

"I don't have to tell you you're under arrest, Earl. You look like you've had a rough morning."

"Do what you have to do."

the Day and the Hour

"Put the Bible down. Turn around and let me have your hands."

Earl lays the Bible on the bench beside him and stands up, putting his hands behind his back. The officer slips the bands of the handcuffs over his wrists and tightens them.

"There's a lot of blood on the back of your shirt. Did you get shot?"

The sound of another siren comes from above. Earl gives him no answer.

"Come on. We're taking the trail up to Deer Drive."

"I'd like to take the Bible," Earl says.

"We'll leave it there. Someone will get it tomorrow morning."

Earl plods up the trail, followed by the dog and the officer. A police car and the FSA surveillance car are waiting as they emerge from the woods. He is delivered into the hands of Officer Filstein of the FSA while Officer Fillmore and the dog get into the other car.

"I'm going to have to blindfold you," says Filstein. "There's a lot of blood on your back. Are you in pain?"

Earl says nothing.

He takes out a roll of tape, removes Earl's hat, wraps tape around his head, covering his eyes, and slaps the cap back on.

"Surveillance, Filstein."

"Surveillance. Go ahead."

"I have Clark blindfolded and handcuffed. Will be at Detention Suites in five minutes. Over."

"Roger. Will notify Cypher."

Although unable to see, Earl knows exactly where he is at each moment by the sounds and the motions of the car. He expects to be encountering Al Cypher when being admitted to Detention Suites. Cypher is emerging from the door as they arrive. Filstein stops, and Al Cypher comes to the car.

"We're having a little problem with security in the Suites," he announces to Filstein. "All the inmates escaped last night—or more likely this morning. Apparently, the earthquake did

264

The Story

something to the system though I haven't found anything wrong with it yet. I'm going to have to put Clark somewhere else until we find the problem. The utility room around back is secured with an old-fashioned, reliable mechanical lock. I'm going to put him in there for now. As long as he's handcuffed and blindfolded he can't do any damage. Follow me."

Al Cypher gets into his own car, and Filstein follows. They stop by a door near the middle of the building.

"All right, Clark. Out you come."

Earl hears the sound of key in lock and of a door opening with a slight squeak. Al Cypher puts his hands on his shoulders and turns him toward it.

"Straight ahead."

"There's nothing in there for him to sit on, Cypher," says Filstein.

"That's all right. He's tough."

"Can't you put him in one of the suites? He can't just walk out in his condition—not with you there."

"I don't want him around while I'm working. He can stay in here. It will do him good. Besides, he's all bloody, and I don't want him messing up the place. ... Coming to the threshold; step high."

Not wanting to touch Earl's bloody back with his hand, Cypher lifts a leg and shoves the seat of his pants with his foot. Earl stumbles forward into the room, and the door slams shut behind him.

Whether due to the effect of his hat or of Cypher's foot, a surge of strength rushes upon Kenneth Clark. He strains at the handcuffs, causing the bands to dig into his wrists, but they remain intact. He moves his two hands over to his right side, and his right hand brushes against a tubular railing. He stoops a little, sliding his left palm under the railing, and while straightening his legs, he pulls up hard with his right arm. The bands cut through the skin; blood drips from his wrists; the connecting band stretches, stretches, and snaps.

the Day and the Hour

Using both hands, he tears at the tape that wraps his head and finally succeeds in peeling it off.

The room is small, without windows. An overhead light is on, controlled by a motion sensor. He is in a narrow space between railings that stand a foot from the side walls. Behind him is the door. The wall in front of him is covered with a chart showing the locations of the sprinkler-system valves and the fire doors. He is in the fire-control room.

Rows of switches for controlling the valves and fire doors are on the side walls. Earl studies the chart. The building is symmetrical right and left, with identical systems in each half. Each wing is equipped with four fire doors on each floor. The switches allow the doors to be closed remotely, from this room.

He reaches up with his left hand and flips the switch for the far door on the top floor. There is a faint rumbling as the heavy fireproof panel is released, rolling on its suspension track. It slams shut, closing off the north end of the wide hallway. A slight shudder ripples through the structure. Lifting his left arm, he runs his bloody hand down the entire outside column of switches. The combined rumble of the massive doors makes a louder noise; and as they slam shut simultaneously, there is a perceptible swaying and twisting on the upper floors. Immediately, before recovery is complete, he raises his right arm and runs his right hand down the corresponding switches on the opposite wall, and the outermost battery of heavy doors in the south wing crashes closed, inducing a slight twist in the opposite direction. Running his left hand down the next column of switches, the next column of massive doors is unleashed, delivering another impulse at the moment when the movement from the previous one is quickest. Again with his right arm he releases the opposite column of doors, and they go slamming shut, augmenting the momentum of the twisting pendulum. Releasing a column of doors on the left and then on the right, the building swings one way and then the other way by ever-increasing degrees.

Additional noises are developing, noises that are not the

sounds of slamming doors. The rhythmic twisting of the building has reached such an amplitude that it has overstressed some of the joints to the point where welds are breaking and bolts are shearing.

The building shudders violently as one of the upper floors breaks away and falls to the next level, pulling structural members after it and crashing to the floor below. Having lost much of its support, the structure above caves in, tumbling down and adding its mass to the plummeting ruin.

There is no mistaking what the noises mean. The fire-control room is surrounded by concrete walls that should provide him some protection, but a tremendous amount of energy is now in play; the floor shakes beneath his feet and the light goes out. Something very heavy has come down and impacted the level immediately above. Debris and dust are falling into the room, and the sound is deafening. The integrity of the roof and walls surrounding him is failing. A fragment of the breakup above, something with sharp edges, knocks him to the floor. As far as Kenneth Earl Clark is concerned, it is finished.

†

"What's that noise?" asked Officer Filstein. He was standing outside next to his car, chatting with Al Cypher.

They paused, listening. Then Cypher looked up and saw that the building was twisting.

"Get back! The building's moving! Run!" he shouted.

Cypher and Filstein jumped into their cars and sped to the far side of the parking area.

As soon as they stopped at a safe distance, a horrendous screech and groan accompanied by snapping and smashing sounds met their ears. Some of the windows were popping out; others were shattering. Panels plunged to the ground, and the upper part of the building descended on the rest like an accordion closing. Only the top floor remained with its windows intact, having come to rest at about the level of the former third floor. An acrid odor filled the air as the wreckage settled. Grinding noises

the Day and the Hour

and hissing sounds continued to escape the rubble.

Cypher, sitting in his car, knows he must wait until the ruins have ceased their shifting and then make an attempt to rescue Earl Clark. It looks fatal for Earl though. Everything that was on the first floor appears to have been mashed and flattened when the floors above came down. He motions Filstein to lower his window.

"I never did trust that building," he shouts. "It was supposed to withstand the big one, and it couldn't take a little bump."

"How do you explain the delay?" Filstein shouts back.

"It was too flexible. It never took much to make it sway. I guess somethin' broke and then it gradually spread. I don't know. **Whoa!**"

The ground shakes; the cars bounce; the heap that was the FSA building is sinking into the ground, the earth having opened to swallow it.

"It broke through into the mine!" Cypher shouts to Filstein.

The whole thing is dropping down, making hideous, hollow sounds as it falls into the cavernous main gallery of the old gold mine. Dust shoots up around it as it descends into the earth. It comes to its final rest with its roof level with the parking lot, antennas rising up like the masts of a sunken ship.

The Story

Officer Al Cypher takes out his phone. The plume of dust is drifting away to the southeast. He gets no answer from his boss. Her phone's location indicator is active, showing it being at her home. He decides to pay her a visit and deliver the news in person; he exits the parking lot of the former Federal Building and speeds down Hill Street the back way.

Arriving at the front of her apartment building, he notes that her car is there. He rushes in through the main entrance, stops at her door, and rings the bell.

Al Cypher unclips his radio and calls the surveillance supervisor.

"Surveillance, Cypher."

"Watchman here; go ahead."

"Where are you located?"

"At the Lakeview where Clark abandoned the car. Unfortunately, he took the key. Over."

"Did you see that the building collapsed?"

"Yeah. So much for the quakeproof design. Over."

"It's worse than you can imagine. It broke through into the mine, and the whole thing got swallowed up. ... Over."

"You mean the whole building dropped into it?"

"The whole thing went to hell. I'm trying to find the boss. I'm at her place. She's home because her car's here, but she's not answering her doorbell. Over."

"Where's Clark?"

"He was in the building when it collapsed. It happened fast. I didn't have a chance to get him out. Over."

"That's too bad. I suppose he had the key on him."

"No doubt."

"Well, It gets him out .... I mean now you've got a chance. Over."

"It'll save the FBI some trouble, and I won't have to explain. ... Yeah. Do you think I've got a chance? I hope so. But we need to find her. Over."

"When they picked up Clark, he was down on the creek trail below Deer Drive. Fillmore said he had a Bible, which could be hers.

the Day and the Hour

I figure he was up to her place. Check the back door. Over."

"Clark wasn't known for packin' a Bible. Stand by."

Al Cypher goes around to the back of the building and finds the door unlocked.

"Surveillance, Cypher."

"Go ahead."

"Back door is unlocked. Over."

"If you don't get a response, go ahead and search the place. Over."

"Roger."

Al Cypher bangs on the door and waits. He slides it open.

"Leila!"

He steps inside the bedroom, noting her phone on the bedside table. He finds nothing of significance in the other rooms.

"Surveillance, Cypher."

"Go ahead."

"Nothing's amiss here. There's no sign of a struggle or foul play. You need to put out an urgent missing-person search order. Over."

"I'm short of personnel. Hooper and Snooper are missing."

"Are we getting help from the town force?"

"Affirmative. They found our cars, parked side by side with nobody around and no bodies. And get this: The parking lot at the Lakeview is full, but nobody's inside. There's a sign on the door saying, 'Believers only.' Apparently, they met for breakfast. Over."

"No kidding? I feel like we're in one of those old End-Time movies. Did anyone check the churches?"

"A few people were hanging around Grace Bible Church when I went by, apparently waiting for Murphy to unlock the door once more. Over."

Al Cypher laughs.

"That's funny. ... Sorry. It just struck me that way. It looks like they were right, but what good did it do 'em? Over."

"I guess those are the hypocrites. I thought they all were, but apparently not. At least they still got a building—nothing a locksmith can't fix."

The Story

"It'll take more than a locksmith to fix ours. It'll set the Reorganization back a couple of years."

"I'd say more like seven, minimum. It'll take a while to clean up the mess. Figure five years just for an impact study. What are you gonna do, Cypher?"

"Do you have any pull with Petunia?"

"A little."

"Do you think she'll have some openings?"

"I figure Daisy is gone. Maybe Daffodil too. Over."

"That would leave her with an all-male force."

"Don't forget Hyacinth Fuller."

"Oh, yeah. ... Would you put in a good word for me?"

"At a time like this? We gotta look out for ourselves, Cypher."

"I thought you were my buddy, Watchman. Over."

"I'm as good a friend as you'll ever get, Cypher. And don't forget it."

"Hey, I'm gonna shape up. Over."

"Yeah? Just because you got rid of Clark, eh?"

"I don't have to worry about him being with her, wherever she is; that's for sure. Over."

"Don't be too sure. If they were right ...."

the Day and the Hour

The Story

About the author ...

I seldom go outside. Travel, sightseeing—these do not interest me anymore. The wonderful world outdoors only reminds me of what I can no longer do. The trails on the sunny mountainside are not for me. No trimming the flying jib, no touching down on two-seven, no gliding among snowy pines. If I step outside and sit under the blue sky, there will come the sound of a motor overhead and the sight of a sail on the bay and looming above it the snowy peak. All these are for the enjoyment of others, not for me. And my friends are dead.

But as long as my mind still finds trails to follow, I will go where they lead, making friends and having adventures in a world of imagination until that too slips beyond my reach; then I will wait in the darkening hour for my Redeemer and the new body and mind that he has promised me. And I will find with him new and old friends. I hope you will be there too.

CPSIA information can be obtained at www.ICGtesting.com
Printed in the USA
BVOW040404020113

309598BV00002B/124/P